.VILLAGE
IDIOT.
.PRESS

PABLO D'STAIR was born in 1981. At the age of 19 he composed his first novel (*October People*) for the 3 Day Novel Writing Contest sponsored by Anvil Press. The novel did not win the competition but was published in the subsequent year - along with his second novel (*Confidant*) - by the infamous and now defunct vanity book-mill Publish America.

In the mid-2000's, D'Stair co-founded the art-house press Brown Paper Publishing with his colleague, the novelist, musician, and painter Goodloe Byron. Through this press and its literary journal *Predicate*, he released the work of more than fifty of his peers along with editions of two dozen of his own books (including *Regard, dustjacket flowers, Candour, a man who killed the alphabet, Carthago Delenda Est*, and the novella comprising *they say the owl was a baker's daughter: four existential noirs*).

Eventually shuttering BPP, D'Stair founded (KUOBA) press, continuing to publish work by his contemporaries. During this era, his own literary output remained prolific but largely unreleased, though several works were made available as limited-edition print projects and in various electronic mediums (including *the purse snatcher letters, the cigarette miscellany*, and the five novella comprising *Trevor English*).

D'Stair spent several years as a cinema critic - primarily for the UK site *Battle Royale with Cheese* - and as an essayist/interviewer for the national newspaper of Sri Lanka's *Sunday Observer* (through which periodical several of his novella and a story collection were serialized). Also during this period, D'Stair began working as an underground filmmaker in the capacities of writer, director, cinematographer, editor, and performer - the cinematography of his first feature (*A Public Ransom*) earned an award in international competition at the XIX Internacionlni TV Festival (Bar, Montenegro 2014).

D'Stair has also written several volumes of poetry, more than four dozen pieces of theatre, written and directed music videos, written and illustrated graphic novels and comic-book series, and written/produced/performed audio essays. His work across all mediums has often been released pseudonymously.

Presently, he lives and writes in Lancaster, Pennsylvania.

Praise for the writing of Pablo D'Stair

"The first thing that occurs to you when you pick up a volume of D'Stair is that it has no business being good. No credentials. None of the usual apparatus that tells you a book has appeared: publishers, agents, press releases. The industry didn't cough this one up. The second thing, once you start to turn the slippery pages, is: how the Hell can such good writing come from nowhere? Who the Hell is Pablo D'Stair, anyway? The final note, the one that makes D'Stair a little troubling, is that this writing is a voice inside your head. Nothing can prepare you for that ... Pablo D'Stair is defining the new writer. There is NO ONE else. As reckless as Kerouac's 120-foot trace paper, D'Stair's independence from all of us needs to be studied and celebrated ... This is revolution. Each word seems to want to wage war. Nothing is settled, nothing is as it should be - and we know as we read and it starts to sink in that this is how things are ... D'Stair's late realism needs to be included in any examination of the condition of the novel."

Tony Burgess, award-winning author/screenwriter
(*Pontypool Changes Everything, Idaho Winter*, and *People Live Still in Cashtown Corners*)

"[The work] is written by someone who cares about language - you'd be surprised at the number of novels written by people who don't. It takes a lot of daring and ambition for a writer to tease out a book like this in such minute detail, and D'Stair is committed ... you stop yourself from skimming because you start thinking you might be missing something - [the work] is too well written to skim ... Somehow again and again you're drawn in ... you get used to the rhythm and follow it because the work is obsessive. We find ourselves in a languid kind of suspense, bracing ourselves..."

Bret Easton Ellis, author/screenwriter
(*American Psycho, Rules of Attraction*, and *Lunar Park*)

"I knew he could write, and I suspect he can do about eighty other things as well - if our minds are hamsters on wheels, then Pablo has more hamsters than any of us ... D'Stair doesn't just write like a house afire, he writes like the whole city's burning, and these words he's putting on the page are the thing that can save us all."

Stephen Graham Jones, Bram Stoker Award-winning author
(*Mapping the Interior, Mongrels* and *All the Beautiful Sinners*)

"Over the years I've stopped being astonished at the multifarious things that Pablo D'Stair can do well. Let's just say it: whatever he puts his hand to he accomplishes and with a style and panache that is his alone ... Original. Idiosyncratic. Off-kilter. Strange. The slap-back dialog, the scenes as accurate as if directed by Fritz Lang. This is D'Stair's world. Welcome to it. I envy you if this is your first time in."

Corey Mesler, author/screenwriter
(*Memphis Movie* and *Camel's Bastard Son*)

.THE
DISEMBODIED.
.PARTS

A RHAPSODY

Pablo D'Stair

**.VILLAGE
IDIOT.
.PRESS**

First Paperback Edition

ISBN: 978-1-0878-8129-4

Published by Village Idiot Press

The Collected Works of Pablo D'Stair

.NOVELS / NOVELLAS

October People
Confidant
kill Christian
Regard
miscellaneous language
Piano Forte
Dustjacket Flowers
Subject
the order, in which the wind
a man who killed the alphabet
Candour
the murder of linen
Carthago Delenda Est
figments of calculation
bread and salt and teeth and tongue
top state secret confidential why why why did you resign?
Vienna London Unreal
we know the death of Archimedes
how February Tolmb explained
TWO NOVELLA - September from its grave; in descending order, alphabetical
TWO NOVELLA - The Unburied Man; The People Who Use Room Five
Kaspar Traulhaine, approximate
i poisoned you
twelve ELEVEN thirteen
man standing behind
THREE NOVELLA - Leo Rache.; Transit; Michel Bolingbroke
VHS
motion in the winter
TWO NOVELLA - The Purse Snatcher Letters; bleed the ghost empty
Trevor English
TWO NOVELLA - Slumber; Tartarus
Lucy Jinx
The Wank Miner
Robespierre
The Ghoul Haunted Woodland of Weir
The Disembodied Parts: a rhapsody

SHORT FICTION/ESSAY/POETRY/MISC.

SHORT FICTION I - while Valerie was no one: two stories; Current Perspectives in
Counting To Ten: twenty-four stories; On Our Current Victimology: fourteen stories
SHORT FICTION II - Seven Stories About Working in a Bookstore; I'm a cigarette: five
stories
Cigarette Miscellany
People in your Neighborhood: ten stories
FRAGMENTS 2008-2019
Voices Restless Inanimate: collected poems
New Fleas, Old Dogs: selected cinema essays

for my father
Dr. Jose Gonzalez-Fernandez

and for my brother
Carlos

.THE DISEMBODIED.
.PARTS

Early one morning the young woman came running into town from the direction of the river. She was soaking wet. She said a big alligator and two little alligators had pulled her in and had tried to get her to eat a raw fish. They were her husband and her sons, she said, and they wanted her to live with them. But she had gotten away.

.ALLIGATORS
from Alvin Schwartz's *Scary Stories to Tell in the Dark.*

.SEPTEMBER.

I ASKED MY DAD WHAT was the big deal about saying 'God damn it' - why'd that twist so many wigs? He shrugged a sixty-three-year-old 'Dunno.' His mind was elsewhere. Equations, I figured. Something to do with his employ as a mathematical researcher.

Nope. Moot arguments about the Speed Limit. He took it on himself, all of a sudden, to vocalize: 'If the Limit is Sixty, that is the fastest one is possibly allowed to go. Not the speed one must go.' Therefore: he concluded his driving thirty, tops, seemed very sound minded, indeed.

After this pronouncement and five minutes silence, I guess he decided he'd better give my earlier question consideration and an answer of some kind. To spare me going through life uninformed like so many of the rest.

He explained how 'Damn it' means 'Send it to Hell.' People of a religious bent, according to his share of experience, get up in arms over God being put on the spot like that. 'God, send this toaster to Hell!' he gesticulated by way of example. 'You've got to wait patiently for God to get around to things like that, in his own time.'

'Pray for it?'

No. No, he didn't mean that. Folks're touchy about praying for God to damn things. 'That's the best way to wind up inadvertently damned yourself, counterintuitive as it sounds.'

I wondered if I would be allowed to say 'God, send it to Hell!' at school. Much as I appreciated my dad's open mind and erudition, his discourse was neither here-nor-there as far as what actually weighed on me.

Certainly it had been the use of Damn which had made the Social Studies teacher so hivey. After all, that dunce Morton had said 'God darn it' right there and then to explain what I should have said, instead. When I'd nimbly retorted 'Darn means Damn and you dang - which also means Damn - well know it' I got in trouble for reusing the offending word twice. 'Flagrantly' Mr. Limerock called it when outlining my offense to the Vice Principal.

Things like this had gotten to be a pesky leitmotif.

Very first week of class, during carpet-time one morning, Mrs. Terre was blathering on about her bourgeoning physical fitness kick, describing her jogging apparel at length, so I was having a chat with some kid I'd never met. Topic got around to movie comedies. So happened I'd recently watched Spaceballs with my older brother so was chuffed to relate one of my favorite moments, wherein Dark Helmet exclaims 'Morons! I'm surround by morons!' A good chuckle was had by us both. But after a blink I realized I'd flubbed the line so tapped this kid's shoulder. 'Sorry - he says Assholes! I'm surrounded by assholes!'

Like some Jack-in-the-box Benedict Arnold this kid jerked back from me, hand raised high, and blurted overtop of Mrs. Terre's story 'Ichabod's saying bad words at me!'

Sniveling little company man!

End of the same week, I was playing kickball during recess. My pal Endie missed an easy catch.

'You hockey puck!' I jibed him.

Nothing demeaning there. Jocularity amongst pals, obviously. But Mr. Simms wasn't having it. Pulled me to the sideline for a dressing down.

'I called him a hockey puck! There's no offense in a hockey puck - or have I overlooked something?'

'In context, a hockey puck is bad.'

'It's a line from Flight of the Navigator! That's a G-rated picture!'

Mr. Simms couldn't be held accountable for what slipped past the censors. 'Because everyone knows what hockey puck means when someone says it how you said it.'

'I'll just stop quoting movies' I mumbled.

INSTIGATOR. AGITATOR. WISEACRE. AND NO doubt worse. I seemed to have the knack for cultivating epithets amongst authority figures of late. The bitter vindictiveness of Fate, a poet might pen. But a realist would see all it amounted to was a streak of honest misunderstandings. These borne of the investigative nature I'd been nurtured into at the hands of both my parents. Not to blame them. Though they were to blame if blame became strictly necessary.

Take this example:

Music class. The period was devoted to rehearsal for the forthcoming

Halloween sing-a-long. A personal favorite of mine, annual-event wise. Indeed, it was the primary reason I remained mildly pleased there was such thing as school.

We were working out a song called The Ghost Of John - kind of a good-natured (if altogether blasé) ditty which contained the lyric *long white bones with the skin all gone / wouldn't it be chilly with no skin on?*

So obviously I was going to lean over to have a private word in the ear of my pal Binion, the purpose of which was (A) to verify whether he agreed the song ought properly be titled The Skeleton Of John and (B) to point out how one wouldn't de facto be at all chilly - not right out of the gate, at least - if one's skin were to be unfortunately removed. 'Think about your muscles, Binion - sinews, organs, fluids.' Painful it would be, without fail! Was I arguing otherwise? But, realistically, you'd die from shock and exposure ages before you'd register whether you'd picked up a sniffle.

Ms. Peabody, all of a sudden, was hissing me quiet - as though I'd been ignoring her entreaties for months on end! When I attempted to explain myself, she didn't hear out my thesis, fully, just stated my explication of the song came off snide and in bad faith. 'And it would be cold - skin is what regulates temperature, Ichabod.'

Or what about this:

Same day, bus ride home. I was explaining the Music class confrontation - understandably impassioned - to a group of other riders. What do I learn the following morning? This constitutionally protected act of communication had gotten me reported by the bus driver!

Charge: being a perpetual nuisance and flouting all attempts to cajole me toward sitting calmly in adherence to some allegedly posted Rider Regulations. The Principal had me read aloud the complaint affidavit. It began 'This entire year, Ichabod Burlap has always caused a disturbance ...' However, being somewhat flustered by the proceedings - I'd been blindsided entirely, after all! - I had, in the moment, not squinted at the paper enough and legitimately thought I'd seen written 'This entire year, Ichabod Burlap has never caused a disturbance ...' As soon as I'd uttered this sentiment aloud it seemed daftly off base, so I ejaculated in honest bewilderment 'Then what the devil was I called in here for!?'

An unmitigated fiasco. Made no better by insisting we all take a breath and admit how the main takeaway for all of us ought be a mindful recognition how it was always best for all parties to take time out for context and a consideration of the individual intricacies of the human psychology.

MY OLDER BROTHER, ALVIN, PEERED into the hall, gleaning the coast was clear or whatever he thought was important, then ushered me, hush-hush, to the far side of our bedroom where we sat to the ground, secluded as possible by the structure of the bunk beds. There were, it was revealed, certain unsettling developments he needed to hip me to.

Hadn't I seen the broken glass at the bus stop those times?

I hadn't, actually.

Well, there's been a bunch of it. Plus cigarette stubs. Bottle caps. 'Also, quite an amount of vulgar graffiti.'

'Yeah?'

A member of Neighborhood Watch had spied the defacement, promptly reported it up the chain, and the Community Group liaison had dispatched a custodial volunteer to paint over it.

In thinking about it, I did remember noticing shapes of brownish paint on portions of the walls and window ledges of the quaint, house-like enclosure set up at the mouth of the development for school kids to wait for the bus in, a decorative shelter for when the weather took a mean-spirited turn.

'That was the closest color they could find to brick on short notice. The drawings were titties and dicks, man. Whole load of cusses, too - it couldn't wait for a true match.'

I understood. Such salaciousness, right at the start of the day, would get at least three overbearing moms I'd heard about hot under the collar. And those ladies had a lot of pull, so best to keep their bread buttered just so.

What this had to do with me was:

Alvin (being in the top grade of the middle school) had gotten wind (via overhearing, at lunch, someone talking about the comings and goings of their older sibling) how a gang of toughs called The Ghostbusters were responsible for these mischiefs. Furthermore, these Turks were making inroads to causing more grief around the development.

'More graffiti, broken glass - that's for starters.'

Word around the campfire (so far as Alvin gleaned from a chat in the corridor between Pre-Algebra and World History) had it how this gang habitually hung round in the bus stop, late at night. Chewed chaw, drank beers, lit cigarettes - all manner of nevermind - until the crazies set in and they started spit-kissing and doodling suggestive pictures to freak kids out in the morning.

'Not that kids care. Kids would like it. But you know what I mean.'

I did.

The purpose of this briefing was:

We were going to put an end to this mayhem, in no uncertain terms, by acting in the capacity of vigilantes. We'd not come out of it without a few scabs, so I needed to brace myself for that. The steeliest constitution I could muster would be appreciated.

What Alvin needed was for me and a sundry few of our pals to put our thinking capped heads together, cobble up some clever stratagems we could incorporate to win in a physical fight if the going got rough.

'Keep in mind' he emphasized 'a lot of The Ghostbusters are tenth graders.'

So there was simply no telling.

ALL OF THIS NEWS, THESE developments, obligations - it put a lot of unwelcome pressure on me, considering I had deadlines to meet.

Of late, I'd taken it upon myself to produce a four-panel comic strip and to have an update posted on the dining room cork-board, daily. Not a humor strip, but a serialized adventure-drama in the vein of Mark Trail (though far less educational when it came to the double-length Sunday installment). Mine was called Hugo Plyankoff, MD and depicted the noirish, quasi-absurdist misadventures of the titular quack-physician-turned-freelance-gumshoe and his generally more sound-minded compatriots.

I had attempted a full issue format, but found it restrictive, burdensome to my artistic sensibilities. As for the dailies: I had been industrious the first day or two, getting ahead more than a week's worth of material. By the second week, my head-start had dried out to a measly three days. By this point, I was in the hot-seat to write and illustrate practically in real-time, live studio audience.

The intrigue was getting meaty, into the thick, necessitating a degree of finesse to appropriately tease out important character dynamics lest motivations seem too superficial. Some forthcoming reveals needed to be timed with class and precision. I also didn't want to slip into endless trap-and-escape, suspenseless episodics. On top of which, I had already killed off Jackson! His dispatch was quite startling, and I'd not yet conceived of a new shocker to raise the ante, there.

Add into the bargain that I was now supposed to be developing plots and ploys to successfully beat up a gang of teenaged bus stop hooligans?

I only had so much bandwidth!

It was a turn of good luck how my interest in maintaining academic standing had dropped off so severely.

Story there?

First straw: Mrs. Terre jumping to assumptions how I might've done well on an above-grade-level math assignment. I'd made no pretense I stood a chance at any such thing. So having to endure the class watching while my paper was graded (Mrs. Terre yapping such assuredness I would join Julie Laport in going down the hall to be shown off like a prize-hog in front of the fifth graders) only to have the teacher's aide shake his head and Mrs. Terre frowningly sigh 'Nevermind, go ahead Julie' was quite the unsolicited toe in the ribs.

Final straw: Mrs. Terre's same jackanape aide (her step-nephew was my growing suspicion) tacitly accusing me of plagiarizing my twenty-four page tragical cat novel by way of quizzing me out on whether I actually knew what a turret was. Gah! How he'd nodded when I'd answered correctly, like as though my knowing what's what was due to he'd done me a favor.

Blowhard.

Yes, homework could all wait or be waylaid outright. What, after all, was the worst case, here? Handful of lousy grades today keeps me off tenure track decades hence? Boo-hoo. Plus: I'd more likely than not fudge something of far graver important than fourth grade vocabulary along the way, knowing me.

But that only helped me so much.

This new threat ...?

The comic absolutely needed to take precedence.

'GOD, SEND IT TO HELL!' I groused, sharp scythe of a hiss and my fist tightening in cow-milking pops. Here's the result of all my conscientiousness and hard work. I never ought to've been working at the dining-room table (of course I knew that!) but it's just so convenient to the cork-board I'd gotten seduced into the habit.

Look at it! There was my just-a-moment-ago finished Hugo strip, all in a ruin. What made it all the more gutting was I'd felt I'd pulled off a real narrative doozy - had even built up a head of steam to nail out the next one or two.

But no, it was not to be. Instead, what went down? I'd set the full sheet of paper to the tabletop, turned to the dry-sink to retrieve scissors with which to cut the strip out (five seconds, tops!) and when I'd turned back - zang! - saw how some spatter of milk droplets from whenever someone recently ate cereal must've been laying in wait, just there! One two - four! - circles of damp blemished the paper (smack dab inside of a word bubble, even!) irrevocably blurring and otherwise mussing the pencil work. Five - six! - six soggy little freckles! And another one right there, where Hugo's erstwhile lover and long-suffering consultant Penelope had been turned into a concrete statue!

It would never do to post a strip in such a shabby condition. I'd have to suck it up. Redraw. Which would be easy enough, in principle. Piece of cake, in fact, with everything already conceived and once-rendered. Except: some of the lucky subtleties to the illustrations could never be precisely replicated, the je n'sais pas impossible to recapture.

Paper stock was too thick for tracing. Unless I wanted to ink the mucked up one, first - and even still it was all a perhaps.

Inking, though, wasn't so bad an idea.

However, I'd need to draw something new to test out the process, first, or risk some further, haste-based calamity. Also: I'd have to wait it out so it'd be for certain the wet spots had totally got back to normal. Otherwise I was presiding over moot court! If even the slightest tad wet, the tracing would tear the original or else moistness would seep right on up through to the new one.

Problem duplicated right alongside the art!

In the end, things worked out peachy. The rub was how the microwave clock proved the process had cost me the better part of an hour.

It was bolstering to admit how I did prefer the re-do to the original (I'd fixed some incongruities with leg size, for example) - but still! Even lumping in the time it'd taken to come up with the conceit of the strip, the original had cost me far less time and effort.

So here's where it left me: haunted by the knowledge I'd earnestly had time to get ahead a few day's-worth and indisputably possessed the right amount of gumption - yet nothing!

Nine o'clock. I'd missed the deadline. Couldn't hoodwink myself into the looney conceit anyone would read this specific Hugo until tomorrow. Mom at work. Brother upstairs for the night, already. Dad doesn't even know this series goes on.

I tacked the strip to place under the index-card labeled Today's Installment, this immediately above the card labeled The Story Thus Far which had all previous strips arranged in columns beneath it.

This one was a day late.

'God, send this toaster to Hell!'

MY BROTHER WOKE SCREAMING. SCREAMING. Then burbling, whining, huddled in a corner to himself, a tangle of his sheet and comforter. It was three in the morning. My mom would've only just returned from her work in the city, a solid hour's drive away. I heard her soothing Alvin where he cowered on the top bunk. Saw her calves, underside of soles, her legs draped over his mattress lip.

Her attempts at hushing, balming Alvin were to no avail. All he was capable of in those long moments was repeating 'It's the picture of dad, it's the picture of dad, it's the picture of dad'. High-pitched, hyperventilating hiccoughs of a phrase. 'It's the picture of dad, it's the picture of dad, it's the picture of dad.'

My mom soothingly assured him it was nothing more than a nightmare. 'Everyone has those' she seemed to all but sing.

'It's the picture of dad, it's the picture of dad, it's the picture of dad.'

I wondered exactly which picture of our dad he meant. Or perhaps he was merely hysteric. Not using the words to reference the real world. Some dissonant horror-show babble only having meaning inside his slumber.

'It's the picture of dad, it's the picture of dad, it's the picture of dad.'

Did he even know what he was saying? Did he care?

'It's the picture of dad, it's the picture of dad, it's the picture of dad.'

There was only one photograph of my dad I could think of. Washed out color. Astride his old horse, Platero. False gold of frame over-crisp. Object heavier than it had cause to be. Down on the overstuffed bookshelf cabinet in the dining room. Kind of shoved in amongst miscellaneous clutter.

'It's the picture of dad, it's the picture of dad, it's the picture of dad.'

Maybe Alvin meant the art print on the wall down in the basement. The one depicting a man (or was it a woman?) on a horse. As seen from behind. Black on white. Sort of a calligraphic quality to the style.

Though why I thought he might mean this painting I'd no idea at all. Having thought of it, though, I now felt there was something terrifying about it. Was convinced it was the culprit to this all. Certain in my blood.

'It's the picture of dad ... it's the picture of dad ... it's the picture of dad ...' Alvin finally stopped saying.

My mom remained in the room dark, absently whispering Shhhh well after my brother was probably back asleep. She went quiet after a time, too. Maybe also asleep. Maybe shivering from the cooling perspiration Alvin had shuddering into her clothes.

I stared at the ceiling, thinking about the skeleton who lived on the other side of it. The skull overlarge, distorted, deranged in its architecture, almost the shape of a peanut. Its name was Muppis. Muppis. The one who stalked me. Would kill me. Only me. Invade my dreams at the merest chance, especially if I slept on my back, mouth open, throat dry, vulnerable. I mentally clicked through every detail of every image of it which dwelt in me. Still-shot made flipbook. Museum of portraits culled from being unable to wake fast enough.

NEXT MORNING WHEN I WAS roused, my brother was in the room, still sleeping away. My dad explained how he had a slight fever so would be kept home from school for the day.

I arrived at the bus stop to discover the older kids were all still present, waiting on tardy transportation. Their chagrin was visible. Why weren't they being allowed the day off? 'Fair's fair' was the grumbled philosophy which trickled over to us grade-schoolers in the dewy grass or under the pine trees where we'd been made to congregate (no way would high-schoolers deign to share the bus-stop house or sidewalk with twerps).

At some point, a ninth grade kid (who I knew from experience was called Dale Beech) took a sudden and flippant stride right on into the road outlining the development, clapping his hands to be certain all eyes were on him, then quite brazenly laid himself down on the pavement, half of him one side of the yellow divider line, half of him the other. It was a third grade Safety Patrol (the one tasked with corralling us elementary-school rabble) who haughtily bolted forward, told him to stand up immediately and to return to one of the secure areas allocated for waiting. While all gathered gaped, she went on to primly make him wise how she would be reporting him, pronto - so he could look forward to being brought up on whichever charges were deemed fit to his offense.

It was Mrs. Terre (of course) in charge of the elementary-school Safety Patrols. And Christ alive, boy howdy didn't she whoop this up! It'd make front cover of Time Magazine if she had things her way. The girl was paraded up and down the hall like a festival! Mrs. Terre related the tale of her bravery over and over to any administrative staff or adult volunteer who came into the room. Carped on it in tones of beer commercial and pinball machine.

No joke, by day's end it was arranged for the girl to have an assembly in her honor during which a Civics award would be presented her by the honest-to-God police officer in charge of the Say No To Drugs program. Officer Wilkes was typically only on school premises for those Thursday sessions, but today he drove his patrol car over, special.

And thus were we all trundled to the gymnasium before being released to await our buses home. Kindergarteners through fourth graders all had to sit on the floor, as was customary. So Indian Style I sulked and zapped satiric commentary to a kid called Patrick as the show got on the road. In no time at all, I was tagged for being disruptive. Made to go stand against the rear wall with the other rabble-rousers.

Patrick? I suspect his grades were too sterling, his dad too PTA, his mom too she-runs-the-bake-sale to not give him benefit of wrong-place-wrong-time. But at least he was a good enough guy to look up at me, ashamed, while I was hauled off.

IT WAS SOMEWHAT OVERDRAMATIC OF Binion to conspiratorially whisper 'Ichabod ... they've returned' when he came into the lavatory where I was busy talking to myself in the mirror. Of course, a bit of over-drama never did much harm. Often, it not only indexed a refined sensibility but, as in this case, was apt to head plague off at the pass.

He was referring, I knew from his tone, to The Disembodied Parts. Those had never 'gone away' for any period of time, though. Yet I supposed I could see where he was coming from. With the school year now underway full tilt boogie, the communal, concerted efforts made to catalogue the vermin - their habits, movements, disguises, weapons - had gone noticeably slack.

Binion told me he'd seen a leg.

'What does it kill with?'

He'd not been able to determine. However, he could relate with certainty how its disguise had been a length of sumac. A thick vine of the stuff.

Which was new and somewhat perplexing. 'Are you positive about that? Sumac isn't an animal.'

But plants were alive, didn't I see? This was the sinister stuff we were up against! And what's more (based on some reflections on what he'd only so briefly observed) he thinks the leg actually travels via roots and can show up any old place at all so long as there's sufficient greenery. It just looks like sumac, specifically, when in disguise mode. Even if no sumac is around. As though someone just left a chopped bunch of it out wheresoever.

'It's one of the legs, though. Definitely. I guess it's the left one.'

That followed, deductively. The Right Leg was well documented to transform into a grouping of thick, overfed crickets. It had double-sided razors lining it, up and down, blades embedded down to the bone, lodged in firmly. Impossible to defend against the fiend. If you grabbed it, your flesh would be flayed to ribbons just as quick as you like! Best just make a run for it was the common wisdom.

'The legs' Binion now submitted 'might work in tandem. The sumac is thick. It can trip you up.'

I could see it all, clear as a bell. Pretty diabolical. His foreboding tone was proving out to be more formally necessary than I'd given it credit. The attributes of these ghouls were metastasizing with alarming speed if all this proved on the level.

Where had the sumac-leg been?

'Over in that guy's yard where we steal his bamboo to make real nun-chucks.'

I had many more follow-up questions, but out of the blue sky and with vigorous aggression Mrs. Terre's toady little aide burst onto the scene. 'You're not supposed to be in the toilet yakity-yakking, Ichabod. You're supposed to be standing against the wall, back straight, listening to Office Wilkes' beautiful speech.'

So I was trotted along, chop-chop, while Binion quickly piped in how he'd show me the new card on the bus, later.

Somehow, Binion was also spared punishment. I saw him blithely return to his place on the floor during a smattering of applause.

I'D ONLY SCROUNGED UP A few of my Reference Cards when I hurriedly gave a look through my desk before grabbing my backpack. Early versions. Most all of them the worse for wear. Every corner dog-earred from being mashed around in the desk's clutter, creases along the centers, kind of grimy with grey-brown, in weird diagonals.

Luckily, Binion had his full set. Endie - a real crackerjack artist! - had his, too. So mine would've been nothing but ancillary duplicates, leaving me free to not even mention I'd brought them. We gravitated toward using Endie's as the official documents, seeing as he kept better track of stats, and that's no kidding. Times sighted. Locations. Confirmed attacks/attempted attacks. Confirmed kills. Clean and regularly updated. Neat and tidily set to the card backs. All his penmanship perfect to the blue lines.

Endie also jotted many miscellaneous tidbits - mythos and hearsay which had been bandied about, no clear primary source but not yet debunked outright so best to keep mindful of.

The card-faces were very fine renditions of the body-part ghouls (arm, leg, hand, foot) taking up the larger part of the space, paired with illustrations of the disguise-animals (squirrel, bird, crickets) set off in the lower right-hand corners (not overlapping the main illustrations so much as blending into them).

HEAD (overweight pigeon): most often seen on powerlines - Weapon, rusted corkscrew (which it bit down on and used like a thrusting spear) - zero confirmed kills, dozens of attempts (including those half-dozen scrapes to Henri, one time, which only through dumb luck hadn't required stitches). The going theory was the Head was kind of The Big Boss and so didn't attack as fiercely or as often as the others - it was, however, in charge of the thinking for all parts.

LEFT HAND, RIGHT HAND (rust-colored squirrel, black squirrel): seen all over the place — Weapon(s), butcher's knife (always bloody) and brass-knuckles dipped in tar and broken glass, respectively.

RIGHT FOOT (mouse or furless mole - two credible sources attested to having seen it as both, swore to their claims up and down with an inspiring amount of passion): Weapon, entirely wrapped in barbed-wire laced with lawn chemicals.

LEFT FOOT (worm that is way too long): Weapon, like a pin-cushion made of needles from syringes - plus: two accounts held that it also 'had a scalpel from the same hospital the needles came from stabbed though it' one account with further addendum how a 'previous victim stabbed it while trying to survive' and insisting the foot 'now stabs people with this, like by stomping on them' (both accounts unsubstantiated and sourced dubiously from kids who were only visiting their cousin for a day or so but had been present at the park while a conversation had been going on, claimed emphatically to have seen the beast - we badly wanted these claims put out to pasture, but were not at liberty to simply ignore them without having done our due diligence).

And now this LEFT LEG, which Binion gave exhaustive description of, as best he could conjure from his brief encounter, and which Endie jotted notes about he would later word more succinctly and add to his card.

'Except I'm not sure how to draw sumac.'

'It's the same thing as a furry rope, basically.'

'Maybe I should draw a collage of assorted plant-life.'

'No. It was just sumac. Until someone confirms otherwise. We don't want to waste time and energies guarding against every last plant we see! There's tons of those! We'd be spread too thin, emotionally.'

We concurred. This was yet another sobering reminder of how easy it was to get caught up and pulled away from one's best judgement in the face of naked horror. Which is why, as we parted, we all renewed our vows to keep up on our other pursuits. The importance of leisure demonstrably paramount.

MY BROTHER WASN'T IN OUR room when I got home. Meaning he was either in the basement working with his airbrush or else something terrible had happened. Before I knuckled down to the day's Hugo strip, I figured I ought to get verification, one way or the other.

None of the above, it turned out. His airbrush was kaput until our dad got home and drove him to Robert's Oxygen to get the canister refilled. In the interim, he was working on a poster-sized rendition of Nexus and Judah the

Hammer standing in the palm of the Merk's outstretched hand. All very prestigious, quite frankly. He was well on his way to the glory and rewards strew upon the professional comic book artist! Or, as he often said, he'd do covers, anyway. Or else limited edition prints for this or that company. 'Freelance is the thinking man's ticket' was his motto.

'What're you using the retractable razor thing for?'

He demonstrated how he would cut a portion out of a sheet of plastic overlay, position it to protect the main image of the poster, leaving only the ink black background exposed (this representing the vastness of outer space).

'To what end?'

Observe: he dipped a toothbrush into a dollop of white correctional fluid, angled it atop the exposed background, shushed his thumb gingerly across the bristles and - voila! - a spritz of stars, all different sizes and densities, lickity-splitly appeared amongst the void. He was a genius and this inventive little maneuver guaranteed it wouldn't be long until the world caught wind of what he had on offer! I told him as much and he replied 'Speaking of which ...' nabbing up and opening my copy of the current issue of Darkhawk, pointing to one of the box advertisements in the Classified section '... why didn't you inform me of this?'

Right there, plain for all to see, was an announcement for a forthcoming comic book convention, right in town. None other than Hugh Hanes would be present. For the duration of the day-long event he would be available for casual conversation, to sign his autograph onto items, and would go so far as rendering original illustrations for an appropriate fee based on size and complexity.

'But most important: he'll be the sole arbiter of an Art Contest, open to all comers'. Alvin tapped the pertinent part of the advert. Indeed, a contest - with a handsome prize purse attached, to boot!

Well, he'd be a shoo-in if this Nexus illustration panned out as all signs pointed to its doing. Positively whiz-bang work!

So I truly hated to have to bring him down to Earth with the glum news a disembodied leg which could disguise itself as a length of sumac was at large and, what's worse, to admit to him how the best intelligence available could only state the leg killed in a nonspecific manner. 'And may be in cahoots with the other leg. The razor-blade covered leg. But only maybe.'

He nodded somberly.

As I turned to make my way back upstairs to get to work on Hugo, he asked if I could start the oven for him - he wanted to cook some chicken tenders. 'Sure' I said, wanting some too, but knew he probably didn't mean to share.

And as I exited, he chimed in how hopefully the sumac leg would dispense with The Ghostbusters, leaving us off the trouble of getting our hands dirty. 'As much as I'm reluctant to wish such a fate on anyone' he added.

No. Believe me, I hoped so, too. I'd forgotten all about The Ghostbusters until then. Really would prefer them to meet a grisly dispatch before I got too dismally behind with the strip.

.OCTOBER.

THE DISCOVERY OF MY BROTHER'S stashed away issue of Appleseed afforded me my first legitimate opportunity in life to give breasts a real once over. The pairs these illustrated ladies sported were rambunctious. The comic had a plot, so far as I could suss out, involving robotic exo-suits and some sort of rebellion. These tenacious soldiers showering off after a tough day of it in the training stocks made the politics seem rather inconsequential, though.

Meticulous, I set to re-hiding the slim volume. Precisely where and in which attitude I'd discovered it - back behind a makeshift blockade of crayon boxes, ceramic art Alvin had kilned in kindergarten, and three stacks of Jughead Double Digests. Was it just so? No. Spine the other way round. Now a tap more this way. That. Slight touch further.

Like defusing a landmine, re-secreting things!

Giving a peek out the window, I found the parking lot was a thick carpet of blackbirds. Or are they crows? If crows, there were murders and murders - a genocide of the rascals! I'd never seen such a gathering. Not a solitary one was moving - no bobbing, tapping concrete or soil with beaks, nibbling under wings. The large pile of trashbags at the lot corner - the collected refuse of the entire neighborhood for the week, pick-up being tomorrow - was entirely redacted. Birds coated the mound, a sharp chocolate shell over frozen yogurt. Overhead was a further thick of them. Hovering like bargain animation. Same three frames recycled through.

Probably nature had a reason for something like this. Even if not, I was mesmerized. Watched for more than an hour before undressing for the bath.

I'd brought an issue or two of Darkhawk along to peruse while I had my soak. Unfortunately, with my mind shuttling between a few considerations, I'd submerged my hands directly upon sinking into the tub, so the mags kept stacked on the toilet bowl, useless. Which may have been for the best. I couldn't seem to tether my mind down to Earth. Listened to the cackle of the four inches of suds as the mound covering me dwindled. The echo quality of this television static sizzle could easily be confused for soft scratches muted by the girth of walls and ceilings around me. Could those birds be covering the house as I lay submerged in the tub?

Such absurd associations hazed behind my eyes. I dozed and imagined for every soap-sud vanishing another immobile and soundless fowl would materialize outside.

But the entire hoard was gone by the time I dried off. No evidence whatsoever of their trespass remained. My memory started playing games with me. Had any of the birds been on the lawns? How was I uncertain? They'd been on the grass of the parking lot islands, the grass by the garbage. But had they been on the sidewalks, even? The shrubs, pricker bushes, groupings of flowers?

Anywhere?

I was more disquieted by where they'd only maybe-been than by the fact they'd been at all.

ALVIN AND I BUCKLED INTO our seats. Our mom was finishing up a banana, hadn't turned on the car, so we kept schtum until the din of her talk-radio got barking.

Alvin handled his poster-board with utmost care, pillowcase wrapped around it like sacrament cloth. I felt sorta crumby, not allowing him the entire backseat to lay it out. Then again, we both had things needed discussing. 'Best get all unpleasantness out of the way en route' he'd suggested, so we could enjoy the comic convention without a headful of wasps.

'You can lay it over my lap, I don't care' I offered.

But - no no - he was fine.

So I set to getting him up to speed on what was distressing me: On Tuesday and then on Wednesday I'd gotten conflicting information about my blackbirds.

'I thought they were crows.'

'They were birds which were black - let's not get overzealous about cataloguing them, eh?'

Our mutual friend Eno (from a neighborhood in the development's first entrance, clean half-mile from our specific cul-du-sac) had been outside the entire day I'd witnessed the swarm. All day and well into the evening. An impromptu flag football tournament followed by an extremely lengthy game of Mutants. He hadn't heard peep about birds of any color, let alone seen a plague of them covering the world.

This had relieved me. I was more than willing to consider the sight a fragment of dream which had misfiled as memory. Lord knows such things were possible.

But the following day after Art class, a kid who resided the neighborhood adjacent mine had, completely without solicitation, asked 'You see all those birds, Sunday?'

'When I pressed him' I explained to Alvin 'he said he hadn't seen them with his own eyes - claimed some kid I've never once heard of had talked about it at some birthday party for another kid I don't know.'

It was impossible to unknot such assertions. Alvin suggested I keep mindful of it all, but not dwell.

As for his news - it was far more graphic and unsettling. And just as was the case with mine, a secondhand element tainted it somewhat. The meat was: Our friend Pinchot (perfectly reliable chap, not given to flights of exaggeration) had intimated to Alvin the horror of accidentally stepping on a baby bird.

'Accidentally?'

'Coming home from Pizza Hut with his dad, late late at night, he felt a gooey crunch underfoot - right there on the walkway to his door. Was a bird, it turned out. Freshly hatched from the look of it.'

What was odd - as I knew for myself, having been over to Pinchot's house, plenty - was how there were no trees overhanging his front yard. A nest on his roof? Except: any hatchling would've had to've been blown some solid fifteen feet to alight where it had. Plus: the slant of the roof made it absurd to suggest wind would unsettle an object in that direction.

'Pinchot felt awful. Went to get paper towels to clean up the remains. Got back? Something like two dozen slugs had clotted over the carcass.'

My mom interrupted, asking incredulously what in Hell we were talking about. 'Is Pinchot killing birds, now?'

'Why're you listening to us? I thought that's what your radio's for?'

But she'd not be so easily diverted into moot chatter. So Alvin (quite impressively) ad-libbed some tap-dance concerning a book some older kid had told him about down at the playground the other day. 'A character is named Pinchot. Pinchot Pinchot, in fact. That's why it's so comical. Imagine the Pinchot we know and love embroiled in such circumstances! That'd be crackers!'

Over-under on my mom believing a word of that?

Not a wager I'd consider.

HUGH HANES, IN THE FLESH, seemed comfortable with me looming over his shoulder. Literally could whiff the peanut butter on my breath while he drafted a medium complexity sketch of The Punisher some conventioneer was plonking down ninety bucks for. Why I was allowed such intimate access? No clue. Hugh Hanes: consummate gentleman. My head swam.

Alvin comported himself with more refinement. Kept near at hand, with a befitting air of dignity, nonchalantly perusing an assortment of the hand-drawn, original comic book pages from issues of titles Hanes had worked on. Clever boy. No percentage insinuating himself on the man. Why risk coming off as though aiming to curry favor with regard to the Art Contest?

I eventually drifted over to join Alvin, shocked to discover how many of the original pages were from issues of Nexus I personally owned. Almost the entirety of the pivotal issue seventy-five was accounted for. The only glaring omission being the two-page spread wherein Stan gets obliterated by Lena Loomis during his duel with Horatio Hellpop.

'Oh I have that framed on my wall at home' Hanes said, having overheard us. 'Not for sale. Any price'

An artist's artist, through and through!

Soon he was deprecating how his life consisted largely of accepting he'd perpetually be the schmuck who followed in the shadows of iconic illustrators like Steve Rude, Jim Lee - a cursed sort, mark of Cain, burdened with the knowledge he was forever the poor man's someone-better. No doubt this disarming humility was the core reason Hanes drew enough water people like me would form orderly queues for autographs. Not to mention: four hundred, five hundred - one thousand dollars a pop for some of these pages! I'd lay even money the man could afford to purchase outright the whole church auditorium where he sat doodling and where two-dozen comic book shop representatives and specialty collector-resellers (both local and from neighboring cities) peddled their wares!

A kind of torture, being penniless in such a climate. I ached as I roamed the seller's tables, gaping at the bounty on display. Forget about original artworks - I couldn't even afford an issue of Badger! Why oh why did this portly retailer (all the way from Baltimore!) have the entire run of the series!? Dozens of issues I'd never once laid eyes on at Collector's World.

I struck a bargain: if I could convince some punter to purchase a pricier item, could I be rewarded a Badger for my efforts.

'Fine.' But the seller made it specific. 'Look over there' - chap holding a hardcover book of erotic prints, did I clock him? 'Get him to make good the transaction, Badger is all yours.'

Whatever song-and-dance rubbish I pitched worked a trick! Off he tromped with his sultry purchase and I dove into the bin to retrieve my due.

'Whoa whoa whoa' the seller chided as I made to dash off with a double-length, prestige format copy of Badger Bedlam 'you said an issue, man! Not a special. Think you can come in here running scams?' Shook his jowly head like he regretted someone so sleazy as me ever darkened his doorstep.

I made some buffoon apologies, trying to paint how it'd been a gag on my part. He glowered while I nabbed a random issue and beat my retreat.

Blessedly, here was Hanes. A true gallant! Let me sidle on back up to him. Stood even closer than previous. That'd get the stink off me so far as anyone who'd seen my earlier humiliation was concerned.

'Oh! He's tight with Hugh Hanes!'

'Obviously we've misjudged his character!'

'Peh! That seller was a real hockey puck!''

Yep. That's precisely the way posterity would record this.

NOT WINNING THE ART CONTEST had soured Alvin's demeanor. It was without doubt true how he said there was no need to hang out in the seller's area, not a dime to split between us. But being skint had never kept us from pointlessly browsing before. I didn't bring this up. Followed him to loiter in the parking lot the few hours until our mom would show up.

'You can go look at Badger or whatever' he shrugged. 'I'll come get you.'

'Naw' I replied, wave of my arm. Felt dismal having my con-man prize, him leaving the venue empty-handed, heart in shambles. It was a tough beat for even a seasoned veteran - couldn't imagine the blow to a starry eyed amateur. He'd been so certain those hot hundred prize dollars would be tucked down his pocket. 'You didn't lose' I ventured, trying on some sagacity 'it wasn't you versus someone, mano-a-mano. Pretty much everyone didn't win.'

But semantics fell flat. Alvin was older than me. Hip to how such hem-hawing was designed for palookas. Harsh fact: We'd seen with our own eyes the M.C. award top prize to some plain-cake sketch of a character from Elf Quest. Not even peripheral acknowledgement of Alvin's masterpiece.

Alvin fixated on how the M.C., in patter with Hanes, had remarked of the winning piece 'I recognize the character, definitely - but I've never seen this exact picture before.'

'Implying what? I traced mine? How am I supposed to trace through Bristol paper!?'

A fine question. I couldn't sort it, that's for sure. 'You got shanked' I said to no response. Added, not without genuine conviction 'Though it's kinda obvious the jam Hanes was in.' What did I mean? A person of his standing couldn't hazard any whiff of impropriety. 'Putting his finger on the scale - meanwhile having a close association with Nexus?' Danger of a besmirched reputation.

Alvin cogitated on this. Maybe he ought to've thought of that. Yes. Clout could be complicated. 'Still could've taken a quick minute, shot me a thumbs-up when nobody was looking. What would that've cost him?'

I was reluctant to side against my new friend Hugh, but had to grant Alvin this. Plus, far better to be politic, let the subject drift, than risk blurting out my true suspicion: I'd queered the deal on account of my big, fat mouth.

My mind churned the incidents around:

Number One: Hugh had been starting a new sketch for some fanboy - just had the rough outline down — when in fervent awe of the notable similarities in technique I'd crowed 'Man! My brother draws exactly like you!'

Number Two: (as if Number One wasn't enough!) when I walked away (not wanting to peel off like I didn't value the bond between us) I'd reiterated 'It's really amazing. My brother draws just like you. He did the Nexus picture. You'll seriously see.'

No reply. Only a fool would fail to recognize the implications.

No. Alvin must never know this.

I'd bear the shame to my grave.

DUSK SETTLED DOWN. THE HALLOWEEN sing-a-long an hour off. I'd have to walk to the school alone. My mom was working double hours, my dad was someplace. As alumni, Alvin could tag along if he felt like. He was occupied at Donovan's, however. Grinding out a high-score in Gunsmoke to snap a verification photo of. Gain notoriety in the pages of Nintendo Power, he hoped.

I couldn't get free of Pinchot's dead bird. Tons of slugs out overnight lately, so a highly believable narrative. Plus, the information was coming from Pinchot, according to Alvin. Add it up? The inherent veracity worked down my nerves. Distrusting my own eyes, even, would be a cinch. But this? It was as though the horror had befallen Pinchot specifically to cover my peace of mind in a damp sack!

I'd waffled between leaving for the school early (short-cutting though the creek while the sun still shone) or leaving as I was (last color sapping from the sky). No choice, now, but going the long way around. In the dark. Past the Montessori school, Community Playhouse, the neighborhood pool. Not exactly a Sunday stroll! Path sentried by tall grass brimming with burrs, tangled weeds where ticks gathered in flocks, telephone lines converging, belching static invisibly from time-to-time, shadows rising in tense fritzes from the mint-white, klaxon light of the Montessori. Disused transport vans peculiar across the theater's parking lot. Pavement in front of the pool an odd consistency, like treading on a picked at scab.

But the creek had seemed frothy with menace, daytime or not. Thoughts of out-of-place glints of sunlight catching on bark, moss, put me in mind of slug residue. Almost made myself frantic over memories of leaning against trunks. Oozing things perhaps taking aim on me. Consolidating into a single plump entity, size and girth of two veiny, strangling hands. Positioning overtop my unsuspecting, uncombed hair. Dropping down. Screwing into my head via eyeballs squirmed overtop of, around, through ears, up nostrils. Dining on me, inside to out, at a glacial leisure.

But able to delay no longer, I took a moment to brace myself at the neighborhood's edge. Glanced to the corner house where my family had lived until I'd turned four. Before something had altered. Before this progress, irrevocable, toward whatever was coming.

Back then, haunts would find me, but haunts would find me to give me comfort. As a walked I remembered: The babysitter sent me to bed early. Misbehavior. I'd cried and cried. Climbed into the crib which still occupied the room, more decorative catchall than anything of use. A noise like clicking. Through the slats I saw a skeleton. Reclined in a squat little chair. Pipe pinched in teeth. Its gaze rested on me, serene. Book spread open, face down, over kneebone. 'I am B U One Skeleton' it whispered. Told me to listen. To listen to the stories it would read.

As I walked I remembered: A week later it was discovered how wasps had built a tumorous nest inside my bedroom window. Could flatten and creep their way in while I slept.

THE SHADOW OF MS. PEABODY'S ballpoint pen made gigantic progress across the gymnasium wall. Flicked on each word of the projected lyrics. Tapped the appropriate syllable count for each. *The worms crawl in / the worms crawl out / the worms play pi-noch-le on your snout* ...

These sing-a-longs, sat in the dark, were the only variety I ever participated in. But tonight I didn't want to be there, amongst everybody. After the third song, I claimed an urgent need for the toilet. A sixth grade teacher, Mr. Slinker, manned the gymnasium's double doors. Alvin had got on well with him and he knew me, vaguely. Let me out, no protest.

The corridors stretched in darkness. Weakling auxiliary lights every fifteen yards along the blue of the painted brick walls. Exit sign red. Seepage from the orange lights of the playground, the parking lot.

I could hear a muffle of song as I loitered at the toilet bowl, not needing to void but figuring I owed the world the play act. *O'Reely is dead and O'Reily don't know it / O'Reily is dead and O'Reely don't know it* ... No reason to flush, I swayed, arms held in pantomime waltz, singing in whisper *they both lying dead in the very same bed / and neither one knows how the other one's dead* ... Squirt of pink soap, scrubbed my hands, attempted with wet palms without success to tame my hair down.

I was reluctant to return to the gym.

Slinker hadn't come poking his nose around for me after two more songs, so I imagined it safe to roam the halls as I saw fit. But my favorite song started up. Decided to hear it out. Pressed forehead to the chilly, grid-lined windows just outside the gym.

There was an old woman all skin and bones
Oo ooo oo oooo

Were those flashlights? I squinted out past the basketball courts, down the hill to the long jump pit, beyond the tree-line separating school property from the wooded area which would eventually join the creek over near my house.

Who lived down by the old graveyard
Oo ooo oo oooo

Definitely. Multiple. Nervous ticking beams of light while a group of indeterminate number made its way through the brambles.

One night she thought she'd take a walk
Oo ooo oo oooo

Who were they? What numbskulls would risk mucking around a creek in the pitch?

She walked down by the old graveyard
Oo ooo oo oooo

Another kid, dressed dark, made a clumsy beeline across the kickball field, burst through some shrubs to join the gaggle.

She saw the bones all layin' around
Oo ooo oo oooo

Clearly older than Alvin. Lank of a tenth, eleventh grader. This had to be The Ghostbusters. I could see no two ways about it.

So went to the closet to get a broom
Oo ooo oo oooo

An abrupt metallic rattle, unmistakable as the gym doors opening, caused me to jump, tense, tuck myself into the wall corner, a louder *oo ooo oo ooo* faded as the doors drifted shut under their own power.

No one. Then Mr. Slinker, failing to notice me, opened the Boy's Room. 'Ichabod?'

And when she'd cleared the bones away

'Right over here Mr. Slinker.'

Oo ooo oo oooo

He must not've heard me.

She saw the church and thought to pray

'Ichabod?' he tried into the Girl's Room.

Oo ooo oo oooo

'Mr. Slinker?'

She tarried at the church's door

I must've been soaked up by some odd blob of shadow.

Oo ooo oo oooo

He passed his eyes right over me. Took a few uncertain strides down the corridor.

And in the aisle she tarried more

'Ichabod?'

Oo ooo oo oooo ...

I SCOOTED IN BESIDE ENDIE.

'Mr. Slinker's been prowling the crowd, casing for you.'

'How do you know?'

'He asked Where's Ichabod? Seemed obvious what he meant.'

This put the kibosh on my scheme to claim I'd been present all the while, no fault of mine if Slinker didn't recall my re-entry. Age playing tricks on him. Immaterial, in the long run. I took a glance around, all seemed calm. 'Endie, we need to talk, man. The Ghostbusters are out, in numbers.'

Endie pointed out how this seemed par for the course, as far as gangs.

In no head for deadpan zingers, I laid a rap on him how this likely meant some big league caper was in the offing, even as we sat chatting so enjoyably! 'They're taking advantage of the whole town being here.' Okay. He had a point. Our parents weren't. And they represented their primary threat. 'But most of them are out on dates, probably.'

Endie gave me the signal we'd been zeroed in on by some second grade teacher so I might wanna pipe down. Ought I risk yet another ejection from assembly?

I wished he'd let me tend to my own affairs, but proceedings were wrapping up, regardless. There went Mrs. Terre, braying about how 'The last number of the night was written by my big hunk of man hubby' (woot woots, whistles, laughter from staff and suck-ups) 'and I like to think it's become a local classic.'

'Because you shoehorn it into every assembly' I mumbled, more to amuse myself than even for Endie to hear. In order to appear attentive, his eyes were strategically glued to the school band lining up.

Yep. That second grade teacher had a bead on me. Wasn't missing a mutter. I turned all attention forward.

'Without further ado - Ghost Walk!' Mrs. Terre exclaimed, abusing her authority to milk some pre-emptive applause before the tune even got started.

I lambasted Mrs. Terre and her toady husband righteously while Endie and I crossed the field in the dark, taking a moment to use the slide before pressing on.

Yes, yes - he agreed the ditty was overall a drub, but what harm did it do anyone? 'And you know it might not've been The Ghostbusters you saw, right?'

Plus, he had another good thought: what were we supposed to do if they were at the bus stop? Nobody had come up with any concrete maneuver, he pointed out, and it'd only be the two of us versus them!

I was about to tweak his nose for being so lily-livered when (A) I realized he was absolutely correct (B) it hit me how I didn't want to confront them either and (C) my foot kicked a flashlight which then skittered to the edge of the grass, struck against concrete.

We instinctively went to our bellies. Rigid. Stared at the grey breath panting from each other's mouths.

Silence. Stillness. Nothing.

Nothing.

My teeth were chattering by the time Endie rabbited his head up, glancing left, right, up (for some reason) and back the way we'd come.

All clear, he shrugged.

The concrete the flashlight had struck was at the top of the entrance mouth to one of the large sewer tunnels. We skidded our way cautiously down the steep incline of this access port. The tunnel gaped, impenetrable, in front of us. Sour trickle of creek water behind. Chunks of cinderblock, piles of quartz rock kids tugged from the sand banks, broken glass, plastic bags - all this rubbish shifting under foot.

'I don't think they went in there' Endie said after a time, the remark inserted flawlessly into my exact line of thinking.

I leaned in. Peering.

'You said they all had flashlights. We'd see the rest of them, you know?'

Noncommittally and not turning back to Alvin I probed 'Literally last night, though? Nickels saw them and you talked to him?'

Alvin was silent, so I glanced up. I'd been expecting some confrontational posture, instead saw he was watching the television, seeming, like me, to be sleuthing out which area of the night sky was being celebrated. He asked me, eyes not averting from the screen 'What was Dr. Who about?'

'Dunno' I said (only honest answer to any episode starring Colin Baker).

He chuckled. Then with abrupt and non-sequitur zest clapped his hands, turned, and proclaimed to me how he was honestly going to start watching The New Red Green. 'And I mean beginning to end - every Saturday night. It's big time stuff in Canada, someone told me. And it might be funny, now that I'm older.' In addition, he was giving due diligence to the consideration he might campaign for Class Treasurer or else take up drawing a political cartoon he'd photocopy and pass around at school on the regular.

Not a certified psychoanalyst, none of these pronouncements could I make heads nor tails of. One thing for sure was they made me realize Alvin was in some sort of acute, diagnosable state. Now was not only not the time to have a serious tete-e-tete, but any of his previous remarks ought only be given minimal scrutiny, as well.

We heard our dad's sluggish trudge up the stairs. And (after a few clicks of adjustment to the thermostat, the walls beginning to whir) he promptly picked the bedroom lock (simple operation, pad of his thumb pressed down, given a little twist) and quite self-importantly informed us of the current time (wrong by forty-five minutes) and how we were to go to sleep.

'We are.' Alvin doused the lights to prove it. Buttoned the television off, screen sizzling, snapping bacon-fat static crackle crackle as it powered down.

We waited in the pitch until we heard the hellion creak of bedsprings groaning under his weight. Another five minutes until he was done blowing his nose and the first snore issued.

Crept to the basement in tandem, finagled the glass sliding door open noiselessly, and wandered over to the long row of poison-ivy tinged picker bushes where often, in our younger days, we'd made forts. Both of us were fatigued so tottered, swayed in loops accordingly, my body shuddering in a kind of numb buzz, now and then.

But we staunchly chit-chatted even through shivers. Slack-jawed and eyes trained skyward through the crosshatch of powerlines. Pointing at and (one eye shut) tracing the flightpaths of planes. Trying to spot UFOs or to convince ourselves one-hundred-percent it wasn't UFOs we were already seeing.

NEAR THREE IN THE MORNING, Alvin dropped his efforts to tune in channel fifty. He'd boasted how there'd this one time been a show called Sweating Bullets which depicted actual nudity. Even despite the brackish static programs on fifty had to be filtered through he'd seen everything some ladies had to offer. I took his word for Gospel. Nevertheless, he wanted to see maybe was it on. 'Just to prove it'.

'There was a topless woman on Rumpole of the Bailey, once' I suddenly recalled and tossed the fact out there, supportive of Alvin's agenda.

Utterly nonplussed, he wouldn't humor this assertion for a second. 'PBS doesn't go in for tits at two in the afternoon, Ick.'

Soon he had channel fifty-four tuned in. Late Night Kung-Fu Theatre was just starting up. This time around the offering was a genuine flop entitled The Incredible Kung-Fu Mission. We tried to the make the most of things, but the picture was such a turkey even cracking wise couldn't redeem it.

'When I wish I was watching Gymkata, something's gone ripe' Alvin summed up derisively.

So our conversation drifted.

As far as kung-fu went, what concerned Alvin was hashing out whether any movie starring a counterfeit Bruce Lee - Bruce Li, Bruce Le, Bruce Liu - was the least bit good. 'Let's put the matter to bed and have done with it, once and for all - shall we?'

But first, a pressing side-investigation: were those people truly named that?

'Like by their moms you mean?'

That's what he meant, alright. See: Alvin smelled a marketing gimmick. Cynical cash grab films, nevermind they were usually such trash they'd not earn back their shoestrings.

But I saw the matter through a different aperture and felt bound to say so. They didn't, personally, want to trade on Bruce Lee's name at all! Quite the contrary: what happy chance how Li, Le, Liu et al. could find opportunities, take their collective shot, hunker down to giving it their all in a gambit to rise from obscurity! Any shenanigans, so far as I could see, were on the part of unscrupulous cover artists and poster makers!

Returning to the main vein of conversation: I submitted The Furious Killer was good. Affidavit evidence: 'I can still sing the song from the disco club fight after two years and one viewing!' Alvin called what he thought was my bluff so I belted out *'Love, everyone love / smile, everyone smile / Dance, everyone have a ball ...'* before the jangle of my mom turning the front door latch broke in and we both shut our traps.

To the sounds of the microwave's hum and rattle-rattle, accompanied by the rising aroma of thawing lasagna-for-one, we zapped the television off, climbed into bed proper, and Alvin switched the radio on, tuning in Q-107.3. As the top of the hour hit (news, sports, weather, plus commercials) I figured Alvin had fallen asleep so positioned myself to luxuriantly break wind, when suddenly, full-throated, he said 'Nate's full of crap a lot.'

I clenched my butt cheeks, hiccoughed, ahemed, and shifted to my side. 'What crap's he full of?'

The jabberwocky Alvin laid out left me flabbergasted! The most shocking morsel of balderdash being how Nate had made claim he'd 'Been chased by a shoulder which can turn into a really big tortoise.'

'A shoulder?'

Trust him, Alvin had not let such preposterousness go unchallenged. What it turned out was: Nate had meant 'the shoulders - both shoulders - and part of the back and the chest' (Alvin related this in dope-toned mimic of Nate's drooly lisp).

'He was chased by a torso?'

Alvin snorted 'I guess.'

And - sure, of course - I sided with Alvin. Yet part of me couldn't shake how it wasn't altogether impossible, Nate's alleged experience. The torso wasn't explicitly accounted for in our records. The going theory? It was sat someplace, like a termite queen, and if its beating heart was pulverized all the Disembodied Parts would shrivel due to no longer having it to re-attach to and suckle nutrients from.

'Exactly!' Alvin whisper-shouted, fist clenched definitive.

'Plus: what does a shoulder kill with?'

And I'd hit square on the other telltale! 'Nate says it doesn't kill as the shoulder - it kills as the turtle!'

Why's it ever bother being a shoulder, then?

'This is what I have to contend with on the day-to-day, Ick' Alvin lamented, voice gravelly, not quite his normal volume, but loud. 'He's either some looney-toon or else causing confusion to get some kinda sick kicks.'

I could see either scenario turning out to be the case. Never had much cared for Nate. Not since he'd that one time tackled me in football when I'd absolutely explained to everyone I was only to be tagged out.

'Either way' Alvin added after another few minutes silence 'talk like that's gonna wind up with blood on its hands.'

.NOVEMBER.

'I KNOW EXACTLY WHAT I want!' I beseeched. Slap-slapped both palms to the glass door of Collector's World. Quite the scene. I felt like primetime television.

But naw, nope, Shine and Cohen, the jolly proprietors, both shrugged, mouthing 'We're closed' and 'Tomorrow.'

Panting, still winded due to the sprint from my dad's car which now idled around the corner, I flattened my money to the glass. 'One minute, sirs' I adjured 'thirty seconds!'

Shine moseyed over after making me sweat it out another beat, pouting while he undid the latch how I was no fun. But over my shoulder, as I went to the bin to retrieve my purchase, I heard him grant 'No, that's not true - you're fun' after which he and Cohen did impersonations of my begging at the door.

It was interesting how they'd take my cash but not ring the sale until morning. Cash register counted down already. Money left on the counter.

The world is odd. ˙

Though what could it matter to me?

Because here it was: The Steve Rude Sketchbook. Volume housed in plastic sheath with cardboard backing. Twenty bucks plus tax (I'd paid to the penny).

My dad had agreed to let me make the purchase, conditional to his inspecting the volume's contents. And 'No' I couldn't even look through it in the car on the drive home.

But I'd looked through it plenty, before. Which is why my fears. Perhaps the amount of nude sketches in the book would have it taken away from me.

Shine and Cohen had been reluctant, in a vague way, to sell it when I'd first broached the transaction but I'd sworn I had parental okay. They'd even phoned my mom to be covered as far civil suits went, forewarned her of the T&A element. 'It's elegant - but they're quite naked' Shine had said, qualifying 'yeah' after a pause while my mom had pressed for specifics 'naked everyplace.'

Thus I'd been building up an eloquent defense of Art and the like. Indeed, I'd got so anxious about this that even before my dad cracked the cover of the thing I'd started in (my erudite defense would be Plan B, only dipped into in the face of belligerence) promising how 'I know there's tons of naked women in it - I promise, I couldn't be bothered. I'm planning to tear those pages out, to avoid any chance of being waylaid from my true aims. Don't worry about my barking up that tree.'

Turns out my dad didn't care a tinker's damn about the nudes. In fact, the old man gave a very well articulated speech, exactly in line with what I was going to say had push come to shove. What he seemed to find a disdain concerning - for reasons which passeth understanding, so far as I was concerned - was how a few pages contained cuss words. He would allow me to have the book, but needed to scribble these words out in order to make the volume less incendiary.

'Uh ... okay.'

Did he think I'd object? If anything, I wanted to point out how - as I already knew what words were being obfuscated - covering them over in ballpoint ink did little to take the curse off anything.

But I kept it cool. Let him thoroughly redact the word Shit from the phrase These pens're really fulla shit sometimes! on the very last page, a word-bubble affixed to an ink rendering of W.C. Fields.

No skin off my teeth.

OF COURSE THE NUDES HAD been my primary objective. Not to devalue Steve Rude's other offerings. My favorite artist, bar none. And this sketchbook was a treasure trove, exceeding my expectations incalculably! Look here at some pages from an OMAC comic he'd done in college! Laid side-by-side with some pages from Nexus issue fifty to show off certain interesting similarities in concept and layout.

But the nudes ... well! How about I just come out and say it, same as anyone else looking might: they were exquisite, the way bumping into a common tongue in Babel might be. The pencil work, pen strokes, the perfection of lines of curves uninterrupted, of lip and hip, shoulders, dimpled lower back. All top dollar!

Oh yes - there were mysteries to unravel, a mature understanding to nourish my bourgeoning talents and aesthetic. Out of my league, entirely, let me add. I had in no way ever attempted to render an anatomically correct human figure before, let alone to replicate the proportions of a goddess.

Hugo Plyankoff MD? The characters in there were rendered as such: small circle for head, oval (or large circle if the character was portly or muscularized) for body. Stick arms, stick legs, hands and feet merely shaded in circles.

Make no mistake - I could accomplish a bunch within the obstruction of my lack of refined talent. But I made no bones about admitting my skills weren't traditional or rarified. No. Not like Alvin. There was an illustrator - and don't you forget who told you so!

The main pitfall I would face with my art-lessons, especially during the initial learning curve wherein I'd have to scrutinize these drawings and fail fail fail, tap my way nearer to anything even resembling a proper woman one scrawl at a time, was how to go about sketching tons of naked ladies without my parents getting hip to the scene and trying to figure out what gives and how to gum me up. They were sensitive to artistic objectives, my mom and dad, no trouble there. But I was not quite ready to put my faith in their choosing not to err on the side of assuming they had a budding pornographer to set-right if they stumbled upon stacks of drawings depicting unclothed women produced by their nine-year old second-born.

Solution?

In the weeks prior to purchasing the sketchbook I'd made a survey of all of the books about cats we had in the house (a lot) and had persuaded my mom to buy me a load of small spiral notebooks (pocket-sized) from the grocery store. The covers of these I had labeled Cat Stuff and made certain, within eyeshot of my mom, to be seen attempting realist renditions of felines and to find countless excuses to show off the works-in-progress to my dad, sometimes going so far as to leave a Cat Stuff notebook on the dining table in amongst his work papers and to playact 'Have you seen my sketchbook?' of an evening.

By now, prying eyes would be inured to these sketchbooks and the remaining blank notebook I'd designated for nudies would slink under the radar.

IT BUTTRESSED MY DROOPING CONFIDENCE when Alvin remarked how he thought I was getting breasts down admirably. He allowed I had quite the knack for a little kid who'd never glimpsed the real deals.

'Except on Rumpole' I reminded him, but he politically acted as though he'd not heard.

Here Donovan piped in 'What about Rumpole?'

Trying to put enough authority in his voice to nip further conversation on the subject in the bud, Alvin said I harbored delusions how some chick had flashed Rumpole.

'No one's gonna flash their personal tits at Leo McKern, Ichabod.'

'Leo McKern has kids! One is even on the show.'

But, very sophistically, Donovan submitted: this doesn't mean his lover specifically had to've flashed him any skin. 'There's all kinds of ways to keep a shirt on.'

I didn't bother pointing out how McKern wasn't party to the scene in question or how, either way, they could've filmed the topless bit in an entirely different take or just asked him to leave the room a minute if it was going to stall production.

Alvin did have a few stern critiques about my rendering of the collarbone. 'You should know what that looks like just from anyone. Naked ladies aren't different from common everyday people in certain respects.'

'That's just there as placeholder for now' I explained. Had to repeat this remark when Donovan mentioned the triangle with a line down its center I'd jotted to designate the vaginal area looked uncannily similar to how he'd drawn chicken feet in kindergarten.

'It's harder to draw that realistically than you'd think. Believe me, I've been studying these drawing diligently and I just don't get it.'

But we had batter fish to fry, Alvin reminded us, imploring me to back-burner my kinky hobbies at least for the time being.

Tonight was the night we'd have it out with The Ghostbusters. Close proximity combat. No holds barred. We were gonna ride down on 'em like gangbusters and by the time we were done they'd never show their sorry tails in these environs again.

'Wabash Moon is our beat!' I wooted, trying for a hoo-rah! from the others but they had no idea what I meant. 'It's from a story called the Juke Box Kid.' This elaboration made no difference to them. 'From that old Shadow pulp mag I bought.'

Oh Alvin recalled that, now - recalled I'd spent forty-eight dollars on it and boy howdy hadn't it turned out to be racist!

'Only the advertisements were racist!'

If I said so, he said.

'Besides which: we were at war in those days! The Japs actually had a secret new airplane called Zero! Were we not supposed to get the word out?'

He conceded the point, took a jab at how another advert had touted 'The miracle of asbestos' - a revelation Donovan mumbled 'Jesus' about although I didn't see what the fuss was.

'Do you even know what asbestos is?'

'Do you?'

'Yes.'

'But did you at my age, I mean.'

Alvin was right, though. We needed to focus. 'We are at war. That's who's at war. In the present. Not the nineteen whenevers!'

Okay. I agreed. Especially when Donovan said keeping ourselves tight and functioning as a unit could be the difference between a black and eye and a regular eye.

Had I ever had a black eye? No. Did I feel like starting tonight?

I had to admit I'd like to avoid it as far as I had control over.

'And what would you tell mom and dad?' Alvin added with a sagacious nod.

I'd probably just tell dad Alvin had done it in a fit of pique. But I didn't tell Alvin this because of the previously made good point about harmony in the ranks.

IMPOSSIBLE TO BELIEVE, BUT MY dad had agreed to let Alvin and I, along with Donovan, sleep out back in the area of trees between our row of houses and the row flanking ours. Up to this moment, his avowed and militant stance was staunchly anti-sleepover. His reasons were many and varied, but could be summed up thus: he didn't trust, believe to be sane, or want to even peripherally have dealings with the adults responsible for progenerating any child other than us.

Alvin had dished it out slick about how 'in school we're reading something by Jack London' and part of a graded assignment was to camp out and 'keep a log of it.'

A clever enough ruse, so far as things went, though I was astonished it had passed the sniff test, utterly uncontested. But here we were.

The plan was: Alvin would head out first, do a thorough reconnaissance while meantime Donovan and I manned the fort and kept up the appearance of a bona fide camp-out. Upon Alvin's return, we'd trek out together and split off for the attack.

I was to serve as decoy. Brazenly approach the gang (nunchucks concealed) as though I were a scofflaw out to get in good with them. Concurrently, Alvin and Donovan would approach from the hill across the street from the bus stop, starting seventy yards apart – they'd pincer in from East and West ('Or left and right' Alvin changed this to, just to avoid confusion) and (knock wood) approach the turned backs of unsuspecting foes.

The Ghostbusters, caught with their pants handily down, would be fish in a barrel for Alvin's bo-staff and the length of pipe Donovan had luckily discovered leaned against a dumpster two days previous.

Once Alvin had set off, Donovan swung on the rope which once had a wood seat attached to it while I ate oatmeal cookies. He was still convinced his plan to arm ourselves with glass bottles was the better bet. He reiterated how (A) these punks would be drinking and (B) all a person had to do was watch any movie to confirm breaking a bottle over someone's head put them down like a champ.

'We couldn't even break bottles against that tree branch, Don.'

'Tree branches are pliable. Plus, things bounce off them.' He did have a point how we'd have the adrenaline of the moment working on our behest. 'I'm guessing they have beer bottles is all - so this way we'd be evenly matched.'

I still wished we'd decided to throw rocks from a distance. But Donovan sided with Alvin how this failed our main objective. To wit: if The Ghostbusters started getting hit by rocks, they'd just run away and have no idea what the intent of those rocks had exactly been. Afterward, how're we supposed to ever dream we'd get the drop on them?

'Reinforcements' Donovan said. 'Other Ghostbusters.'

All poppycock, so far as I was concerned. But Alvin also made the good point how once you throw a rock you lose control. Someone might turn all of a sudden - Whacko! - lose an eye. The same isn't true with nunchucks, pipes, and bamboo staffs. We'd have a lot of control with those. We didn't want to blind these Visigoths. They just needed to find another bus stop.

I COULDN'T RECKON A POLITIC way to float to Donovan how hitting someone with a rusty pipe might not be advisable, in application. Could lead to infection, if nothing else.

We were stealthing our way past what was known as the Little Park - the most popular of some half-dozen play-areas dotting the development - en route to the bus stop.

Alvin'd been away a solid hour. Were he wheezing his last, rolled into some ditch, bag of lawn clippings slashed open, dumped to obscure his makeshift grave, we wanted to have shown at least a minimum effort toward rescue.

Not that I was truly worried. Alvin would've known to play possum, act knocked out before he'd actually been knocked out had he found himself outnumbered or the tide otherwise turned against him. We'd all discussed this. An Official Strategy. Secondary application: act knocked out so the person fighting you turns to attack someone still viable, then stand up to catch him out from behind, unawares.

The bus stop.

Deserted.

Silent.

Cold.

Something in the air smelled sweet the way garbage could.

'I'm certain they haven't killed him literally, Ick' Donovan reassured, queasy voiced, as I twirled my nunchucks, peering from my concealment behind a damp woodpile outside some house's backyard fence.

But where was Alvin?

Where was anybody?

We opted to make a wide, strategic approach. Back through the Little Park, up the hill into our pal Quincy's neighborhood, across the road at the development's third entrance, crested the hill by the office buildings under construction. We kept ducked down. Sprinted the field. Got round to where Alvin had said he'd do his sentry work.

Nobody. Nothing.

Bus stop deserted, even yet. Mint orange streetlight falling chill on empty brick.

Hop-skipped over and stood inside the house-like structure.

Zero beer bottles, cigarette butts, candy wrappers, signs of struggle, bloodstains.

'It does smell a little like cat piss' Donovan observed.

He probably meant dog piss. Would've been more accurate, anyway. Why split hairs, though, seeing as I got his drift?

Suddenly: Donovan yelped, backed up, this nudging me forcefully enough I slipped and stuck against the rough brick where two walls cornered. The see-saw clanging of his dropped pipe and my shoe's scuffing kept me from hearing exactly what he was saying - pointing through the window at the curved brick wall with the neighborhood's name affixed and a groomed patch of shrubbery on its other side.

Donovan leaned to the window ledge, taut, and I stiffly joined him.

A ruckus of mulch.

'There - there, there, there! - do you see 'em!?'

Flickering of shadow accompanied by skittering clickity-clack - some animal dashing across the road pavement, disappearing down an only half-grated sewer drain.

Silence.

Silence.

Donovan said we needed to beat it, no gag - didn't even bother retrieving his bludgeon.

He was calmer once we neared my house, but I hadn't yet got any semblance of a proper debriefing. Was clearing my throat, addressing myself to motion as though to indicate I needed answers but ... 'What in Hell is that?' I hissed, instead.

From some eighty yards off, we scoped the beam from a flashlight slicing left-right, right-left, up-downing and diagonaling the area by the rope-swing where we had our camp. And while it would've been sounder to have hung back, gathered facts, some kind of shock response numbed both Donovan and I. We strode forward, casual as can be.

My dad trained a flashlight on us, leveling the light in our eyes longer than was strictly necessary, the gesture not seeming tender or parental.

Where had we been?

A fair question.

I suggested we'd been just over at the park a quick minute 'because we thought we heard fireworks and wanted to see if we could get a look from the top of the slide' very glad Donovan was no longer armed, seeing as I was already having to add 'and these nunchucks are something I found, by coincidence'.

Cue Alvin making his way, bo-staff twirling ever so carefree, whisper-bellowing 'Turn off that light, morons - and stop talking or you'll wake up dad.' Comic beat. 'Oh hi dad.' Comic beat. 'We were just talking about you.'

I WAS IN THE SCHOOL library, voting for Ross Perot. The man had quite a constituency, so far as I could tell. Handily secured the election, only a few kids tossing folded slips of paper into the box supporting Clinton. Evidence suggested they did so merely to give them an excuse to say 'Bubba' as many times as possible during the day. It was clear these children didn't even know that wasn't their so-called preferred candidate's surname. And if these were the sort of followers the man was looking to garner with his lowest-common-denominator charisma, well, I could see why talk-radio had it in for the guy!

I'd been hipped to Perot by Frank, a man who lived three houses down. He was wont to invite neighborhood kids and their sundry moms and dads down to his basement to flaunt the neat things he adorned his life with. Satellite television. Super Nintendo. Gun Safe.

'Vote for Perot. He's self-made. Has a vision. Those others are dynasty politicians, bamboozlers. Don't be bamboozled' he told me once, taking a break from mowing his lawn long enough to endow me this wisdom.

'I won't' I vowed while he tugged on the choke and the perfect crisp of gasoline coated my nostrils.

I'd learned later on how the rest of the nation hadn't been given the dope so straight and thus the country was poised to steer onto unbelievably disastrous tracks.

A kid who wanted to be my pal but frankly was a tad cloying for my likes took full advantage of our being seated together (we were to work on a cut-and-paste) to strike up some banter. He wasn't a bad guy, turned out. We had a lot in common. He wanted to learn Jeet Koon Do, I wanted to learn Jeet Koon Do. So I was glad to rap with him how there were advertisements in the back pages of Inside Kung-Fu for various manuals or videocassette courses. I knew I was lazy as a carp, when all was said and done, but had convinced myself that since I didn't want to be 'good' and by no means 'noteworthy' at the martial art even the most lackadaisical home-study would serve my purposes.

The kid agreed and put the matter succinctly enough: If Bruce Lee was the best, then learning from his personal playbook, even if I only wound up a thousandth as talented as the man, should put me on the same level with an intermediate student who took themselves seriously, stuck to a disciplined schedule, but only availed themselves of more commonplace instruction.

But before this kid could get convinced we'd reached the bosom-buddy stage, I excused myself on some pretext of remembering about a book I was supposed to borrow for my little brother who went to another school that didn't have it.

I'd developed a stern addiction to Archway oatmeal cookies, such a fiend I carried them in my pockets and snuck bites no matter if the time was opportune. I'd eat the cookies stacked two at-a-time because the effort and ache to my jaw of working the chewiness into swallowable slop was exquisite. True, they weren't as delectable as the hard oatmeal cookies my dad would bring home from the National Institute of Health, but there was little I could do about this seeing as that specific variety of confection was only distributed directly by the United States federal government. Plus: even if I asked him to bring a lot home I'd be lucky if he remembered any.

Just now, I ducked down the Biography aisle, tearing an oversized bite into my maw. At the window was Donovan, motioning I should join him in the hall. Mouth full, I just shrugged, sloshing of mastication soundtracking the pantomime of his insistence, my head tilting to indicate how he knew as well as I it was notoriously difficult to finagle a Bathroom Pass during Library because the entire class always stops on the way to and from.

So he motioned me to stay put while he glanced around for purposes unknown. Finally, he pulled what turned out to be a crisp dollar bill from his rear pocket and used a crayon plucked from the cart outside the near-at-hand Art room to write: Last Night - Cat and Opssum [sic] - together.

When he'd cottoned to I'd read this, he flipped the bill over and started scribbling.

I took a bite from a new cookie pair.

The reverse of the bill read: What parts even are left??

BEFORE WE BEGAN, WE ASSURED Donovan, who insisted on raking up graves, that 'Yes, our dad's a kook. He sounds like Dracula, yes, he has a fluid relationship with logic, yes yes, but he's garden variety nuts, nothing to file a report over.'

Here's the shot: Donovan, on the night of our Ghostbuster busting campaign, hadn't been allowed to return to his own house after my dad had terminated our camp out. Indeed, he was made to sleep on the sofa while Alvin and I had been sent to our room.

'No, seriously, it's one minute that way' he'd said.

Not a chance.

So I suppose I could see why it lingered on his nerves.

But how did this make me or Alvin the answer men or issuers of apologia? As though either of us could explain the thought processes of a man who'd been older than both of us combined by the lead up to the second World War!

Alvin declared enough was enough. 'Facts' he insisted 'we need facts!' We couldn't allow some random chatterboxes or sewing circles to confound our efforts viz the Disembodied Parts.

Okay: a cat and an opossum? Was this the thing?

Alvin could vouch for the cat - he'd seen it when he set up his stake-out.

'No, there was no sign The Ghostbusters had been recently devoured.'

Both he and Donovan independently described its color as 'marmalade', which would've eased me out a heckuva lot more if marmalade was an actual color.

This could be the mandela effect for all I knew! Same with the opossum. It was the opossum I'd probably seen - but what had I seen? Could've been the cat.

'It was both!' Donovan demanded. 'Pressed right up on each other like they were conjoined or stitched that way!'

But the twenty-thousand-dollar question: what parts? There's only so many parts to a human body, after all!

Checklist: head, torso (taken with a grain of salt, but nevertheless), arms left and right, hands left and right, legs left and right, feet left and right.

'That's a person!'

'What about a dick or a butt?'

Is this where the hands on the clock had come to? 'Here lie The Ghostbusters: Jolly-Rogered by a disembodied dick!'

And what, praytell, would a dick kill with? Had anyone thought of that?

Plus: where were the corpses, eh? Upwards of a dozen Ghostbusters just vanished into the thin night air?

'The butt could've ...' Donovan made a gesture of turning his hand from palm-up to palm-down '... absorbed them' and finished off with a kind of slurping sound.

'The butt could have absorbed, bare minimum, seven-to-ten teenage hooligans? This is hysteria talking, Don! What butt could pull a feat like that? Absorb them where?'

He supposed I had a point. Yes. He conceded I certainly had a fair point.

And on top of that, well, it's difficult to imagine a butt arming itself with something.

'But there aren't other parts left.'

'Except' - and keep in mind how he hated to say this, oh Donovan truly hated to say this - 'what about what Dale Beech said that time?'

'Dale Beech is probably a Ghostbuster, himself - he's certifiable!'

Alvin concurred, but wanted to get the shot.

In summary: Dale Beech once claimed there to be two bodies - a male and a female.

'Which gels, frankly, with something Winshaw said.'

'Oh Christ Jesus' I groaned 'Winshaw!?'

'Winshaw's your friend, Ick.'

'He's not my friend. He's just someone I one time accidentally swindled out of seventy-five cents - that's different than friendship!'

Focus! What had Winshaw said?

'He said it all started in the Civil War'.

'Alvin' I had to call halt 'do you have any idea how many things Winshaw claims have to do with the Civil War?'

On the other hand: didn't the Civil War dead roam the train tracks over in Fern Glen?

Hmn ... Well ... The Civil War dead did, yes, in fact roam the train tracks over in Fern Glen.

Didn't those same tracks connect over by Criswell Chevrolet?

They did.

'Facts!' Alvin said, fist-to-palm. 'Facts are facts. I'm all for speculation and interpretation so long as we don't forget that speculation's speculating or what interpretation's interpreting.'

'Facts' I mumbled, testing the word out.

'Unless I'm wrong' Alvin sighed, end of tether 'you tell me.'

THE SHAPE, HEFT, THE RELAXED give of this woman's buttocks was eluding me artistically. Steve Rude made his penciled sketch seem at once weightless and stoutly, three-dimensionally thick. Where the woman's flesh touched with the floor she posed upon - how did he capture that pressure?

Page after page after page of my stabs at rendering the same image as he had produced flanks without curve, a buttock squared, almost Lego-sharp whereas he managed plush melt and delectable suppleness.

I was hesitant to make fugitive, studious glimpses to the backsides of class-mates, teaching staff, grocery clerks, or members of the female populace at large. The few times I did, with nary an exception, there was nothing re-motely rectangular or right-angled about the anatomy.

Same problem with shoulders. And Lord help me, I'd never solve the mys-tery of how to render an armpit with any semblance of grace.

'You could probably draw strong people' Endie said as I gave up this twen-tieth time in-a-row. He meant my renditions of breasts, especially if depicted near underarms, seemed quite muscular.

I was briefly chuffed. Imagined gaining a notoriety for my depictions of hulking ladies until he — and this he had on authority from his older sister who worked in nursing - explained how breasts couldn't be muscularized or shaped through cardiovascular or isometric efforts.

'They just kinda sit there and you're stuck with them, she told me.'

I wished breasts looked different. Like something else I could already draw.

Endie, sweet soul, kept on trying to buck me up. So I felt a little bit callous telling him, much though it was appreciated, the bromides could be put on ice.

'Listen: there's something I need to ask you to do with me. And we could easily both wind up dead. Or worse. Is that okay?'

He wanted clarity on how we might die. But sorry - his guess was as good as mine.

The situation was: he'd seen, same as I had, The Ghostbusters go into that sewer. I wouldn't go so far as saying it was faulty intelligence which stated they still used the bus stop because 'Maybe they have splinter groups' or 'maybe just other people use the bus stop at night - who knows what who saw.' But we'd seen them go into the sewer, ourselves.

My money? 'They stumbled into something way above their weight-class down there interested in far more than spit-kissing them.'

Everyone else was chasing bogeys - 'I'm sorry, but I call it how I see it' - and some demonstrable proof of the macabre horrors of the subterranean could go a long way toward consolidating our survival efforts.

Endie couldn't argue with that.

'It'd help us and would even collaterally save nimrods who won't help themselves.'

This is how it would have to be. I saw no way out. We would have to, Endie and I, venture down the sewer and return with proof positive of The Ghost-busters' ghastly fate.

'We're talking upward of umpteen corpses. And who knows if some of them have been partially devoured or been laying in slop-water all this while going goopy.'

I needed to impress upon Endie how even in the best-case scenario (our returning unharmed, physically) the shocking memories we'd be letting in would imp us the rest of our lives.

But what alternative? Blithely go our way? As though an ancient, lurking terror which might well consume our neighborhood entire wasn't standing in the dark, right behind us, breathing down our necks!?

'It's not The Ghostbusters I care about - they made their beds and if there's any good in the world their demise can serve as a cautionary reminder to other know-it-alls who'd follow in their misguided footsteps.'

Endie nodded. His assent didn't strike me as entirely committal but I'd not mention it as this was a lot to be taking in, especially with us probably only going to be alive another three-quarters of an hour.

IT WAS LIKE THERE WERE two echoes, two chills, one from inside my nostrils (the breath coiling into a whistle in there, resonant, tuning fork) the other stirred by our movements, whispers, our entire presence exhaling back off from the rough, dense curve of the tunnel's unlit concrete.

We kept our legs spread wide, our hands touching the walls, arms raised a bit, rather as though we were juddering letter Xs rather than human beings. Little need to keep such a pose - what moisture there was amounted to a modest slick akin to a semi-liquefied fruit roll-up, grimy dribbles along the exact center of the floor.

Odd how this wetness would dry out entirely for a length, then suddenly be present again - thick, thin. Whatever it was, it was nothing much like wa-ter. In fact, certain side-pipes dripped like runny noses and the plink of actual water was as one would expect, the puddles mild, appropriately deep, no evidence any thickening would occur, a gummy damp be given longevity.

Were the center slicks even water, then? What else? Mucosa?

There was something membranous about the stains. I could tell Endie felt it, too. Our X shape maybe the same unconscious recoil from an instinctually perceived danger. After all, we hadn't discussed the pose and I was bringing up the rear, had only noticed Endie's orientation after a good length of travel, mine not in mimic of his.

The tunnel narrowed. At first imperceptibly. Then making its slimness known by an ache in my low back. More cobwebs were present and some-how they all had plant life caught in them, no presence of drained insect husks.

Why would the tunnels get dirtier further in? What leaves, weeds, would get down here and under which circumstance? Why this scent like the rusted underside of a car becoming denser and denser?

There would be a tunnel-joint coming up. Ahead of us it glared in the ap-pearance of a gigantic eyeball, our blinks making it seem as though a gargan-tuan entity was blinking and with each bat of its lid down all around would go black - perhaps really we'd never blinked at all.

I supposed Endie, like me, was imagining this joint to be our destination. I figured he, like me, was both relieved at the tunnel getting wider, taller again. Relieved and disquieted.

It was evident as we got used to the quality of light or as we passed areas where street gutters allowed in ambient illumination how the tunnel shrank even narrower further along, after the joint area.

Our walk had an air of peristalsis to it. Due to my squinting and the rising aches at my shoulders I felt masticated. And, frankly, the refrigerator aromas I couldn't quite single out particulars of made my head feel oblong. My per-ception could easily be convinced we were traveling straight down rather than immediately ahead.

'Wait wait wait' Endie suddenly hiccoughed, hissed.

My head bonked the tunnel roof, teeth clicking hard enough that if my tongue had been between them it would've been snipped off at the tip as though by a cigar cutter. 'What?'

'Wait.'

I waited. 'What, man?'

He turned and looked back behind me the way we'd come. 'How far are we?'

Not far - what was he driving at?

He wanted to know where the joint (just ahead now) would let out.

'How would I know?'

'Are we under the park? Or under the road?'

Now this was a genuinely fine question. I tried to gauge if we'd journeyed far enough to be past the tennis and basketball courts. Didn't seem like it. Yet - yeah - I got what Endie was saying. 'Why is there a joint to the tunnel there? Where's the light coming from?'

'The road?'

'Wouldn't it be coming from the other way?'

And did we remember there being a rain gutter?

I didn't think so.

Had we started going sideways?

Endie was ahead of me on that. 'No, man. I can see straight out to where we came in.'

If the tunnel had a bend, we'd not be able to see out to the creek. If the road was so near, we'd hear some intermittent traffic, right? We could hear the burble from the creek, birdsong, lawnmower, laughter from behind us - but only to the terminus of our own huffs out noses in the other direction.

We both stood, listening to each other listening.

'Where are we?' Endie finally said, exactly as I easily might've.

AT OUR FEET LAY EVIDENCE enough to sway the sternest skeptic. My insides curdled, yet I'd admit a thrill my hunch had proved out. Splayed open, face-down, were three pornographic magazines. More were nearby, sludgy in a tilting stack, fusing to each other. A lump of scintillating cartilage.

Endie's nerves showed in his fidgeting lips, the way he worked at his shoulder cramp.

'Of course it means The Ghostbusters were here!' I snapped when he tried to comfort himself with rhetorical What-ifs. 'You could dispute this?'

Yes or no - we'd seen a dark clothed group of older kids with flashlight sneaking through the woods?

'Yes.'

So that's for starters. Later: an abandoned flashlight, nearby this very tunnel - real or make-believe?

'Real.'

'This is causal reasoning - my dad's crazy for it. The Greeks invented it, he says.'

Endie was sobered by this and I proud of my old man's bookworming.

So what do we discover on inspection? The suggestive and outright smutty visual materials one would exactly expect The Ghostbusters to horde! 'A lot of them're tenth graders, don't forget.' Maybe Endie'd lost sight of that for a moment, but his synapses were popping proper, now. 'Lookit' I deduced at him 'these magazines were clearly discarded in a hurry - most of them only half-read!' Thus, we factually conclude: 'Whatever happened here was quick, merciless, and final.'

Should we get out?

The question hung heavy. Endie's eyes unfocused over the illicit mess.

We'd be okay for the time being. The mags were damp. Everything must've gone south ages ago. 'No one chucks this kind of stuff down so callously without fine call to.' In a way, it was pitiable. Those hapless goons fancied they'd lucked onto the ideal hidey hole. 'Little did they know how dearly it'd cost 'em.'

'We take the mags, right?' Endie asked, obviously knowing of course we did. I think he felt asking took the curse off being pegged grave-robbers.

He poked the more-or-less ruined stack with his toe. I urged caution. We'd best to let them dry if we wanted to salvage the boodle. 'A clever man'd tear each page out.'

'Why's that?'

'No pages'll stiff together as they dry.'

Endie looked up with growing respect for my cool head and resourcefulness.

Meanwhile: I didn't much care for these small tunnels going off in three directions from the joint.

Endie saw me looking. 'Why're those small, all of a sudden?' And see how rich with viable spider webs. Laced all around with the snot glop, too. 'This place was like an on purpose trap, all along - don't you think?'

Or a nest, I thought but dared not utter.

Gathering all my bravery, I crouched low to cock my head, glare down one of these thin apertures. Too small for me to wriggle through, even were I to attempt.

'You'd get stuck even if you used a skateboard to scoot on.'

I concurred.

The stack of semi-ruined mags began tearing no matter how gingerly we lifted it. How the heck were we supposed to get these home, broad daylight, moving point-six miles-per-hour all the while? Parents had a tendency to notice things like that.

Go home for plastic bags? Backpack?

'How much daylight's left?'

'Oh a bunch - it's not even noon, probably. We could make the trip, get back.'

'What if they're gone? Someone stumbles on in here while we're absent?'

It was a possibility. I hated to say so. But, again: logic.

Would we be able to face our reflections, blowing an opportunity like this?

'You live closer, Endie. I'll stay here. Just hurry.'

He would.

Also: maybe he oughta come back armed.

.DECEMBER.

OUR MOM, POOR WRETCH, WAS worked like a mongrel in the Word Processing department of some high faultin' law firm in the nation's capital. Cut from gritty homesteader cloth, though, she spun this burden into gold so far as Alvin and I were concerned. Now and then, when an overnight shift was lumped atop her typical slog, she trundled us along to the office with her.

The drive was through dank city streets, tunnels lit mint-green, each longer than the previous (and 'If you hold your breath to the end, your wish is granted'), then down a corkscrew parking garage via an altogether secret agent entrance (spikes to perforate tires were she to make one wrong move).

Twentieth story of an otherwise empty office building.

Computers had Space Invaders, desks had jars of paperclips which resembled multicolored starships we could war with, knocking the destroyed ones down holes meant for monitor cords seeking plugs.

Three different kitchen areas - satellite Mars bases we would helm. The favorite was a spook-house venture through the corridors, well worth it for the prize of free packets of lemonade powder, hot chocolate, crushed ice for sodas we'd down with take-out pizza from Luigi's.

Around the corner from this was a room which must've had a business purpose, though we couldn't reckon what. A sofa. Some chairs. Television with VCR, plus it got way more channels than we had at home.

Tonight, we'd brought rentals along - American Ninja II: the Confrontation, Bloodsport, Rapid Fire - so no complaints on the entertainment front. However, we were too invested in working on our design for a video game to tuck into those flicks, quite yet.

The brainwave had been Alvin's. In an issue of Nintendo Power there'd been some concept art reprinted to tease a forthcoming game called

Earthworm Jim. Impressive stuff! Like literally playing a cartoon, if the graphics matched up to the sketches.

But it was plain to see we had ideas equal if not superior. All that stood between us and a lucrative licensing deal was committing a finalized proposal to poster board.

We were going for something Oriental Heroes-cum-Golgo 13. Obviously, it would be the fisticuff aspect of the game (with a series of moves available to each character such as had never been unleased upon the world!) which would drive it into the hearts of the masses. But we wanted the deeper respect of the more selective populace, those philosophically inclined gamers who went in for the convolutions of anti-heroic assassins.

'You should almost be sad when you beat a villain' was Alvin's clever twist on the tired tropes of the industry 'because they always seem to have more developed motivations.'

Who would disrespect such an insight? We could prove it out simply by stating our own preferences!

And I could not get over myself when Alvin beamed how it'd been my assertion 'Our hero actually dies in the last fight, no matter what!' which would elevate our game to Cult status.

You see: in his death, a greater triumph is found. True, the world descends into several generations of darkness - but the simmering memory of his self-less, indefatigable heroics (irrelevant how he'd had his own interests driving him) eventually birth a rebellion which 'doesn't merely save the world but births a new one, entire!'

It's what I'd always felt in my heart: the true desire of Nintendo players was to be martyred, become legends felled by impossible odds - godheads who even when someone else triumphed where they'd failed still felt inferior to!

This was the scale and intellectual complexity we were capable of - positively zeitgeist altering. And with the processing capabilities of the Super Nintendo and Sega Genesis there finally existed devices which could support it.

WE DISCOVERED RUBBER-BAND GUNS, DESIGNED in replica of Revolutionary War pistols, in some random attorney's office. Alvin somehow knew what they were on sight.

And thus did an immediate game of stalk-and-kill begin.

The corridors, private rooms, kitchenettes, cubicles were illumed by perhaps one out of every sixteen of them, scattered hurdy-gurdy, having a lamp lit, the simmering hum of a computer monitor, or a blue On button to a private coffee pot left glowing.

I'd taken shelter behind a Xerox machine flanked by two long filing cabinets. Not so wise. Even when Alvin crept by, entirely the fool to my concealment, I was so jammed in I couldn't aim the pistol - even if I could've, I'd no clean line of shot.

It'd be ages until he backtracked to my location, so I wriggled out and began slithering along walls, hands and knees, peeking around every corner before taking it.

The comfort of the television room, the kitchen, the bright main office where my mom toiled became solar distances remote. And every creepshow and gibbonous thought the offices had bred in me seemed front and center. Regret. Such foolish things I'd let myself in for. My own memories turned septic and rose to drown me. The very curves of my mop-water hair seem vulnerable flesh.

Remember? How once (Alvin not with me that time) I'd braved an episode of Tales From The Darkside, cloistered in the sofa room? Forget Alvin and his Mickey Mouse play guns - some personage requiring revenge from beyond the grave may've had a bone to pick with one of these legal beagles or paralegals! How was I to know what depravities they might've got themselves embroiled in? A reanimated carcass could be making its steady progress to tear limbs from limbs, securing its bury-my-bones final rest. If such a creature happened upon me why would it spare my life at the risk of wandering, malformed, anguished, for eternity? Give up its chance for vengeance and succor? Hardly! I'd be mincemeat.

The only weapon I had in my arsenal was the chance that (if it were anything like the corpse which'd made its way down the chimney in the episode I'd seen) perhaps it would let me go if I raised a fist and yawped 'Viva la revolution!' in macabre triumph, mimicking the ghoul as it stood over its final victim.

A fool's hope. What were the odds of so specific a monstrosity lurking at Gibson, Dunn & Crutcher?

Sweet relief when Alvin zapped me clean in the side of the face.

'Let's team up and fight pretend things' I suggested. And Alvin was game for this, perhaps knowing otherwise it'd be at least fifteen minutes spent seeking me out in some new arcane hiding spot.

We swiped ammo from a supply annex and went at it another jaunt, Alvin only remarking 'Should we be cleaning up?' after we'd returned the weapons to their original spot, our game complete.

Could it get our mom in trouble, these rubber-bands littered willy-nilly?

'I don't think they know she's here.'

Odd how I'd never considered this. If something happened to us, it might be Monday before we were found.

Also: if they knew she'd clocked in but wasn't there when rubber-bands were discovered everywhere, wouldn't their first thought be concern for her well-being rather than disciplinary action?

'No one would think to pin this mess on our mom - it's simply outside of her character' Alvin concluded.

We made inspection of a few other offices. The side of one's door was practically the sharp of the corridor wall's corner, its interior murkily adorned by a breathy green haze off its computer monitor, a powdery gloom made concentrated by the wood slats of its window blinds being shut fast.

I had a flush of the creeps, so loitered at the door while Alvin gave some drawers gentle tugs. His skin tone was washed out entire, his eyes seemed solid black. 'Hey, Ick ...' he said, voice a throaty wrinkle of concern.

On the monitor screen - each letter of each word appearing one-by-one, one-by-one, one-by-one - was the phrase Can I go home now? This same sentence again and again and again and again. Computer green letters, like digital clock digits. Can I go home now? Can I go home now? Can I go home now? as though miserably, hopelessly, desperately being typed out.

'Who's writing that?'

Can I go home now? Can I go home now? Can I go home now?'

Once in the hall, at a hurry, back toward our mom, Alvin theorized 'Could be someone's trapped somewhere - might think they're getting the message out someplace else.'

In a basement? Another building, nearby? What lawyer keeps hostages? Why? To suppress testimony? Elicit it?

I played this game of Let's Guess in order to keep my own certainties at bay.

Whoever was typing, they'd never get home.

Can I go home now? Can I go home now? Can I go home now?

An echo of something, someone already gone. Speaking right to us because it, he, she knew we would be there to see.

I BLAMED IT ON HOW I always got car sick. Except I didn't always get car sick. This was just one the ways my mind found to angle things. A little retro-continuity never hurt anyone.

The city was deserted and my shivers were from fatigue. Bobbling in my mind was a memory from another time at mom's office:

I'd gone into the oddest of the three kitchens. The one with the smelly fridge. With the copy machine. With the television above a disused bread-maker and dozens of file boxes plopped against one wall.

Had it been Dr. Who? Had it been that strange Nightmare on Elm Street series, nothing to do with Nightmare on Elm Street, Freddy Kruger merely a wise cracking host figure?

On the screen, people had been killed. Vaporized. Only their clothes left. Strewn in the shapes of their wearers. Spilling from the sleeves was a crystal-line, powdered substance. Salt, thick as glass shards, flimsy as sand.

Would that've been what'd become of The Ghostbusters? Did it explain the lack of bodies? Would it hurt? Slowly dehydrated down to calcified resi-due? Or petrified suddenly? Shattered by falling over?

... What about their clothing?

... Could've easily been tentancled down those floor tunnels ...

I had the rear seat, Alvin up front. My mom had on the radio. Some pro-gram. Corn Between Your Teeth. A down-homey disc jockey, voice sopo-rific, introduced this or that comedy sketch. Cheech and Chong. Some song. Basketball jones.

I drifted. Knew I was conversing, but the words were soggy, molasses. Did my best to prove I was awake by focusing on things out the window. Blinking red light at the top of an air-traffic tower. Cathedral which shone like a theme park ...

... The city turned into blank highway. Long and striped in dotted lines like fancy trousers, slick with orange from streetlights drooping in postures of parched daffodils, green signs with white letters I couldn't decipher, road names, avenues, boulevards, parkways. Were we this near to home or that?

As soon as I thought I was asleep though, I knew I was awake.

And Alvin had asked mom 'Why's it called Corn Between Your Teeth' just as the announcer purred gravelly 'This is Corn Between Your Teeth ...'

I'd wondered this, too. Needed to know. Had pictures in my head of bumpkins all slack-jawed.

'I don't know' mom said and (it seemed uncertain, a guess) 'because it's irritating?'

... Because it's irritating ... Irritating ... Irritating ... No. I wasn't sure. Is that what she'd said? What I'd heard? It made sense and didn't. Or had she said 'To have corn stuck between your teeth is irritating'?

I had images of this in my head. Cartoonish yet unsettling. Corn and teeth both off-yellow, streetlight orange, malignant tumors growing their own be-nign ones ...

... I'd refused to eat corn anytime it'd been served me. But would lick the butter and salt off the cobs my dad served. Loved the two little corn-cob shaped spears we were given to hold the things. My mom sometimes used a fork and only on one side ...

Later, in bed, I lay and wondered what it would feel like to be paralyzed. Forever.

Would you understand? Understand forever? Why would being paralyzed give you any insight on that?

I told myself my legs couldn't move. I lacked the power to command them. Even if I wanted to. With all my will.

And I got confused.

Was I really unable to move my legs?

I wasn't moving them.

Was this pretend? Is it pretend if I can't stop? If I don't stop is it real?

I either realized I'd brought myself to tears thinking this or woke up and remembered I'd dreamed making myself cry by pretending I couldn't pretend myself out of paralysis but could, oh so by accident, play pretend myself into it.

MRS. TERRE WAS ACROSS THE classroom in conference with a nice enough Science teacher, the police office in charge of the anti-drug program, and her usual toady. I couldn't help being unnerved by how often they made glances and gestures (small, but enough to not be hidden) in my direction.

A girl called Rita must've noticed me noticing them and so (causing me no end of grief) kept looking over at the gathering, over at me, over at the gathering like we were some abstract table-tennis match.

'Are you in trouble?' Rita slow-motion and hoarsely whispered. 'Are you going to jail for drugs?'

I made a face indicating where she could stuff the question. But in the same instant she flitted eyes back toward the quartet, my own automatically following. For some inexplicable reason it was exactly then the toady and Mrs. Terre, in a perverse tandem, began motioning me over, giddy, almost kissy-facing like I was their new kitten.

'And here is our little author' Mrs. Terre gushed, maternal gesture toward me like we'd ever once got along. The cop was clocking me, giving the thorough up-down-all-around, as the Science teacher bid the group adieu.

'What's it all about?'

After the New Year, the anti-drug program was kicking into high gear with two whole weeks dedicated to nothing but it (overtaking the time slot usually occupied by Silent Reading, just before Lunch and Recess).

'Terrific. Why tell me?'

Mrs. Terre, air as though she was finally providing me the insulin she'd withheld, said 'There's going to be a writing contest - all grade levels.'

I made generic gesture I'd noted this, but enthusiasm was scarce when I looked within to drum some up. Not that it sounded bad. No typical five paragraph essay kinda thing. No, no. The officer explained 'It can be poems, stories, memories - you could even write a play.' I was skeptical, still, but satisfied when he, the toady, and Mrs. Terre in synchronicity assured me there were no length limits or specific points of propaganda to slip in. And the winner got a prize, but they were playing the particulars of what close to their collective vest.

'I've heard a lot about you' the officer told me, probably not meaning to utterly send me into a noiac fever 'and I really look forward to seeing what you come up with.'

Mrs. Terre winked and the toady gave me a double thumbs-up.

Endie was of a mind this had set-up written all over it. 'And why does Officer Wilkes have a dossier on you?'

'Oh why did you think!'

'What's he? Your stepdad? Wants to get you on the straight-and-narrow?'

'There's no one straighter or narrower than me' I cock-crowed. Though any attempt to display this by simply living as I desired and allowing it to be observed in the natural play of things got mercilessly thwarted by tattle-tales, busy-bodies, and ratfink nephews of homeroom teachers who, now that I thought about it, had been cozying up to me an awful lot, of late, never lacking a personalized remark of encouragement when handing back a Spelling test.

'You'd think with a badge like that he might wanna go catch a proper crook. But no. They'll probably comb over my manuscript, looking for psychological insights that won't hold up in court but can be used to smoke me out or something.'

So: I was gonna enter the contest?

'Endie, it wasn't an invitation - get with it, eh?'

LATER IN THE TOILET, MICA and some other kids I hardly knew were pencil fighting. They paused on my arrival, demanding to know since when was I a narc. Nevermind how they'd been hipped to me getting cushy-cushy with the resident copper - they were just informing me I'd better not dream of pulling slick undercover work against them because I'd been outed and better not forget it.

I gave appropriate assurances they were way wrong about me. I could understand how rumors got started, what it all must've looked like, but I wasn't turning States Evidence so no need to stop their illicit gambling on my account.

These were not enemies I wanted to cultivate. I laid it out - keeping vague, seeming aloof to it all - how it was one of those wrong-place-wrong-time deals and I'd just needed to set the poor old traffic cop on a false scent while keeping up appearances for myself at the same time.

'Something big went down. A parent called a Tip Line and dropped my name. Said they'd seen me around. All routine stuff, guys. Wilkes is on emu duty, you know? Scrap-to-scrap.'

So: I promised I wasn't gonna turn Dale in?

'Dale?'

Dale Beech.

'Dale Beech?'

For the graffiti on the Montessori school's wall.

I made a croupier gesture of hands clean, stepping away from the table - now they were into territory and affairs I neither wanted to tread nor knew peep about.

'You better not say anything, now that you know.'

'I don't know squat, man. I wasn't even here.'

It piles up and piles up! This was exactly what I meant! Who could've predicted, waking up today, eating a frostingless Pop-tart, I was gonna become embroiled in this degree of cops-'n-robbers? I needed a scorecard to keep track of all the players involved, even already! A flow-chart to keep myself clear how I was to comport myself with each.

In Art class, Binion let me unburden myself, shook his head almost in pity, and agreed it was a tough beat which'd take the wind out of anyone's sails. 'If they get caught pencil fighting, even randomly, you're probably toast.'

He was right. What was I supposed to do, though? Serve in the fulltime capacity of lookout for them? Run interference whenever they were trying to win scratch-and-sniff stickers or scented erasers off each other?

'And say it occurs to them what a barrel they have me over? Put me on payroll but without having to offer me diddle for my time?'

Yeah. Binion agreed even more than before. It was absolutely worse than he'd thought.

Cops. Teachers. Pencil-fighting racketeers. Videogame development. Writing contests. And to top it all off having to bear the burden of knowing the fate of The Ghostbusters yet knowing twice over how I'd never be believed were I to air the story to the public.

How the devil had I become the nexus of so many questionable and altogether otherworldy happenstances? 'Didn't anyone ever think maybe I have ambitions of my own? Projects I'd like to kick off?'

The failure of Hugo still pressed on my heart. I'd meant to cook up another comic but hadn't had the time.

'But you're getting better at drawing nudity.'

This was my entire point! What good did it do me if I never got to really delve in? Even when I worked on it at school, while meantime I ought be reading Jar of Dreams, I had to eventually draw clothing on all the figures or my goose would be cooked!

Even in Art I was made outlaw.

NEEDING JUST MYSELF AND MY head, a trustworthy few hours, I'd ventured out, pat after school.

Recently, a bunch of kids had reinstituted our off-and-on adventurer's club, The Pack Rats. Same as usual, it was the discovery of disused pornography which lead to our coalescing under a common name. An area of pricker bushes we'd used for headquarters in the past had been re-hollowed. Communal hidey-hole. Rules and Regulations. All in it together. At least, if history proved out, until 'mysteriously' the mags vanished, often with much window dressing - as when, one time, a kid called Davy (who we no longer associated with) dramatically took the blame, claiming his parent had followed him one day, found the loot, confiscated it, adding in how he'd nobly taken the full weight of responsibility, refusing to name collaborators.

Such bugs and goblins in our lives!

I almost laughed recalling this, all while giving a half-hearted leaf through an issue of Hustler which featured a sleazy Batman parody called Sprat-Man. This featured a cartoonish, mild BDSM scenario of Batgirl being caught in a florescent web The Jerker had set up. All very lowest common denominator innuendo. Yes yes ... a 'Booby trap.' How droll.

Leaving off the mags, I wandered out further. Kept to the untended fields which in the summer would turn patchwork with the odd resident's caged-off gardens. Soon I was out past the Odd Park (belonging to the third entrance, set smack where the development name technically changed and the houses became inexplicably and demonstrably higher quality) and the power lines were no longer strung along wood poles, instead laced through four-legged metal structures with dangerous looking transformer boxes barnacled to them.

The few times I'd run away from home, this long stretch of fallow, dirt-and-weed expanse was the furthest I'd gone. Even here, present day, it felt properly the end of the map, a natural, ninety-degree, bottomless tip awaiting me if I kept on another two hundred yards.

In reality? No. Through those trees were some more posh neighborhoods and the other Elementary School. I envied the students there, the families, the lone dreamers like me, able to live out their days in the manner intended by evolution.

Soon, my moping run of self-pity was interrupted by the sight of Monacci. He hadn't clocked me, so I crouched to conceal myself.

Ah, Monacci. Our relationship had always been a complex one. I had nothing against the kid, but he was such a prevaricator I'd drifted out of friendship's orbit. Absurdity after absurdity had to be gone along with for the sake of his feelings - eventually the pressure got too much, I'd not wanted to be labeled weirdo-by-association, my credibility torpedoed because he felt the need to put on outrageous airs to get the time of day off any old bystander.

Last time I'd seen him had been summer. He'd been on the dirt-patch portion of the area where we sometimes played baseball. Hands and knees. Motioned me over. There were fresh, mountainous anthills, the brown dirt taking on a copper tone, extremely fine to the finger's touch, like talcum. He was drooling slow, weighted loogies in order to destroy the structures, drown the residents. Some need to posture as God, I supposed.

It was funny, him in this field. Of all places. Of all days.

I watched him roam lonely circles until, as though in response to some hidden signal, he took off running. Then I roamed the same radius he had, studying the dirt for signs.

What was I thinking? That his most ridiculous story had maybe been true?

He claimed he'd been running through this field, tripped on a tree stump which it turned out was phony - a hinged door 'opened upward like a submarine' to reveal a 'two-mile deep ladder'. According to him, he'd descended, wandered five hours through a cave 'lit by radioactive torches which never went out'. Discovered the place.

The Secret Movie Theatre.

The only way to obtain a ticket was to survive a trial-by-combat. The seats had straws built into them on the left, an endless supply of any drink you desired. On the right, popcorn or candy replenished in perpetuity.

And the movies he'd claimed to have watched there! 'Sequels that won't exist for decades, Ichabod - like way way later sequels than are out now.' Batman Eleven. Looks Who's Talking, but with an alien baby. Cool Runnings Part Eight!

'Right, Monacci - the continuing, heartwarming hijinks of those wacky Jamaican bobsledders.'

He'd bristled at my dismissive tone, seemed near tears. 'These movies are from the future, Ichabod. They win a ton more times!'

IT HIT ME IN A jolt how not only should I get home, or at least near-to-home, before it got much darker, but how if I missed my dad coming in Alvin might've already conned him into going to the bookstore by the time I put in my appearance. A trip to the bookstore was exactly what I wanted to con the old man into!

So I began a light jog, singing as my huffs huffed out 'Basketball jones ... I got a basketball jones ... I got a basketball jo—' when for some reason, at just that moment (one moment further, who knows what my fate would've been!) I glanced down. I'd had a sense. Instinctual. A thought half-formed like 'There might be piles of sticks' or 'Don't deer crap in this field all the time?' had commanded me to slow. Stop. My left foot had been raised, about to begin its descent. But I'd glanced - in exactly enough time to see the tortoise. My body contracted, expanded like a spring mechanism, the force generating a slice of pain and cramp, whipping me upward, unfooted into a teeter, a tumble, a crash into the dried, wheat-thick stalks, seedpods, and burrs.

It was a tortoise, no gag (or a turtle, my jangled nerves would have no idea how to sort the difference). The lout was humongous!

I begged my mind to be playing tricks. Oh how I pleaded internally to find myself suddenly laughing and calling myself a dork, a dolt, a dotard! Couldn't it all have been illusion, some odd trick of peripheral, corner-of-my-eye blur? It'd be all I'd ever ask to be able to finish my hurry home, tell the story of what a chump I was, scaring myself to death, Alvin finding it all a hoot, the ordeal becoming an inside joke between us for ages to come, a new nickname maybe.

But no.

The dead sober truth was I'd almost stepped on a bona fide tortoise. Tigereye, marbled shell. Large as a mailbox cut in half at the belly.

I could tell I would have scrapes enough to scab later. My leg convulsed in a static Charley Horse and I was reluctant to so much as tense it outstretched to help ease out the tedious ache.

Overhead came the unmistakable flap of a bird as it lit to the powerlines.

'Exactly the opposite of what a bird would do!' I fantasized myself insisting to no argument from Alvin, later, safe, secure, away from there. 'Think about it: I'd been running, singing, making a racket, and now had smack fell down to further the compounded ruckus. Birds fly away at that - they don't suddenly land! Not the all-natural birds.'

The tortoise didn't move except to, I thought, open its eyes, a glint of light catching in the milky cataract I was certain I could make out in the last of evening's light and from under the buzz of one of the lampposts lining the wood fence separating field from properties which lined it.

I should call for help. Don't die of shame, you chucklehead! Don't be complacent in the face of your maker! There must be families seated around tables, at televisions, Nintendo's clang-clanging kapows, kabooms, crack crack crack of shots taken at ducks and dogs giggling as ducks flew off unscathed.

My scream died stillborn. Not even in my throat. Rotted to a heat like that of a coming bowel movement down my belly. Because when I turned toward the fence I saw squirrels, skittering along its top and along its second slat. Squirrels. One. Two. Squirrel squirrel. One two three four. Squirrel squirrel tortoise bird.

Surrounded.

The squirrels, understanding they had me, stood to haunches.

The tortoise shuffled.

The bird shivered its wings like clearing itself of water or beginning to transfigure ...

... and somehow I managed to find myself running, snot nosed and hiccoughing, until I was to the locked glass door of my basement.

IN THE NORMAL COURSE OF events, I would've been miffed by my mom's little trap. Under the specific circumstances, though, I not only didn't feel put off, but found it a welcome and comic distraction, so played my part in a freewheeling, puckish manner. This, I think, proved helpful to the overall tone which (as afterward Alvin reflected) probably could've broke bad for me, big league.

I was just in the door, freshly composed, wanting nothing but to get to my room, strip, then sink into the cocoa-butter scent of bubble bath, when my mom called 'Hey kiddo - I need you to take this basket' from around in the living room where she'd been folding clothes.

No sweat. I made a footloose entrance, all grins.

Then she sprung her snare.

On the piano bench I saw my backpack. Every zipper pouch open. Innards gutted, arranged in distinct piles dot-to-dotting a half-circle (or the tip of an arrow, depending on how one made the trace). My schoolbooks and various bric-a-brac to one side - nothing's nothing about those. Next over, a pile of brown paper lunch bags - lots of 'em. And finally, a small, blue, spiral note-book - the words Cat Stuff written heavy into the cover stock.

'No no no' my mom said primly as I stammered how I could explain what-ever it was going to be I'd be required to explain, that I was sorry, so let's simply move past it, assume the lesson learnt.

Here's the shot:

My mom had received a letter of concern from Mrs. Terre. This letter, in precise, businesswoman terms, explained how Mrs. Terre, as well as a few other faculty and administrative individuals in conjunction with the lunch-room staff, were concerned about me on several fronts (concerns attested to by some parent volunteers, for effect).

Firstly: a number of papers requiring parental signature hadn't been re-turned to school - this charge also stating a lack of accountability for filling out the Calendar Worksheets and how some permission slip for a trip to the Chesapeake Bay I very passionately did not want to go on was overdue.

Secondly: it had come to everyone's attention how I was never seen eating at school, except for 'sometimes, it seems as a source of entertainment to other children, a vast number of salt packets'.

I was braced for a 'thirdly' but apparently the thirdly was nothing to do with the letter, so after she'd said 'Thirdly' my mom paused then said 'Well, just Firstly and Secondly, let's start there.'

In reverse order, I supposed, because she gestured at the lunch bags, pres-ently.

I had to plead guilty. She had me dead bang. Approximately three-dozen lunch bags, had to be (most of them well flattened by the weight of everything else in my backpack having been tossed in on top of them) were on jury-dis-play, just there.

'Ichabod - you have to eat. And these are disgusting!' She removed a few articles of evidence - peanut butter sandwiches, the bread molded to occult shades of blue, grey, green, and an orange only observed in tree-frogs by cer-tain explorers. 'Your dad makes you these sandwiches because you won't eat school lunch. This is such a waste.'

It was. I confessed. But look at me! Strapping enough. 'I always make Chef Boyardee when I get home.'

Not good enough.

Fine, then - I promised I'd eat the lunches dad packed. It'd be easy enough to remind myself to just throw the bags away. My laziness was to blame for all this song-and-dance.

Not so fast! I was going to be observed, daily. Either I ate the sandwiches or I would have to start buying school lunch and sitting with an aide.

Diabolical! No wonder she was in such demand with lawyers.

The signatures, permission slips - she gave me a mulligan, there. 'I thought your dad checked that - he doesn't. From now on, I want your homework done, binder out for inspection. I'll check it before I go to bed each night.'

I nodded. 'Now, let me explain about the Cat Stuff. Dad knows all about it. Gave me the greenlight. All very tasteful - not a scrap meant to be scintillating or smutty. Nor do I flash it around to philistines. I'm not some slick pornographer, I assure you.'

She was smiling, leafing through the pages, giving off a kinda you're-not-in-trouble-for-this vibe. 'Can you keep this particular artistic vision at home, perhaps? At least until' she gave a nod at the lunch bags, the papers, the binder 'we've got normal life under control?'

ALVIN HAD BEEN KEEPING TABS on the hiding place our mom had used for Christmas presents since forever. Was pleased to inform me it was stocked up, if I cared to have a look. He'd been the pink of courtesy, hadn't so much as given his nose a poke in yet so we could do it together.

'Where were you all day, by the by?'

'But mom's home tonight' I bulldozed overtop his question.

Obviously he knew this, so rolled his eyes, slandering me a yutz and a simp. 'And she'll sleep like a headstone right after she's done watching golf. That's when we strike.'

I figured he'd known about the backpack fiasco, but he convincingly stated it was all news to him. So I took a minute out to bring him abreast, broadstrokes only.

'You're rich, man!' he said, gave me a hearty grip to both shoulders and a paly jostle.

'Rich?'

'Wealthy. Loaded. Rolling in it! How many bags did you say there'd been?'

'Something close to thirty.'

'And you'd never even opened them?'

'Something about the way dad makes a sandwich bugs me.'

Alvin concurred. 'Or' he suddenly took a hiss breath, seemed to be bracing against a gut punch 'did mom already take the money? You say she had the sandwiches on display?'

'The blue blazes are you on about, Vinny?'

This entire day was wearing on my last nerve, I swore to God! It's like I was in stuck in one of mom's All My Children episodes.

Alvin motioned me calm. Dig it: didn't I know dad puts cash money inside the lunch bags?

'Cash money?'

'Hard currency, Ick - you've heard of dollars and cents, right?'

But this made bonkers sense, if any. Each morning, a brown bag had Alvin written on it, a brown bag had Ichabod written on it. Sandwich and a plastic baggie of peanuts was the full spread any time I'd bothered to peek.

'Why'd he put money in if I'm not buying lunch? Entire point of packing is to avoid having to pay money down.'

Here's where Alvin explained why he'd be taking half the boodle. Listen: going back to the historical start of the bagged-lunch decision, Alvin had been gaming the system. 'Dad wouldn't buy us juice boxes or Kool-Aid for reasons he never made apparent, yes?'

'Yes.'

'So: what's he think we drink?' Pretty much I assumed he thought we only drank milk. 'Precisely! And he's not gonna pack us a glass of milk, eh?'

'He'd point out physics makes it unfeasible. Plus the fact it'd get warm, possibly sour, would make it a health hazard.'

So Alvin had finagled a flim-flam wherein he not only got the old codger to pony up money for a drink each day 'But I inflated the going price! When's he ever gonna bother checking?'

Suddenly, this was the smartest plan ever made by someone not technically an astronaut facing mechanical crisis. 'How much does he put in?' At least a buck-fifty!? More often than not two bucks, because he probably doesn't have coins!? 'He put a five in!? A five? Wait - to last the whole week?'

'Naw - just one day he must not've had small change. Next day was two bucks, again.'

Mom hadn't mentioned anything about this money. True, I wouldn't put it past her to take full advantage, pocket it, cost of doing business - but it couldn't be overlooked there existed the honest chance luck would pan out she'd been so repulsed by the stabbing sweet, condensed aroma of fungal growth she'd turned her head away and never much bothered with closer inspection beyond pulling out a rainbow sandwich or two for visual aid during the trial portion of or conversation.

'Alas!'

'Alas what?' Alvin said, draining pale to match my livid intonation.

'The bags - they're outside in the trash pile!'

No no - didn't I see? This was good!

Here: he would go down to the basement, ostensibly to work on art, and would unlock the door. 'You, meantime, gather up some other trash, take it out, and bring the money bag around to the back - then go back around front and inside so no one will get wind of anything fishy.'

TWENTY-SEVEN BAGS.

Two of them, yes indeed, had crisp five-dollar bills within. One, rather inexplicably, had thirty-five cents (five nickels, a dime) though Alvin made rhetorical reminder how life is a funny thing from time-to-time. All totaled: forty-nine dollars, thirty-five.

'Which I should technically get loads more than half of, seeing as I could've taken it all.'

I didn't much have it in me about contesting the point. 'Go ahead. Take thirty bucks and the coins. Fair's fair.'

Alvin, never one to waste breath when scooting along without remark was advantageous, divvied the loot based on this pronouncement.

There was bit of a deflation when we discovered the Christmas presents (back behind random empty picture frames, horse tackle, and bottles of old medicinal soap which was likely toxic by now, leaking poison into the air like radium) were already wrapped. Mom was becoming defter at keeping one step ahead. Of course there was little logic to the matter, as Alvin and I soon sat discussing with the television on (set nearly mute to a repeat episode of Mama's Family which, even if new to us, could be very easily interpreted on pure visuals) one of his coats stuffed into the crack between the floor and the door bottom to keep glow from emanating out.

'If she knows we know where she hides them, hide them someplace else. Hiding them in the same place but wrapping them seems a peculiarly aggressive action from a mother to her sons - if, again, she knows we know that's where they'll be.'

And sure, a large part of me wanted to let this disaster of a day dribble out in these good-hearted expressions of brotherly intimacy. Sleep. Wake up. All this behind me. Go blow this found money on frivolous back issues of some bizarre later work by Jack Kirby. And OMAC! I mustn't forget to actually get some OMAC since Steve Rude loved it so much. And now I'd have new money every single day. And I'd find a way to fake it about the sandwiches.

Yes!

Let this be the day's curtain. Let me awake with a head light and a soul empty of Earthly concern.

'Alvin ... we might have a bigger problem than we'd been reckoning.'

Did he remember Monacci?

Who could forget Monacci!? Alvin whipped through a litany of some of his favorite Monacci moments, relishing in particular the retelling of a time the poor sod had caught a pass in football, a clear line to touchdown, started staggering sideways, toppled over, fumbling the ball before collapsing in a pile of leaves, thus allowing Quincy to score for the other team.

I tried to contain my own laughter at the memory of us all, agape, trying to make heads or tails of Monacci shouting 'Unnecessary roughness!'

'No one was near you, Monacci!' Alvin reenacted and I piped in, mock-Monacci-voiced 'It was the wind! Unnecessary roughness on the wind!'

And then he'd stormed off home!

'But ... yeah, what about Monacci?'

I told him about earlier. The field. The tortoise. The bird. The squirrels. 'And in all that bramble there could've been sumac, man. Could've been moles, long worms, fat crickets.'

But I didn't need to sell Alvin on anything. And for a moment this relieved me near the point of tears. Until he said 'What if that wasn't Monacci?'

'It was Monacci.'

But hadn't I said he'd run away for no reason? Exactly before I'd been surrounded? 'What if it was all of the parts? The entire body. Luring you. What if it had combined, but made itself look like Monacci?'

All he'd been doing was walking in a circle ... and in just the spot where I knew he'd said the entrance to that nonsense movie house was ... 'How would the parts know about that? Do they have access to my memories?'

'We can't take anything for granted - especially not when all the pieces slide right to fit. After all, we're talking about, just for example, a leg full of razor blades that once snuck into the tool shed out back of Nils' house!'

We sat in silence, watching a soundless commercial for Ora-gel, another for Listerine, another for Waxi-Maxi.

'That spot though ...' Alvin finally uttered, whisper almost drowned out by the flickers and static hum of the television screen '... it's like they were circling ... congregating ... as though it was the unholy axis of some energy.'

I knew what he was driving at. Wished I'd stayed in the Pack Rats reading Sprat-Man.

'Do you think the nest's near there?' he finally verbalized.

And I closed my eyes. The black of the insides flitting bright, gone, shaded, shaded, bright, gone as the television stammered.

'No' I said, normal voice, then quieter 'No ... I know where the nest is. I've been there.'

.JANUARY.

THIS WOULD MARK THE FOURTH time I'd heard Mrs. Terre's story, inside a week. It certainly didn't become any less atypical or unsettling in the re-telling, though no one else much batted an eye. Indeed, while she'd initially addressed it to only us students, as though relating some torn-from-the-headlines fable, it was other faculty, volunteers, and administrators she addressed in subsequent recitations. This audience phenomena was something I'd become quite interested in. She could go on repeating herself from now till Kingdom come, so far as I was concerned. Research. Plus: if she was yammering, she wasn't asking me to spell or define things.

The tale repeated with uncanny verbatim, as well. In summary, the matter went thus:

Once upon last Thursday, Mrs. Terre had been using the toilet facilities. No, not the one's for employee use only, but rather the same privy any child, first-through-third grade, might use of a day (Mrs. Terre had had reason to be down that wing of the building when nature called, you see?). Whilst she'd sat voiding, not a care in this world save the business at hand, who should enter the echoing, faintly bleach scented confines of the lavatory than two young girls, sixth grade - names withheld for the typical legalese, though it had taken zero students more than zero minutes to do the requisite journalistic legwork required to ferret out the identities.

So: these girls, the story goes, immediately set to mischief by way of the one saying to the other 'Let's see what little kids are in here and freak them out.' A good opening tactic as far as terrorism went - victims already captive, let them sweat knowing their card's about to be punched.

Unfortunately for our young vipers, when they decided to use the closed toilet bowl in the stall next door to their would-be victim's as stepstool so they might pop their heads over divider top, it was only Mrs. Terre they discovered. 'They immediately tried to apologize and leave' Mrs. Terre explained 'but I told them No, young ladies - this is what you wanted to see, so now you may stay there and watch.' And true to her word - this was Gospel, the hooligan's had confirmed it without ever varying their shock-horror narrative - Mrs. Terre made them observe the whole Broadway production: tinkle, spray, grunt, pinch, tissue tear, wipe, panties up, skirt smoothed down, and toilet's shebang! Afterward, she'd made them write an essay explaining what they'd done and why they should never dare dream of enacting similar mayhem again.

Me?

I couldn't get the sound effects from Monty Python's 'Do you embarrass easily?' sketch out of my mind whenever this tale reached climax (even this time had to suppress a chortling, stifled guffaw) - the bad job, of course, being how I also couldn't help thinking of Mrs. Terre's pipes and faucets at full toil and cannonade every time the sketch came on.

Anyway: that was it. Mrs. Terre's Just-So Story for this modern clime. How The Camel Got It's Hump or something. Rikki Tiki Tavi.

This other adult she told the yarn to (didn't know the man but he seemed very comfortable hearing this kind of saga in front of a roomful of children) nodded and, like all the others, spake as though the official, cliché moral 'Be careful what you wish for' before (I liked this guy) taking a step away, thinking the better, and deciding to anoint the story with a more ancient, biblical justification viz 'You reap what you sew - something they ought to've been brought up to understand.'

DESPITE BEING ASSURED 'ANY FORMAT' was allowable for this anti-drug contest, there'd been a snag when it turned out comic books were given the nix. After some failed sophistic volleys with the gatekeepers (e.g. 'I'm writing the same story, simply using pictures in addition' this yielding 'It's kind of cheating - picture is worth a thousand words, but you didn't necessarily write them, eh?) I'd cut my losses, re-grouped.

I retained my advantage, head-and-shoulders above any competitor, because I'd take my long history and experience in the comic book realm and translate it to penning a stage script. Officer Wilkes couldn't police my mind, after all! I could write the story all in dialogue, exactly as I would a comic, picturing it as panels on pages, boxes of exposition like stage direction, and he could go his merry way thinking he'd won the day.

I really took to the role of playwright. Within a week of the censorship I was over it - even thankful. After all: it's higher-brow to write plays. We weren't even old enough to yet be studying the format! None of my contemporaries had read one, let alone wrote in the medium, all dramaturgically painstaking. The closest any of them might've come were the practice vocabulary dialogues for afterschool Spanish class - but those weren't plot heavy and often relied on color-coding and checking the illustrations on the board for context clues.

Afterschool Spanish ... I shuddered at the thought. It'd been humiliating when I finally got caught out for how I'd been ditching it since the first day. But I harbored no regrets.

And this piece was gonna be pure class with a poison-pill punch to knock these dang fools' socks off!

In a funny way, I owed much of the cautionary satire of the piece to Mrs. Terre. Her fetishism over jogging apparel despite having regressed to mere walking. The cultish hive-mind of the higher-ups listening to her potty tales. There was something more than natural to this if philosophy could find it out! All I had to do was connect the dots to the pulse of popular culture. And the deftest method for that was aliens and the such. Alakazang - I was cooking with gas!

Though much would depend on precise wordplay and character developments (often subtextual) the scenario itself was a four-alarm fire! Dig:

A smokeable drug of unknown origin is being introduced around the neighborhoods ... kids starting to act strange, conforming lock-and-key to popular notions and trends ... Non-druggies would question them only to be met with chestnuts such as 'We like it because it's cool - it's cool to like cool shows and cool shoes, man.'

Meanwhile?

Parents were forming gaggles who'd jog or do callisthenic exercises in groups ... more and more often inviting each other to potlucks and communal yard sales whilst simultaneously seeming gung-ho about tricking kids into Fun-Runs with the promise of community picnics after ...

... A growing sense of noiac unease underneath it all ...

But it wasn't smoking drugs nor getting fit physiques that were the bogeys - it was conformity itself! Indeed - and this was my piece de resistance! - when the heroic junior-deputy and his plucky younger sister find like-minded people to help them smoke out the masterminds behind the indoctrination ... it turns out this squad is yet another false flag operation set up by the actual alien interlopers!

'Get them all to conform to something - it doesn't matter what or how many things - then pit them against each other! The very chemicals in their minds which cause individual identity are the drug which will undo them!'

Endie had been listening, rapt, but kept sinking lower in the bus seat as I boomed and gesticulated. I got his drift. That miserly bus driver and his over-inflated sense of civic adherence to the letter of the law, send its spirit to Hell!

Slunk down and whispered 'But you see how this proves my point, right?' Endie nodded, grit teeth.

It was a bit much, the play. I could admit it. But this was early in the pro-cess. I'd thin the soup out. Get it streamlined.

He had to admit the thesis was a corker, though!

SOMEBODY HAD BROUGHT A KITCHEN chair - fancy, capable of rock-ing - and set it up inside the hollow of the snow-boulder we were using as a fort (twice the height of the tallest of us, length-and-a-half of this same person laid prone). I admired whoever it was for having such lenient parents. Though Alvin had been correct to mention we could probably bring out an-ything from our house and 'our parents wouldn't exactly call in the Federal B.I.'

'But this is a nice chair' I said, noting how the back rest had all its slats.

The other nearly two-dozen participants in what was shaping up to be a day spanning, multi-neighborhood snowball war were scattered to the winds, setting up temporary fortifications of their own, caches of snowballs left stra-tegically around, preparing ambushes, the whole nine. Early word had been circulated how Hubert was going to be attacking from the treetops - so he'd have a truly rude awaking when a temporary truce was drafted between all teams in order to pummel the blazes out of his birdhouse butt.

The inside of the snow-boulder was calming to me. Womb noise. I had, in the week it existed, often ventured out to it on my own. I'd lay on the ground or relax in the chair, gazing skyward or else running my mittened palms over the interior of the cavity's round, enjoying how it got denser, icier, sharper each day. One time, I'd dug a portion of the wall out and hid a candy bar inside. Now, I couldn't find the patch and felt animalistically clever.

Though it was important to the overall wellbeing and physical safety of everyone, I'd hoped Alvin wouldn't ask 'What's the word from Winshaw' when, as though by dark sorcery, he asked 'What's the word from Win-shaw?'

Okay. Dig it: I did talk to Winshaw. He did lay a rap on me about the Civil War origins of the Disembodied Parts. 'But we might wanna be careful tak-ing him at face value.'

'I thought he was your friend.'

For the last time: I was not his friend. Once upon a time I'd genuinely believed the sawdust which popper-fireworks purchased from the ice cream man were packaged in was extra gunpowder. I'd struck a deal to sell said gunpowder to Winshaw for the low low price of eighty-five cents. 'He offered that exact amount and I just said Fine because there didn't seem much point bargaining with someone who would say Eighty-five cents.' Anyway: Winshaw had thought it was gunpowder too, until his mom hipped him wise. Then he'd woefully shambled up to me and said 'Ichabod ... you cheated me.'

To reiterate: this is different than friendship.

Returning to the matter at present. Listen:

I'd seen Winshaw roaming about and so struck up a paly rapport - 'Hi' 'Hi' that sort of thing. Knowing I'd have to get more low-down to dredge any usable intel up, I'd accepted his cordial invite to help with something in his backyard. What this translated to is not what a layman might've reckoned on. 'Vinny - he had the carcass of a groundhog on ice. Had a drift of snow where he was keeping it under wraps. Like nothing's nothing - as though showing me a work-in-progress, read me? - he continued with trying to saw through the poor bugger's gums to pry out the front teeth.'

Wait, Alvin needed to understand something: 'Why're you friends with this character?'

Har har har. I allowed him his fatuous moment of mirth there and then got back to the beef.

But unfortunately (though Alvin was offput by the corpse desecration) the rest of what Winshaw had imparted seemed to confirm a lot.

'He said the haunted bridge - over by the Nature Preserve?'

I was forced to admit 'Yes, he'd said that - why?'

It so happened Alvin knew a great deal about this haunted bridge over by the Nature Preserve! Even how to get there on foot. 'Follow the train tracks. Wow. Everything seems to fit.'

I'D PEELED OFF FROM THE war-faring to enjoy pouring the Kool-Aid Kool Burst I'd found hidden in another group's supply cache onto the snow, eating tasty handfuls. Soon I got to enjoy the seclusion, hidden away in the denser, dirtier brambles near the creek. I fantasized being a deserter. Finished with the life I'd known. Consciously divorcing myself from the shame I'd be forced to perform were I to return to my kin. I'd forge a new path. Like some holy man. The cold gripped me firmly, completely, such that I had numbness in feet, teeth chattered, my energy level dwindled, and my clothing was notably sodden. In such a state, not much feeling like resuming the game (my thoughts occupied with the best routes I might take home, unseen, whereupon I'd slither into the bathtub) it was simplicity itself to pretend I was no mere deserter, but instead was gut shot, dying, time losing cohesion, meaning, thoughtscapes such as only those breathing their last could experience and which would be forgotten if somehow I were found out by the medics, nursed back to health.

I heard a tinny cough. Like a contained echo. Heard clear sounds of lumbering, shoes scuffing cement.

Why had it never occurred to me how near I was sitting to another entrance tunnel to the sewer? Just around the bend, really. If not for the hill rise and the sharp drop toward the creek bed, I'd be face-to-face with whoever it was had just belched, farted, scratch scratch scratched at what must've been a fancy cigarette lighter such as Endie's dad used. Thup-thup and whirling crackle of heavy weight shifting foot-to-foot on the pebbled bank of the creek, a sharp of thin ice cracking, and a loogie hocked. A moment later, just in the area of passage I had window of, Dale Beech stepped into view, removing cigarette from mouth to turn my way in a gruff cough.

Putting on the aw-shucks charm which won him so many hearts, he gave a bang-bang gesture at me, a Bob's-your-uncle touch of hush at his lips, wink of his eye, and a two-finger salute. Rather than continuing on, he double-took at me and said 'Say ... your name's ... somebody, yeah?'

'Ichabod.'

'Like the horseman without his head, eh?'

Well, like the schoolmaster haunted by it - though I didn't bother correcting his cite.

'You're a troublemaker from way back, that's how I've heard tell.'

Was I? I shrugged.

Say, did I want a cigarette?

Naw.

Well, if I ever did, I could count on him. 'That's my hideout' he said, meaning the sewer.

I nodded. The poor dolt. But I couldn't summon words for a warning, felt a childish squirm of embarrassment over how he'd either laugh or pretend some serious consideration to my face then go slander me a bet-wetter around town if I told him my concerns.

'Mica's got a big mouth' I for God-unknown reasons blurted out instead.

Dale was all ears.

Oh ho! - so young Mica had ratted him to me, wasn't that a curio!

'I think he's too stupid to know he did, though - was looking out for himself and his pencil fighting.'

This won a guffaw which cleared birds from trees and got something in the brush scampering. Dale said Mica didn't have much pencil to fight with. I nodded a chuckle like I grokked him, Roger-Roger. 'You got my back though, eh?' he asked, gesture of cigarette and then a wave away of my needing to answer, we were already on the same page and he wanted me to know it.

'I thought The Ghostbusters hung out in the sewer' I pressed to seem worldly, then playacted a gee-whiz like 'Wait - are you with The Ghostbusters?'

Another bulbous chucklehead peal of laughter. But he stifled it. Went low. Like imparting something just between us. 'Ghostbusters're yesterday's news, man - ding dong, dead and gone.'

I nodded.

He stared at me. Blank faced. Paused. Smiled. Winked. 'We're taking over, eh?'

CERTAIN THINGS AT THE GROCERY store, from what we'd observed on trips there with my dad, were okay to take and to consume without paying for. Not because he was a thief or endorsed pickpocketing, generally. Far from it. My dad was medical doctor. A mathematical researcher. A scholar of science and physic. A Utopian, we figured.

The items which had become rote to purloin, a part of the shopping experience, were: a small carton of chocolate milk and cookies from the bakery. The cookies: most commonly it'd one of the decorative Smiley Faces (yellow icing was typical, though from time-to-time variants did appear) - either that or a bag of assorted fancy tea-cookies paid for by weight.

I could understand why my dad played fast and loose with civics. The store went through all the trouble of having the bakery place the selected goods on a scale, printing out a sticker with barcode which would ring at the appropriate price. It seemed eating the confections was plenty encouraged - all kinds of people did it. Most of these, perhaps being dim members of the generic populace, would set their empty bags on the conveyor belts with the rest of their goods when time came to visit the cashier.

But why not merely deposit the bags in any number of the trash receptacles found conveniently throughout the establishment? Or slip them behind a magazine or a packages of diapers?

I could see the seams of a genuine philosophy in my dad's antics. What leg would a store detective have to stand on if one tried to impinge on the old man, get him fitted for cuffs?

'If you want me to pay, have a cash register at the bakery.'

Yep. I could see my dad nimbly pointing this out, unbending to any protest which failed to thwart the streamlined reasoning without resorting to sophistries. After all, he'd once spent forty-five minutes in Socratic debate with someone who'd dialed our house to do a telephone survey. That time, the matter had been: for each question he was given the options Strongly Agree, Agree, Disagree, or Strongly Disagree.

'There should be an option of Somewhat Agree and Somewhat Disagree.' No - those were not the same thing, he'd patiently insisted. 'This would be synonymous with I agree a bit more than I disagree versus I disagree a bit more than I agree though without making a bed with either mindset.' Added into the bargain, there should be an option called Neither Agree nor Disagree. But (he intimated right after the call while relating every detail of the conversation to Alvin and I) he'd not wanted to short-circuit the poor surveyor's head.

Yes. He was a doctor's doctor. Hippocratically, it must be conscionable to take these cookies and chocolate milk. Very first line of the physician's vow, I could semantically argue, had me covered there. Or were they calling my dad a quack! He'd been roommates with the chap who'd made the first English translation of Borges - so let any swine dare challenge his devious twists of fabulist logic at their peril!

Of course, I understood the limits, wasn't raised like some farm animal with no control over my appetites. I couldn't well open a soda can, gulp it down, or unbox animal crackers, have a Nestle's Crunch bar.

The world was quite simple when looked at for what it was. It's people make things complicated. 'People makes things complicated, don't they dad?'

He touched my head and said very meaningfully 'That's okay, Icky Person.'

BUT MUCH AS MY DAD'S laissez faire support of the noblese oblige expected of grocery magnates pleased me, the unique aperture through which he viewed the world could become some real corn between my teeth at times.

There was a repetitive scenario in which I'd ask him could I buy something from the bookstore and he'd say 'Yes' of whatever item I presented in specific. Then, as was typical in the two hours plus I'd spend loitering the shop while my dad stationed in the cafe working on his important papers, I'd discover something else which tickled my fancy. Often shored up by the fact the new thing cost considerably less than the first thing, I'd inform my dad I meant to purchase it instead and he'd unceremoniously renege on his offer to stake horse me for either. No amount of argumentation would budge him at such times - it was as though he became a monolithic automaton of denial. His justification would never be explicated further than 'I don't have money for that.'

This led to much disgruntled merriment between Alvin and I. A famous caricature developed in our joint satire concerning how the codger had gone well off his rocker, literally consulted with the drawings of presidents on the bill faces. Washington, Hamilton, Lincoln would either nod him the okay to proceed or else sigh and inform him 'So sorry old boy - I can't be used for a magazine, I daresay! I'm only for Penguin paperbacks!'

This pitfall was front and center as I perused the shelves of J.B. Dalton discovering sets of old time radio shows. Little wooden crate packaging. Four cassettes to each. Original illustrations circa the era of production decorating top and reverse of each. The Shadow. X Minus One. I Love A Mystery. Suspense.

Wondrous! Magnets tugging the metallic of my very soul!

It'd been my penchant of late to read the fantasy novels of Mercedes Lackey, Tor editions of H.G. Wells and Robert Louis Stevenson, and certain original crew Star Trek novels-or-novelizations. I had two of these last type of volume in hand - World Without End and Kobayashi Maru - which my dear old dad had already vouchsafed I could buy.

But would he go in for this audio entertainment if I tried to pull a swap? Or would he feel it frivolous natter?

His advanced years made this a tough contemplation.

In the normal run of things, I'd observed how parents were battle-lined against new-fangled entertainments like movies and video games. But my pop was decades longer in the tooth than most other kids' dads - was older than a good many grandparents! Would 'radio' be some whiz-bang, modern day balderdash to him?

I needed to spin-doctor my presentation of the switcheroo cautiously. Or else I'd have to steal them, risk of being apprehended with a parent in store a real consideration.

No! It was too thorny an escapade to even consider.

But I couldn't get to the mall myself - not without much effort expended and danger of vehicular homicide befalling me at the highway onramps.

'Dad - if I can pay you for half when I get home, could I get these (Suspense, The Shadow) instead of the books?"

No outright veto. He asked to inspect the packages.

'Here's what: I'm writing a play right now and it struck me how maybe it could be rendered a radio drama, as well. Radio drama is something I've become increasingly interested in as a medium, you see?'

After the longest three minutes of my life (why did he take off his glasses to read the package when he could read better with his glasses on?) he told me he'd get them. I was to remember to pay him when we got back home, though. Which he'd forget all about by tomorrow. By the weekend. By the following week, this same time, tops.

'I will. Thanks dad.'

———————————

IN THE BATH, I ENJOYED observing subtleties in the aging wallpaper. The faint lines - indicated more and more by a build-up of grit and mildew over the years - where one strip was applied next to its neighbor would this time line up, that time not. My favorite spot was where the misalignment was so near to being perfectly correct I could convince myself I'd only dreamed it wasn't a flush fit. The pattern was some kind of swirl design boarded by laurels and dots. There: just a whisker too low, a tsk too much to the left. Yet sink down into the chocolate warmth of the tub water and it looked aligned.

Couldn't I walk away from this all? Couldn't I forget the Hellmouth which might be spawning cavities beneath me - the very pipework which was now topping off my bath with another burst of hot water touching down into some goblin innards of succumbed sewer line?

My friends - did they even take it seriously? Enough I'd stake my life on it?

Say some diabolic hand had got in here, stashed itself behind the toilet tank, lay waiting for me to drift into slumber ... rusty serrations lusting to stretch across my throat ...

Which of my compatriots would burst in here to prevent it? How long would they mourn?

Then again: say Endie were being strangulated by a left foot or something, this very minute - could I help him? And when I couldn't, would I spend the rest of my days weeping with garment rent?

I did have things to do, after all!

And who's gonna believe me I go on about what the likely culprit was?

I had no evidence. The Disembodied Parts were meticulous in their deniability.

How bad could dying be?

... the bath was turning me morbid.

I pulled the plug and left the room, hardly toweled dry.

It was always a pleasure, opening new cassettes. Four. I would savor them. Remove the shrink-wrap from Tape Two only after both sides of Tape One had been listened to. Listen to the episodes in the order they were presented. No need to guess from titles which story I'd be more fond of. These all seemed fabulous.

'Suspense — The Columbia Broadcasting System's outstanding theatre of thrills! Roma Wine is proud to present ... ... Suh - spen - suh!'

Orson Wells gave preamble to this first episode. The Shadow himself! Mister War of the Worlds!

'The following story is a thriller - if it's half as good as we think it is, you might call it a shocker ...'

And so began The Hitch Hiker ...

... and so adrifted my soul into a new ether, milky and plump, pulsing like a birth sac ... sounds taking shape, time becoming meaningless, the dark of the room, even though not absolute, going thick and tight like an ink spill, thin and vast like an ink spill's spread ...

'Hello ... Hello ...'

Chills.

Terror.

Hopelessness.

Who was this hitch hiker? How was he able to follow this man?

'If a fella were to drive along - say at a nice steady clip of forty-five miles per hour, you see? - couldn't someone else, say traveling seventy, eighty, always manage to pass him by, be waiting up ahead?'

'Well, sure - but who would wanna do that?'

Bernard Herman was the composer of these jarring intrusions of strings and cymbal, according to Orson. Their strains danced macabre with the subtle mutter of sound effect, voices as though far away or right in close.

'You didn't see him?'

'See who?'

'The man in the road - he was there ... I tried ... tried to ... to run him down'

'Run him down? Oh let me out - let me out!'

My chest was stammering. So hard was my pulse I had to sit up, lay down, sit up, lay down with its percussion. No longer at the adrenaline of the radio play, however. No. And no longer at phantasmal horror or concern for what fiend body-part might be salivating over me out there in the dark. Severed head as bird, breathing down my neck. Squirrel in the attic, waiting to transfigure, brandish its brass knuckles, dip them in tar, roll them in glass shards. No. It was in recognition. This was my calling, by God! Radio drama! Like in the Golden Age!

How bad could dying be? - had I asked that?

Oh what a dope! I had much too much to live for to dwell in the doldrums. Much too much blood to curdle!

IT WAS SHREWDLY COLD. DEW still fanged to the portions of grass which no longer housed iced patches of snow. An almost growling crisp to the crunch of our feet as we made our way out of the neighborhood, Alvin, Endie, Binion, Nickels, myself.

The route we would venture was not without hazards. A five-lane road would need be traversed to get to the motel behind the Denny's and the car dealership. From there, we could punch through some fencing to get onto the train tracks.

The relative laziness of the weekend's early morning would be cloak against any odd parent who might be about, able to mark us where we'd no right to be. Who knows whom and for what purposes frequent that dingy Red Roof Inn? Nevermind neighborhood nosiness, even. People out for a quaint drive might feel the urge to pry their snouts where no snouts were welcomed. The motel staff might report us as hoodlums if we lingered too long at the fence.

A police report was the last thing we were cruising for. So this would be a precision operation. And we were more than up to the challenge!

First, we stopped at the Shell Station for Slush Puppies and candy bars. And before you knew it, we were traversing the tracks, shielded from the below highway's traffic by high concrete barriers which Nickels (very worldly bloke) explained were to defend hapless commuters from possible derailment. Binion said his mom once told him those walls were to keep the train noise contained, but we all told him to think about how little sense that made on multiple levels.

As we marched our way along, Binion and I became keenly invested in speculative talk about what the various graffito might mean. Who did the spray painting? Wherefore? How often? We were playing the questions for yucks, goofballing through first our nervousness then, as the walk droned on, our boredom.

But Nickles was a bona fide fount of information and soon joined us, Alvin and Endie closing ranks for the free lessons as well. Many of the markings were rubbish, it seemed. Meaningless. Idiots who didn't understand there's little point spritzing cement with atomized paint if it has no import or mystique. These were the name-icons of various gangs. The Diamond Farm Crew. The Billionaires.

'The Ghostbusters?'

Nickels seemed genuinely puzzled, now he had reason to think about it. He didn't seen any tags representing them.

I kept my chills to myself. Perhaps their erasure was not only physical. Something miles beyond murder. All trace of them being scoured from recorded history in any format. How soon until I (and maybe Dale Beech) was the only one left who recalled their moniker, their deeds, their end?

Nickels explained how he frequently walked these tracks because a friend of his lived in Franktown. Probably this was the main reason he had accompanied today as Sherpa.

He pointed up ahead at one of his all-time favorite tags. 'It's a history lesson. A lot of these are.'

Prerak killed the Serial Killer.

Very quickly spewed words, it seemed. But a sanctified, obvious pride to them. And clear of all other graffiti for quite a length, as though the scrawl were universally venerated.

'What's it mean?'

'It means Prerak killed The Serial Killer.'

'Who was the Serial Killer?' No one really knew, it seemed. 'Except Prerak?' Sure. Prerak knew, obviously.

Endie felt puckish and said 'I suppose nobody knows who Prerak is either - except the Serial Killer?' a real tongue-in-cheek pronunciation of Prerak (Pree-rack) class-clowning like he got the point, big league, and was fronting off.

But Alvin said, proper pronunciation 'Naw - Prerak lives in those houses back behind the mall. He went to school with Sullivan.'

We digested this information.

Binion threw the remainder of his Slush Puppy (all sugary liquid by then) over the concrete protection. And though there was no need to worry, regardless if it hit one of the cars we heard buzzing below the bridge we were passing over just then, we all ran away, booking a solid five minutes before slowing to cough and catch breath.

'How did Prerak kill the Serial Killer?' I asked, not really meaning for anyone to answer.

But Nickels said, as though reciting a fact from a well-thumbed textbook 'With poison he got off of mousetraps.'

NOW WE'D COME ALL THE way out, it was occurring to us we didn't know exactly what we were looking for. Nothing about this patch of train tracks particularly screamed Civil War. Plus, we were confronted with how anemic the scant facts we had about the dead soldiers actually were.

We knew: ghosts of Civil War soldiers. We knew: around here.

'Is that all we've honestly got?'

Alvin was taken to task, as this whole turkey-shoot had been his bright idea. Though, he was right - he'd merely said there were such things and it was funny how Winshaw had also mentioned the Civil War.

What a crazy miscue, when it all shook out!

Myself, and by extension the others, had likely assumed Alvin's going to bat for Winshaw's crackpotism meant Alvin had the straight dope in scholarly detail about these ghost soldiers. All the while Alvin, knowing he only knew his factoid because he'd pulled it from a listicle, assumed my, and by extensions the others, deciding to go ahead with this long march meant we had between us enough details to flesh out a meaningful account of what Civil War dead would have to do with anything.

Endie was correct when he said (A) Civil War soldiers don't necessarily need to haunt exactly where they died and (B) if one took a statistical view of life, certainly some of the Civil War must've gone down here. 'And absolutely somebody died. People've died on every inch of the Earth if you take since the beginning of time into account.'

This all passed the sniff test. Except: would train tracks have been in play by the Civil War?

No.

They might've been.

'Since when's it been with trains?'

Didn't any of us ever pass a test on this?

I offered up how John Henry was a steel drivin' man, but confessed I couldn't vouch for it being true, per se, or being germane to a specific time and place pre or post-Civil War. Nickels and Binion made some incredulous claims which were neither here-nor-there as they referenced events of The Revolutionary War and World War One, respectively.

'When was the Civil War?'

Alvin called for reason: let's forget the pop quiz and focus! 'The story goes: they come out in the fog. Or at least when its chilly. Or maybe all the time. Right near that bridge over there.' He meant the little one which traversed the thin, winding, one-lane road, outlined by thick and especially spiky trees.

Who had seen these ghost soldiers, personally?

Marvin and Carlye and Rickets had, according to Albert and Finn.

Good folks, the lot. Yeah, we all nodded mutely how they could be banked on.

'Look around for bullets or medals.'

Ghosts always want something. Maybe these spooks were looking for such trinkets, wanted them buried somewhere so they could achieve their final rest.

'What else ought we be looking for?

It was a good question.

'Canteens. Coins, maybe. If it looks Civil War-ish just nab it so we can all put our heads together, give inspection.'

On the tracks? Or in the woods?

'They walk the tracks.'

Which may or may not have existed in their day.

'Maybe that's why they can't find the medals they dropped.'

We poked around a bit and listened to the backyard sounds from the nearby housing development. Scents of someone cooking out in the middle of the day.

'Any chance we know any kids live around here? They must have the skinny on whatever goings on there are.'

Alvin and Nickels didn't think so. The rival swim team to our swim team all hailed from this development. Those guys were boneheads, an indisputable reality which Alvin made a point of illustrating by way of assorted anecdotes.

'Why're you friends with Winshaw, again?'

I chuckled and took this on the chin. But in truth, I was starting to the warm to the kid. Wished everyone would leave off ridiculing him about his groundhog corpse. It did have cool teeth. I could understand wanting them. They were something people had wanted. Teeth. Things like that. Look at history.

HOW QUICKLY REVERSALS STOCKPILE.

We'd come all this way in the cleverest fashion, let's grant that. However, come the stroke of midafternoon we'd yet to take the first stride of our return trek. It'd be coming on early evening when we squiggled back under the motel's rear fence. Lordy, wouldn't the roads be swarmed! No way we'd avoid getting our pictures took, dead bang!

Now came the rain clouds. Winter had gotten us complacent. Overcast skies the norm. Snowfall had lulled us into feeling impervious to run-of-the-mill downpours.

Roads'd be jam packed plus everyone paying extra attention out their windows for safety's sake. Or else to have scapegoats to front off a grudge about viz 'Now these punk kids're darting around!? I'll see them strung up for this!'.

Not to mention if the deluge lasted hours. But we'd be soaked to misery, freeze ourselves into fevers by quarter-mile up track if we got hasty. So we'd scurried for cover into the tunnel beneath the bridge – the tunnel which Alvin only suddenly had the presence of mind to mention was, itself, haunted.

'We should be fine. Only trouble comes if you park a car down here after midnight, kill the engine, turn out the lights. Nothing to do with the Civil War.'

Some relief there. But it turned cold comfort indeed when I spotted the leg in amongst the rubbish at the road shoulder. A leg. 'Someone explain why there's a leg right there' I will never forget my composure in demanding.

'It's a fake' Binion put out after a journalistic, bent forward squint.

As though context helped matters!

It was, no doubt, a prosthetic leg. Phew and all, but ... 'It's a prosthetic leg in a buncha roadside trash, in a haunted tunnel, under a haunted bridge!'

'Near some haunted train tracks' was the better descriptor, Endie pointed out. 'The bridge itself doesn't seem specifically haunted.'

We were thankful for his cool head. 'But we should come to some consensus about this leg, just to avoid future controversies.'

Hypothesis One (via Nickels): 'Maybe they didn't need it?'

Hypothesis Two (via Alvin): 'Right?'

Hypothesis Three (via me): 'Are you kidding, man?'

Hypothesis Four (via Binion): 'Might've been a prop for some theatre piece, the run's over.'

Endie, again our compass, pinned a tail on the donkey by clapping, gruff 'Say whatever of those things prove out. Still: how'd it get here? You throw your fake leg out of a moving car? Take it off because you're fed up?'

'Okay' Binion offered up 'Dig this: In a moving-truck - leg fell out while the guy's changing residences - driver unaware. It's his back-up leg, only, so he hasn't noticed.'

I understood the game being played here aimed to calm us. Inundate with minutia, pile up banal details to make this bizarre spectacle present as feasible. But I couldn't get behind it.

'Fell from a truck? Fine. Still: It's there on the road, yeah? Complete stranger out walking sees a leg?' I pantomimed ushering the limb to its current spot with a push broom, dusting my hands a sarcastic job-well-done. 'Frankly, I think I'm learning more about how your mind works than I'm comfortable with, Bin-bag.'

The jocularity underneath all the barbs caught on, soon enough. Useful to stave off the shivers, buck against the suffocating dread.

My final summation: there's no getting around how it's not reasonable for a prosthetic leg to be chucked in a pile of empty Mr. Pibb cans.

I was serious. But let the laughter go. Let them have their cocoon of rhetoric as we whistled past the graveyard.

THE OLD MAN WAS LYING. A bald-faced confabulation. But my hands were tied. I couldn't outright accuse him of deceit. After all, I'd need him to buy me Roy Rogers hamburgers in future. Which he probably knew. Was testing me some way. My dad was always pulling such wily tricks. He knew I knew he was lying. 'Let's find out what kind of metal the kid's made of' - tent me to the quick was his angle.

I explained it all to Alvin when I got upstairs. How dad had promised to go to the drive-thru, bring home a bag of bacon cheeseburgers for me. Gets home, doesn't have 'em. Understanding I'd point out how simply he could turn the situation around by hopping back in the car - zip zip - he then makes the bonkers claim Roy Rogers had closed.

'Didn't say they were closed as in they'd not been open at all, today. No, no. Alvin - he said they literally closed as he was driving up.'

Quick look to any clockface would get this parent, so-called, thrown in the brig for perjury. But Alvin concurred I was right to mind my manners about it. And to help me over the ordeal, we jointly concocted a song using the pre-programed melodies on a chintzy Casio keyboard which had been laying around on the floor since forever. Salsa, in particular - as close as we could find by way of a proper nod to dad's Argentine blood. We had ourselves cracking up, before long, with our on-the-fly lyricism.

'I said Oh no! / they closed at seven forty-five! / Oh my poor son! / They closed right before my eyes!'

We promised to make a recording, but in our hearts knew such spontaneous magic would never be recaptured in a studio setting. Quickly moved past the promise, no muss no fuss.

Things settled into chatter about our new focus - namely, we'd like to take a crack at a learning a genuine martial art. I remained partial to Jeet Koon Do. Bruce Lee was a hep cat, let no man say otherwise. 'And he was in a gang when he was young' I said, not meaning a thing by it except to sound scholarly. Alvin made kind of a yuck face and reminded me not to judge iconic, game-changing superstars by their youthful peccadillos.

Main point: we didn't want Karate. Or anything Japanese. Not because we had it out for the Japanese or principally found fault with their contributions in many fields. No. Movies had simply proffered proof positive Japanese martial arts were based more on loud noise, stiff muscular posturing, and a load of harebrained machismo, while Chinese martial arts were nonchalant, seemed tighter fit to our tastes. Not to mention we preferred the outfits. Cloth shoes a la Tiger Wong were just the thing for what ailed us.

We'd brought home books from the library (Karate, Kung-fu, and Tae Kwon Do) but the stark, stiffly performed images in the photographs in concert with densely written instruction was no kind of way to educate.

'These are such scams' Alvin bristled. However, he liked them as models for drawing. And we could find no fault with the leotards the women were decked out in.

'Dad's not gonna let us take kung-fu' I had to remind Alvin. 'He abhors violence, even when violence is artful and has a meaningful historical lineage.'

Alvin said he'd been working it out with mom. She went to the gym to swim and jog and whatever all, didn't I know? Well dig it: the beard to our activity would be: she'd signed us up for 'exercise class'.

Pretty good cover-fire, I had to admit. I'd never known our mom to be particularly shrewd what with her perpetual insistence we be honest, law-abiding sorts. Good for her.

'The female of the species' Alvin imparted. I nodded because I doubted he'd be wrong about something like that.

Though it was all moot until we found a decent dojo. The Yellow Pages had Karate on the brain, seemed like. And when we'd tried to physically walk to the one king-fu joint listed, all there was was an old guitar shop which, itself, had been shuttered for ages.

BY MID-DAY SATURDAY, DAD HAD made it all up to us. He was cemented in our good graces immortally on the strength of how he'd simply shrugged 'Okay' when we'd asked could we ride in the trunk on the way to rent some movies. To ice the cake, he agreed to go inside to pick up the tapes so we wouldn't have to get out of the trunk in the parking lot, either.

Unprecedented as this victory was, we decided not to let the grass grow underfoot. Figured if we rolled the dice, phoned ahead to have the tapes waiting at Check-Out, we could finagle some R-rated flicks, into the bargain.

An element of chance to this proposition.

First blush? Sure - dad was an elderly guy - why would a clerk question if R-rated was okay? The law was on our side, there.

Human nature though! Dad might say he's picking up for his kids, clerk might assume kids meant young children, be some work-a-day do-gooder and thus inquire whether dad had given our selections his blessing.

Also: while it was hard to believe he would, dad might ask the clerk probing questions about the thesis and content of the films. We didn't have to worry about him seeing anything untoward on the boxes, as the artworks would be in the aisle - but while this helped us in one respect, it might stoke his omnipresent curiosity about the world around him.

Regardless: a thing worth doing is worth doing whole hog. Alvin made the call. Requested Lionheart, American Ninja IV: The Annihilation, The Perfect Weapon, and No Retreat, No Surrender.

The trunk ride was magnificent! Fifteen minutes in amongst some thick wires we didn't know the purpose of, an old briefcase, some manila envelopes, and a not-quite-empty bag of industrial salt with a tire iron shoved in it.

We gabbed about a back-up plan in the eventuality dad popped the trunk, told us the films were inappropriate. Figured any strategy was moot, though. Dad would merely decide to not rent the things, drive home, and tell us of his veto only far too late. Not even to teach us a lesson. He was simply a mercurial algorithm of a person, at times.

He did open the trunk, quite unexpectedly, before going in, though we couldn't sort out why. He acknowledged us wordlessly, we squinted through all the sunlight, kind of glowered, then he shut us back in.

Alvin wondered what would've happened had there been a fender-bender. 'Dad would play it cool' was our consensus - no need to mention his offspring stowed in the trunk and no doubt he'd trust us to have his back.

A bad wreck, no survivors?

Well, good luck to the poor rookie cop assigned to sort out what would quickly become quite the baffling crime scene! They'd never get to the bottom of it!

It was akin to being invisible, overhearing candid conversations of people getting into the cars nearby us. For a jape, Alvin banged on the underside of the trunk lid and made muffled sounds of kidnap.

Silence from the young couple we'd heard chatting.

When they resumed their debate, Alvin made gurgling sounds and noises almost in the shape of words, whining and whisper toned.

Silence from outside. Then: 'Hello?'

We both froze. Eyes fused open and locked, tensed knees clicking against each other's.

'Hey.' Sound of the trunk handle being attempted - thankfully the old man had locked it fast! 'Is someone there?'

Alvin was holding his breath so I did likewise, though regretted it because I was terrible at holding my breath and now feared a bulbous exhale.

'Is someone in the trunk?'

'There's no one in the trunk' a girl's voice incorrectly asserted.

'I heard something in that trunk.'

'Can we just go get some fries, Evan?'

Enough was enough. Alvin and I, in hushed tones, agreed to wait this gaffe out. Keep cool and we'd be home free in no time.

Suddenly: key to the trunk lock and my dad handing us three tapes.

'I did not like a movie to be called A Perfect Weapon.'

'The Perfect Weapon' Alvin corrected for sake of accuracy.

'You cannot have weapons.'

Sure sure - could he close the trunk, though? Who knows what this was all starting to look like to prying eyes.

DONOVAN SIMPLY WOULDN'T FACE UP to the facts. 'The Hudson Hawk videogame's a conjob!' We'd never even got the Start screen to come up! Okay. Those few times. But just stuck on the title image.

He continued blowing into the cartridge, the console slot, undeterred. Had to physically wrest him away because Roscoe needed to play Spy Hunter. He aimed to prove once-and-for-all how 'After the boat you get in a chopper.' We'd been calling this bluff for ages. Took our seats to smugly watch him not even survive to the boathouse, let alone get airborne.

I liked to play Elevator Action followed immediately by Spy Hunter. 'It's like they're sequels!' Elevator Action guy survives his pop-gun decent down apartment building, hops in that car - zang! - Spy Hunter picks up the narrative.

'You should send that to Nintendo Power!'

True. The world'd be improved from this observation. Except the mag was getting so Super Nintendo centric my keen insight'd be ash-canned as nostalgia bait.

Alvin must've tagged some subtle shift in me following this discussion. Come evening, he entered the bedroom where I was at work on my play, told me to join him in the basement.

'Do you feel the world's phasing you out, Ick?'

Blink ... blink ...

'That Nintendo Power thing' he meant.

Truthfully, I'd not kept it in mind. But felt some need to perform an existential shiver befitting the artist my brother's tone took me for. 'There's still so much I could say about Abbadox' I sighed, light-hearted.

So we riffed about the advertisement for that game in the back issue of Quasar which'd made me so excited for it. 'Battle inside the belly of the beast!' And to continue the talk-therapy, Alvin moseyed down memory-lane, too, recalling how hard we'd taken the piss out of the first advert for Mega Man.

'Trouble in Monsteropolis!' he mugged in dork-voice. Yet? Mega Man was a stone classic. 'Life's funny.'

True. However: I didn't feel we'd been off-base to mock it, in its time. The illustration of Mega Man looked nothing like Mega Man in the game proper. How were we to know?

Then: like a switch swatted into activation I started railing on about the roiling qualms which'd been lacerating me. I'd been keeping them to myself. Trying to swivel them into an unreality, a childish fixation. Was the world blind? Was I some palooka for thinking of the wellbeing, vitality - the very survival - of the general populace? 'Everyone's a bunch of lemmings, Vinny! Dumb as grubs! If they can't help themselves, how can I help them? For that matter - how can I count on it they'll help me?'

Alvin made no gesture suggesting my histrionics were out-of-order. Watched while I spewed it all out.

Where could've a prosthetic leg come from? 'Let me tell ya: yanked off a living, breathing cripple!'

Who'd leave it under a bridge, no regard to decency? 'The free-roaming leg that screwed itself into the stump!'

These Disembodied Parts could be reconstituting into whole bodies! 'They probably aren't real animals or body parts, Alvin! Those're just convenient vessels for misdirection! Easy ways to attach to and take over hosts!' It was all there for the looking! Walking amongst us - nodding, waving, gripping, walking - could be the full evolution of the seedlings we knew. 'And

what good's a sixteen-bit Castlvevania gonna be to anyone if none of us are
any of us by the time it comes out!?'

Abruptly, this pent-up screed of angst hit a wall. I was spent. Hardly remembered coming to the basement. Didn't recall the contents or substance
of my rant - if there'd truly been any.

Was about to laugh when Alvin said 'I'm glad to see you see.'

SO HAPPENED I'D BEEN LISTENING to the radio same time Donovan
had. I'd been in my mom's car on the way home from her piano lesson, Donovan'd been - well, I dunno, his bedroom probably.

So: out we trudged to Circuit City, Donovan hopeful of securing his big
break, though with no real through-line to his thesis for accomplishing this.
'Just gotta be ready to make a splash when opportunity comes knocking' was
his mantra. 'Worst comes of worse? I'm the same as when I started.'

No one much could argue with his stoicism.

Here's the shot: a local man (not to our neighborhood, city, or state, but
to somewhere) strolled into a branch of this electronics chain, set to using the
display keyboards, and performed live a hilarious song he'd composed. Beers
In Heaven. By happy trick of chance, his performance was captured by someone testing out a camcorder. After a bit of technical tinker-smithing, the audio was plastered over airwaves to environs near and far.

A star was born!

I'd dug the song, personally. And ever the curious sort, I'd pumped my
mom for information. Wanted to appear as erudite as possible in conversations such as this one, walking with Donovan. She'd clued me in how it was
a send-up, based on a song called Tears In Heaven by some old-guard bigwig.
'It's very sad' she told me. 'His young child died by falling from a hotel bal-
cony.'

I didn't exactly know what to make of this. After a moment spent trying to
sort through the complex human reactions to grief, I (as non-judgmentally as
I could muster) had asked 'If this guy's kid just died, what's he doing in Circuit City being some kinda cut-up?'

Question paid off: now I was able to explain to Donovan how she'd meant
whatshisname's kid had died, not the guy who wrote the funny song.
Though, we both felt, it would've been whatshisname's private business had
he wanted to deal with his tragedy through the balm of parody.

Donovan was living in a land of his own delusional creation, was my honest
opinion. What're the odds two celebrities would break onto the scene via
Circuit City? 'It's a pretty specific venue for an origin story, man.'

But this was his point, exactly! 'Everyone's thinking Circuit City's been burned through, so wannabes have moved on. While they twiddle their thumbs, I pull the slick move of going where everyone'd least suspect!'

Not bad. Seemed correct, his theory this'd make his performance come off twice as spectacular, just by dint of whodathunk?

After fifteen minutes I needed to get out of the chug-a-chug, obnoxious atmosphere of the shop. And all Donovan was up to was browsing the still-overpriced discount cassettes and ogling the CDs as though he'd ever come close to affording any.

I gave him the power handshake and split.

Detoured to Collector's World where Shine was relating a dream he'd dreamt which'd given him a great idea for a short story or film treatment.

'I'm in a restaurant and I sit down in a booth. Notice a man keeps staring at me. But when I look closer, I discover his face isn't a face, just a collection of geometric objects which, corner-of-your-eye, resemble a face. And he proceeds to tell me how the end of the world is coming - and it's based on my anxieties.'

This sounded crackerjack to me! A surefire hit! He seemed glad for my support, explaining it'd been a while since his first (and as of then only) story had seen publication. A piece titled Weiner's Losers. I asked, but he didn't impart any particulars to me.

On the way down the plaza steps by the payphones, I bumped into a kid called Wayne.

'You hear what happened in the Montessori parking lot?'

No. What happened in the Montessori parking lot?

LITTER OF CANDY BLUE WINDOW glass in a grapey clump like deer droppings. This must've been where the victimized car had been parked.

No law enforcement on the scene to eavesdrop anything official from. All I had was Wayne's hearsay account: Some brazen hooligan, middle of this crisp sunny day, had hefted a piece of cinderblock retrieved from the weedy clumps skirting the tree-line, smashed the window up a treat, and bilked some woman off her purse which'd been rested on front passenger seat.

Touch of victim-blaming from Wayne (a la 'Here's why it's best to secure your belongings blah blah blah') which I found quite out-of-order. This was an educator of children! Obviously her attentions were on things of graver importance. If anything, she put an abundance of trust in the better angels of the everyman. This is a laudable stance to impart to youngsters. Though, yes, she might wanna temper her lessons, in future, not oversell her pie-in-the-sky outlook. However: even granting that, her continuing to suggest to kids that not everyone they meet is a snake-in-the-grass was nothing to browbeat the woman for.

Cops? What good were they gonna be? Buncha whistle-while-you-work flatfoots, you can quote me! I saw it from a country mile off: took statements, poked their toes around thinking Abracadabra! the culprit would return to the crime scene to gloat. For all I knew, betcha they had a duck-blind set up, scoping me, figuring I was in on the scheme. Even better? They'd pin lazy blame on The Ghostbusters! Treat this as another statistical tick proving the counties descent into gang-law.

Cops watch too much television, there's my two cents.

Nothing better going, I decided I'd do some freelance digging.

Start with this broken glass.

Imagine I were the crook - well? I'd know the landscape, wouldn't I? Have a route planned to book it, double-time.

Quickest way to escape? Into the creek, sub-path next to the bridge.

Lo and behold - what do we have here!? I dared someone to tell me with a straight face the scuff mark on this rock wasn't clear result of that footprint in the slick of mud, right there.

Put it all together? Boom - crook steps in mud - Boom - touches down on rock.

Where to next?

Obvious leap onto the creek bank. Dash through the water to throw possible dogs off their scent. Which would mean they'd be banking for the hill, just ahead.

Pay dirt! I was a natural! Look at this evidence! The very purse - strike me blind if not! Only nonessential things left inside the sopping cavity of it - compact, lip gloss, ruined receipt papers - but gimme a break! I didn't need to have the owner present to confirm - what other purse was it gonna be, right here, today of all days?

I was jittery with accomplishment. Wanted to whoop and holler.

What's the next move?

Scuzbag must've pocketed the valuables ... then would've either gone that way or ...

... I froze ...

Silt from the slow trickling water stuffed in around my foot sides, weaseled to my flesh through my sock fabric.

In the water - in the water! underneath the prim warble of its surface - was a footprint in blood.

A footprint.

In blood.

I gaped, unable to process. Except wasn't I looking flat at it, sure as I was alive?

... A footprint in blood ...

... Toe pointing thataway ...

...Thataway ...

Toward the sewer gullet. Dale Beech's little hideaway. Which was (facts were facts) the more reasonable escape route than up into a public field where anyone out walking a dog could drink you in.

I turned around a few times, trying to sort out a way I might be seeing things askance.

Any other footprints?

Nope.

Smashed glass.

Footprint in mud.

Scuffed rock.

Depression of leap down.

Into water.

Maybe twelve healthy strides.

Blood.

NOT BLIND TO HOW FLUMMOXED I was stammering, Alvin pointed out how two aspects of reality lent a touch of incredulity my story. In no particular order: there was no bloody footprint and Dale Beech couldn't have had anything to do with it.

If not Dale, who? All the pieces fit when he was painted onto the canvas.

Let's start with Dale, then. Here's the scoop: while I'd been out all morning playing pat-a-cake with Donovan's dreams of local-boy-makes-good, other kids in the neighborhood had found a treasure trove in the form of lengths of firm yet pliable plastic tubes. With some ingenuity, they'd fashioned these into bows-and-arrows. Taut string or yarn was utilized to bend the longer lengths, then pieces were broken into shorter increments to serve as projectiles.

A raucous good time was had splintering into factions, planning campaigns of violence against one another. Until: some wet-blanket member of the community gestapo found something amok with this and telephoned everyone's parents. 'There's a directory the Neighborhood Watch has - I dunno'.

Someone (Alvin said a name I failed to recognize) was silver-tongued enough they'd bargained the gaggle of mothers into allowing the bow-and-arrows to remain viable, provided they were only used for a ramshackle archery contest.

'What's this have to do with Dale, Vinny?'

He's coming to that. 'Context is important, Ick.'

Suddenly: who should come stalking down the sidewalk? Dale Beech. Armed with a bow-and-arrow he'd fashioned out of a genuine tree branch same as an honest-to-God survivalist might. Dale had spent the morning shaving smooth smaller sticks and hollowing out divots at their tips where he could affix thumbtacks or those needles that come with dress shirts.

'When was this?'

Hmn ... So, he was right ... That business only ended thirty minutes before I'd soggied my way home to gather witnesses. Impossible Dale could've committed a crime, made a getaway, and gotten himself killed all inside a half-hour ...

And where was the foot-print? Washed away?

But that was the entire thing: I'd stared at it for certainly ten minutes and at the very least longer than it should take a footprint made out of viscera to wash away. Thus my assumption of the supernatural at play.

'And' it now seemed to strike Alvin 'it must've been there awhile before you arrived, too.'

Yes. Thank you! Now he was getting into the spirit of the thing! 'It's our most tactile and indisputable evidence yet. The only shame is we don't know which body part did it so we can't update the card appropriately.'

'Only thing more definitive would've been if you weren't the only one'd seen it.'

True. Though we agreed I'd done my due diligence there, considering the specifics of the incident.

Even best-case scenario: someone had slasher-killed a purse-snatcher. If so, that's not too terribly good to have going on in a suburban community.

'A vigilante?' Alvin spit-balled as we gave a final poke around. Perhaps. 'For all we know' he continued 'the slaying was justified. Combat. It may've come to much the same had we been made to tussle it out with The Ghostbusters that fateful night.'

Which, odd as it was, had never occurred to me as a possible outcome to that affair.

I was being a child. How long had I been such a child about all this?

There must've been other people who, like us, had taken a look at the moral decay encroaching ever so insidiously into the bucolic environs of our development and decided they were right fed up. 'People get fed up.'

'People do' Alvin nodded, letting a sigh down his nose.

Also: other gangs could've moved in to fill the power vacuum left by The Ghostbusters ghoulish demise.

Or like those Japanese soldiers out in the jungle, maybe some autonomous cell of Ghostbusters survived. A more malignant breed, willing to stoop as low as they could. No idea their war was over.

TO SAY I WAS TENSE would be to wildly undershoot the mark. The situation itself was traditionally nervy, being a matter of the heart. Stir in my penchant for subtlety and I had to fend off pangs on multiple fronts.

Would Nikki profess feelings for me I'd no reason to believe she harbored? Perhaps yearnings as tight-bottled as my own were toward her? Would she notice the symbolic, personalized invitation I'd included on the envelope containing her Valentine?

Say she sidled up to me, asked if I wanted to accompany her to a sock-hop of some kind? I honestly didn't want any part of things like that! I simply loved her and didn't see why there had to be more to it.

But who's to blame? Wasn't it me who'd concocted this goofball gesture?

Odds were she'd not notice. So I played it cool, doodling on the grocery-bag brown cover of what I realized wasn't actually my Math book. No. Nikki wouldn't notice a thing. I'd been too romantically understated, not in any way aiming to impinge on her autonomy, place her on the spot, or even have her realize how she made me fall aflutter to pieces on a daily basis.

Her hair was white-blonde! Her name had two Ks in it! A minx, by default. And she was very good at memorizing things, too - how she'd caught my eye, in fact.

She wouldn't notice, because I'd been careful. Lookit: on her envelope, on the underside of the licked adhesive flap, I'd written, in feather-light pencil Nikki, I actually love you and don't know if you love me back but hope so.

Inside? Nothing to give the game away. Store bought, dime-a-dozen card with a Starburst candy affixed to it with scotch tape. Same as I'd given everyone.

It'd go like this: there she is, watching her collection-bag fill up, chatting with Elise about whichever natter. She wouldn't even read the names on each card. Who does? In fact, now I wanted to keep my eyes peeled, maybe find a sly method of getting rid of the envelopes once the cards were exhumed just so she could never discover the notation.

Wouldn't it be awful? Three weeks, a month, over the summer or something she finds me out? Right when I least expected! And boy oh boy I'd have to answer for it, wouldn't I?

Binion, when I confessed all, pointed out I was manufacturing my own trouble. 'Life doesn't go like in the books we're assigned.'

'I don't read those books.'

He knew this, but his point still held. Though, he admitted, Snow Treasure was a bit over-the-top. 'Nothing at all goes like Snow Treasure, full stop.'

Intrigued, I asked what was Snow Treasure?

'Kids hide Nazi gold in snowmen. I think it's an allegory.'

I didn't know what that meant. Allegory?

'It was a vocabulary word last year! I thought you still got good grades back then?'

My god ... That was true, wasn't it? Third grade. Such a Johnny-on-the-Spot. Big things writ on my baggage ticket, baby! Mr. Southern had noticed, even given me a special copy of Maniac McGee which'd come with a cassette of the author being interviewed.

How had it gone from there to here?

Binion had no idea. Had his own fish to fry. But when I asked which fish, he was reluctant to go into it.

'Come on, man – what's the shot?'

Just some concern over Field Day. It was months off, but he had the sinking suspicion he was no longer the fastest kid in class. I could see what he meant. The only person whose speed was commented on regularly was Bishop Wexler.

'And he can long jump. And climb a rope!'

A formidable rival to have. 'We'll think of something' I said, touching his shoulder.

He knew we would. Just wished being fast was still easy. Like when it wasn't anything at all. Just what he was.

TROUBLE WAS, I WAS IN no kind of the mellow head required for love. Plus: I was fooling myself if I thought someone as posh as Nikki would even be interested in feelings so pedestrian. Love? Such outré grandiosity was the realm of plebian scriveners like me, not porcelain godheads who bathed in buttermilk!

It was avowed: I'd get this anti-drug script polished off, hook-or-crook. It'd gotten into an atrociously half-baked state and was due by the end of the week, besides. And that was only with having been given an extra week on the strength I was clearly being groomed for some purpose by John Law.

Right off the bat, I needed to ditch the ethereal notions contained in the early draft. Meat and potatoes. Maybe salt, butter, pepper. But leave off the garnish and slaw! Retain the driving pulse, excise the navel gazing meant for people too timid for the chilling jolts I'd offer.

Alien's invading us ... skins exuding a 'new drug' which eventually skews epidemic ... infecting an entire community ... stoned out PTA moms stalk the night streets, force feeding jazz cigarettes to their offspring ...

I daresay there's plenty of punch packed in that!

Even setting aside the implications and uneasy parallels to the contemporary epoch, the piece was a bone-rattler apt to keep any sensitive reader abed at night - and how!

Just look at this scenario:

A kid no older than myself has witnessed his adoptive mother inhaling a drag off a purple cigarette which doesn't get shorter as it burns - the smoke is mustard yellow. She doesn't exhale! Rather, he watches smoke leak from her eyes, linger in almost erotic coils in the air in front of her. Then she breathes it back up her nostrils before finally shushing it out through lips so tight they whistle - whereupon the smoke returns to the cigarette tip from which it had emanated.

No one would soon forget bearing witness to a spectacle like that!

Yet here goes his parent, tra-la-la like nothing ever happened and - holding the evidentiary cigarette all the while! - telling the kid right to his face he's imagining things, strong-arming him into disbelieving the evidence of his own senses!

'You're dreaming this, Piper - this is something you're making up - when you wake up tomorrow it will feel real ... but it's a dream ... today is a dream ... a dream ...'

She starts bearing down on him! Does he flee? Does she suddenly act normal?

Who cares?

Cut Scene! Pick up elsewhere. Some liberal pops in timeline and perspective only augment the medicine-head quality of the narrative. After all, we can't burden ourselves down with tick-tock reality at the expense of sensational kicks!

By eight o'clock I had twenty-six pages completed, not a dingleberry among them. Though in reading some dialogue aloud I was annoyed how often I'd used the words And, That, and Nevertheless. Seeing how my mom was on deck to type up a clean draft for me, I figured I could write a general editorial note suggesting she elide as many recurrences of these words as possible. I'd lay emphasis how I trusted her discretion in substituting other words, if she felt appropriate, so as not to seem perversely dictatorial.

All that remained was to stick the landing.

It was self-evident no deus ex machina existed. Neither grace nor sudden wonder could undo what had been done - I'd seen to that! The heroes of the piece were due to be garishly subsumed into the hive-mind of the cigarettes (which I'd made explicit were sentiment creatures, replete with circulatory systems and brainpans).

Yet ... I couldn't help thinking it would be more of a gut punch if the leads actually died. Leave audiences with a pranging uncertainty whether they were better off for it or the ones who'd suffered the most.

They can't survive and stay the same.

It's either unbecome or perish.

But its kids. School administrators might take it the wrong way if I handed such a document to the cops, theater piece or no. Price to pay if they wound up with egg on their face after going to bat for me.

Where did my artistic priorities lie, here?

MAYBE SOMEONE WITH AN INSIDE lane could advise me why I'm the whipping boy of Fate.

Dig: I'd been so cocksure of my clever mnemonic for spelling Orchid I hadn't bothered even studying the other words, all week. I'd bragged to Binion 'It's spelled O-U-R-C-H-I-L-D - which is Our Child, see? Child - Or - as in Also Known As - Kid. Our-child-or-kid. Ourchild.'

Let's admit: he'd done his best to set me straight. Alack, hubris blinded me to counsel. The dismal results of the exam would require a parent's signature? Well, Mrs. Terre could go pound sand on that count, baby, no fooling!

So: nobody's business but mine, I sulked in the bus' rear seat, turned over the test paper, and made sketches of various school supplies. Ruler. Protractor. Pencil. Pen. Bottle of white glue. Last but not least, I jotted a rendition of lower grade-level paper - two solid lines, dotted line between them. On this sketch (purely for my own kicks, no need anyone else should be concerned) I'd written out various cuss words (in all capital letters then all lowercase then in sentence-case) as though to satirically imply how strictures such as 'good penmanship' inspired youngsters to seek out these terms as rebellion.

All the jolly while I knew I'd need to get rid of the paper.

Debarked from the bus. Crumple crumple - chucked the doubly-sullied document in behind some tall bushes. And I trudged on home.

Upstairs, I took a load off. Read some comics. Stared at the ceiling.

Got a burst of energy, so decided to go for a bit of a tromp, maybe use the swings at the park with the tall slide, climb one of the trees.

But wait: a knock at the door downstairs. My mom answers.

Must be my imagination - sounded like a young girl conversing with her.

Heart in my throat for an absurd instant ('It's Nikki! She's noticed my surreptitious love note!') I soon came to my senses enough to understand it was that overzealous Safety Patrol.

My mom thanks her kindly.

Door shut. Latched.

Could I come downstairs?

Something afoot. But for the life of me I couldn't think what the shot might be. No way to prepare for whatever blindside.

And blindside it was! There in my mom's hand was the very Spelling test I'd drawn on and thought to be rid of! This was like living in a haunted house! The denouement to one of those Edgar Poe stories Alvin was so nuts for lately.

So I laid down a rap about I knew I needed stricter study habits, what a true-blue knucklehead I could be at times, so forth. Solemnly swore I'd do some flagellations, give some alms, go forth and sin no more.

Ah. It was actually the illustrations on the back which were the rub, here.

My move? Play the part of the dumbfounded innocent. 'The glue bottle?'

Champeen of dry wit, my mom paused a solid beat '... Yes ... the glue bottle ... for example ...' before she went on how she was a smidgen more concerned how I could 'perhaps avoid the four-letter words while at school?'

First: why's no one questioning this Safety Patrol imping me to the point she's truffling out litter I fling away, shaming me on my own front stoop? She moonlights as the neighborhood priss, is it? Clock overtime pay for her efforts?

Second: 'Four-letter words?' A peculiar designation if ever I'd heard one! 'There's lots of nice four-letter words. Like ...' my mind oddly went entirely blank '... uh ... like ...' I finally managed 'Flag! Nothing's the matter I wrote Flag - or are you suggesting there would be? Or ... uh ... runt?' Hey! And not to mention: 'Ass only has three letters ... Unless I spelled that wrong, too.'

ALVIN DECLARED THE FINAL DRAFT of my anti-drug play an in-your-face knock-out, truly an example of high-octane virtuosity! If it didn't garner top prize, he'd never trust the artistic or intellectual tastes of the vice-squad again.

This was the earnest pick-me-up I needed. Soon was back to my stoic and energetic self.

I explained I'd no intention of making a radio play from the script, despite its prescience as to which direction our world might be heading.

Oh I agreed wholeheartedly I needed to get to work on something for radio. No one need worry on that count a moment longer. Already I was developing a four-part serial in the style of I Love A Mystery. Having spent the week listening to the multi-episode story Bury Your Dead, Arizona I was convinced long-form drama was the wave of the future.

For the prologue: I envisioned setting the atmosphere with either the Moonlight Sonata or something by Rachmoninoff. Then: Bleed in sound effects evoking sluggish, torrential downpour. Layer on some honks, pedestrian chatter so we understand we aren't on some moor or Dixieland swamp, but rather a sodden modern city, some dismal-time-of-year.

A strangler stalks the tenants of a skid-row housing block.

How was the killer moving to-and-fro unnoticed? Were there multiple killers? Who could be trusted? Was anyone investigating? Could the authorities be counted on to act in the best interest of the populace? Were there insidious motivations for keeping the death toll at peak?

Holy smokes! Alvin could hardly believe the scope of this! Promised he was all in if I needed another member of the voice cast or help generating sound effects.

Meantime, he had developments of his own we needed to celebrate.

Due to some past association with a girl whose mom was big kahuna in the community, deputy-marshal of the pool, Alvin had been tasked with designing a logo for the swim team. His icon would be heat-pressed onto various athletic wear - t-shirts, hoodies, speedo swim trunks, anything aquatic athletes were keen to acquire.

'It's gonna be officially copyrighted and everything. Plus: I get paid - matter of Contract Law and intellectual property.'

'You're a professional now!' This was unprecedented! At thirteen-years-old!? Certainly he and I and countless others had taken magic markers to a shirt to wile away a bored moment, in our day - I could open the closet, pull out the red sweatshirt I'd drawn The Badger's emblem on to prove as much! But Alvin was taking the game to dizzying new heights.

I wished I had any worthwhile insight to give, but my comprehension of design fundamentals had stunted around second grade. This is why I admired Alvin so much. Me? Always content to follow my nose, bet the outside of the table, treat life like an easy breeze. Alvin? He'd knuckled down to his craft. A clear trajectory. Crayon to pencil to mechanical-pencil to pen to airbrush to whatever got images on swim trunks.

Yep. I was awed by him and not shy about letting on how!

Maybe he'd design some packaging for my radio thriller?

He'd do his best.

'Only if your schedule permits' I insisted. 'And we'll steal a bunch of blank cassettes for copies. See if John and John will let us sell them on consignment down Collector's World.'

'What do you mean steal?'

'What?'

'You said steal cassettes?'

Had I?

'Where are you stealing from?'

'Circuit City ... Giant ...' I stammered, Alvin's expression impenetrable '... or have dad get some ... I don't really mean to say steal.'

'Okay.'

'I just meant: this is Art ...' did an Elvis hip-swivel, Yosemite Sam guns with my fingers pew-pew '... any means necessary, right?'

.MARCH.

SPIDER-MAN'S VISIT TO OUR school had been rumored for a fortnight. Everyone had their own opinion on the matter. I leaned in the direction of thinking it wouldn't happen in a strictly literal sense. Rather, some manner of suggestive 'evidences' would be strewn throughout the corridors for the student body to gleefully stumble upon. Makeshift webbings with educational pamphlets about Phonics, tooth brushing, or booklets filled with mazes scotch taped to these stage-dressings.

Say it did come to pass, though? Blasé-blasé was my attitude.

But Endie, Binion, lots of folks had faith and were revved up. Look at it this way: the puppet-show about epilepsy had come through. Moreover, it was confirmed a Harlem Globetrotter would be addressing us before the year was out. Add that up? Why not a visit from Spider Man!?

Binion surmised I'd grown into a sour-bellied curmudgeon due to the anticlimactic response to my script. Oh don't get Officer Wilkes or Mrs. Terre wrong - they were tickled by the work I'd put in, you bet they were! However (per Officer Wilkes) 'It's over the heads of a casual audience' and (via Mrs. Terre) 'We're giving it special mention, because there was also a three-page limit.' Special mention? Nothing beyond a feeble nod during the Say No To Drugs graduation assembly (and frankly the nod was snide, at best).

The winning piece? Some phony baloney after-school special propagandist melodrama. Studious girl watches her well-meaning older brother forget to study for college entrance after 'peer pressure' got him 'toking grass' one night. She wrestles with the moral dilemma of squealing on him.

The fact the Safety Patrol snitch authored it and the libretto was lifted from a story Mrs. Terre had been regurgitating ad nauseam about how fascinating it'd been to hear her junior high school sons' aghast reactions to a classmate's plans to smoke cigarettes was all the evidence of a rigged game I needed. The two-page piece of maudlin quackery received a medal the round of which was big though not quite so much as its flunky author's mouth.

So, sure - Binion was on the button. I was a grouch. But society was to blame.

The day we were pulled from class to gather on the soccer field for Spidey's arrival I was in a distinctly foul heart. Gun to my head I'd not be shifted when clearly our Vice Principle, donning a baggy, homemade, dyed cotton web-slinger get-up, appeared atop the single-story school's roof. Two auxiliary security personnel on loan from Community Recreation Services were on hand to steady him. He waved some half-dozen times while fanfare re-sounded. Dropped a gym rope from the ledge and carefully lowered himself to the pile of mats in place at ground level where he was further assisted down to the pavement by a Math teacher and the elderly Custodian. Almost as soon as he'd appeared he was ducked through the doors near the Art room while several administrators made gestures to stoke abstract applause from all gath-ered.

Same day, final class period, we had a substitute who clearly knew how to game the system. No lesson plan, just a film projector wheeled in and Carry Me To The Sea started with no explanatory preamble. No complaints from me! Film was a personal favorite since first grade.

Right when the carved Indian was watching a forest burn (I was then occu-pied forcing the hole in my sock wide enough to get my big toe through) a slice of overhead lights snapped on, causing me to wince violently. Squinting, I turned to remark the liquidy blur of Spider Man in the doorframe. He ex-toled 'Stay off drugs!' in a clumsily disguised, fabric-muffled voice, flapped the light-switch down and was gone by the time I next blinked.

BAND-AIDS HAD CAUGHT ON LIKE wildfire. Three out of every seven kids plastered with 'em.

I'd welcomed the trend, at first. Even been on board when creative sorts worked in ace-bandages. Frankly, I was kinda jealous I'd not thought of this first. Alvin'd been shocked, seeing how much I dug Fist of the North Star. Would've been an excuse to front off I was Kenshiro!

'Speaking of - Wally says he has the actual Fist of the North Star game for Genesis' Alvin then mentioned.

Nope. In no mood to discuss anything Wally-related. Good on him were it true, but wouldn't be worth the headache to verify.

A week into the Band-aid fad - when neon, oddly-shaped adhesives the more well-to-do parents sprung for to insure their poseur offspring could act high on the horse started appearing - I was sick to the teeth with it. Thus, when morning announcements made explicit the trend was being cracked down on, I breathed a sigh of relief.

'Band-aids are for legitimate medicinal use. Any Band-aid will be removed for authentication of injury. If legitimate, the discarded adhesive will be replaced by the school nurse. Absolutely no Band-aids will be permitted on the face, barring exceptional circumstances.'

Monacci must've thought what everyone had on their minds was 'What's Monacci's take?' because, Lord in heaven, didn't he fill two days embellishing a crock how the ban was a good idea.

Why?

Because in his 'other school' (we'd known him since first grade, so he insisted 'Where I went to kindergarten!') a similar fashion craze had gotten in everyone's bloodstream and soon 'People started wearing casts - then people would wear two casts, four - come to class in hospital beds - until one kid used so many bandages he looked like a mummy and almost suffocated when he flushed the toilet and the gauze got caught, dragging him in!'

Normally, we'd have a blast playing newsroom fact-checker to each atom of Monacci's lunacies, birddog him until he was railroaded out of town - however, a series of high-profile lunchroom scandals captured the popular imagination enough we didn't bother.

A cricket found in the wrapper of an orange ice-pop?

Disturbing.

And on the heels of this, someone named Lester brought a cow-tongue sandwich in for a gross-out, barfed after one bite, never to return.

Side-effect of letting Monacci go unchecked?

Here's what:

According to a kid called Simon, his older brother had pulled a prank of putting Saran Wrap on a urinal in such a way it remained invisible to the naked eye. Unsuspecting kid takes a wizz? Mist of urine drenches their entire mid-section!

Obviously we now all wanted to come up with pranks of our own! Most were riffs on Simon's brother's brava concoction (plastic-wrap over the lunchroom trash cans, people try to dump their trays, hilarity ensues!) But what did we care? Simple pleasures.

Except here comes Monacci! So struttingly assured he could pull the wool over our eyes he sullied all enthusiasm for the new venture. Smack off the starting gun isn't he spinning some yarn how he'd once 'put tin-foil under the seats of the kindergarten toilet bowls' and 'thirty kindergartners got so covered in poop the fire brigade was summoned!'

Why the fire brigade?

'They took off their clothes and were running around the halls crying!'

What's the fire brigade got to do with that?

'The police were busy because three pumas escaped in the next district over!'

And ... what's the fire brigade got to do with it?

'The kids'd spread poop all over! It looked like they were diseased! It was in their eyes so much they were going blind.'

So ... why call the fire brigade?

'Ambulances were busy because a shipment of grapes was poisoned at the supermarket - this was on the news! Fire brigade was all that's left. They get deputized as police and doctors combined when they going gets tough.'

Sure, Monacci.

'Plus: how're cops or doctors gonna get poop off three-dozen kids? Fire trucks have hoses. Think!'

I TOOK TO THE ROLE of radio producer, writer, star, and editor in a straightforward and commanding way. I felt downright austere, my psyche embracing with gusto the fracture into distinct, self-contained personalities for each aspect of the craft. They'd all get their own names, I promised them - would be listed in the credit booklet I'd realized in a brilliant flash I could easily make out of common, everyday paper. As many accordion folds as I felt like if I used an unobtrusive sliver of tape to connect one sheet to another.

Maybe I'd include the entire script of the episodes in there! Except it'd take forever to transcribe it all. And I might get bored having to write so tiny. True, my mom could type it up for me at work. But it might be more trouble than it was worth, having to explain the dimensions and layout of each panel.

In any event, there was also the public library. Xerox machines I could utilize. Not to mention: there wasn't so much a script as an outline I'd then improvise scenes from. I didn't want things too complicated. Didn't really matter much what was specifically said in a given sequence provided it clocked in under a minute.

Gotta keep things brisk. Idea to idea to idea. Dwell only when atmospherically imperative or there's some subtler point of moral philosophy I couldn't count on the astuteness of a general audience to pick out without a touch of spoon feeding.

A lot of dialogue, as with the plays I modeled mine after, had the dual purpose of expositionally setting a scene ('Hey Patsy ... you see that door over there?'

'*That green door by the fire hydrant with the dog tied to it?*' '*That's the one.*' '*I see it*') and hitting necessary character beats (*It's cold in here ... I've always hated the cold*' '*Even as a child?*' '*Yes ... yes ... even as ... a child*').

Cadence was paramount. The difference between what seemed a clunker on the page and being the quotable of the century might come down to a pause, a gurgle, an emphasis. These things could often not be predicted. Verite was the name of my game.

Even within the first three scenes of The Bread House Strangler I had, on the fly, improvised lines which radically altered the trajectory of the tale I'd started out in mind to tell. After all, the central hero cannot be a down-on-his-luck Dr. Winchell Sykes if I suddenly have a character say 'It's ... it's that doctor!' 'Doctor Sykes?' 'He's ... Glenna, he's dead!' 'Strangled?' 'Strangled ... The poor fool. But still ... he'd been running from himself so long.'

A lot to unpack there! The more I thought about it, the juicer this last utterance got. Why does this guy know so much about this doctor? Running from himself?

Five wholly distinct interpretations of this remark sprang to mind!

Medical man winds up residing in some flop house apartment? Not to mention how this seemingly random character stumbling upon the body seemed markedly suspicious if you ask me! Especially since the body is gone by the time the police show up!

More than meets the eye ... I'd have to remember to milk this later.

Maybe Dr. Sykes could still be the hero. Used the fact he'd been reported dead to keep his investigations incognito! Just as easy? He could be the killer! These witnesses, so-called, might be in cahoots, having him quote-die-end-quote to eliminate him from all possible suspicions.

There was no telling at this stage of the game!

Say I'd gone ahead and had a whole script wrote out, ahead of time? Then I'd be stuck, wouldn't I? Here, I could trust in my gut. Build a true sense of suspense off the fact the players were so genuine in their uncertainty because not even I knew what to expect!

ALVIN STARTED SLEEPING IN THE basement. If he had specific reason, he played it close to the vest. It suited my needs dandy, regardless. Allowed me to arrange a stable studio, keep production ramped up. Nothing worse than losing time on a daily basis in set-up and tear down.

Radio drama was a funny animal. My recording method took a bit of trial-and-error to jury-rig. Layering primary scene, background, sorting what needed to be pre-recorded versus what needed to be performed real-time.

Music I plucked from the Public Domain - classical and jazz tracks off my mom's CDs. But the 'atmosphere' the 'ambiance' of a moment was not so easy as it sounds!

To produce a night club scene, for example, I'd use one radio to simulate the music playing, then would have to record myself doing both sides of a conversation on one tape, put that tape in another radio to have it playing while I recorded myself doing both sides of another conversation, then put the tape of the both conversations into the first radio to be background noise while I recorded a third two-sided conversation with the now previously recorded two two-side conversations as background - repeat until it was a bustling cacophony, as though dozens of pleasure-seekers were there cutting loose. A similar thing was required for action set during a charity dinner, on a jam-packed train car, or a quaint street corner where townsfolk congregated.

Important effects such as the engine of a car driving I'd use my voice to simulate, humming a vroom sound, doing a re-record with one vroom playing background while I made another so that by the time I had five vrooms layered I'd eat my hat if someone could tell my mock-up from the sound of an honest motor vehicle.

Some corners were cut, to be sure. But in the final mix I doubted they'd be perceived. Especially taking goodwill and suspension-of-disbelief into account. Example? My parents wouldn't allow me to purchase a cap pistol, so I'd resorted to the click-click-click of a plastic toy weapon for gunplay.

Once the two background radios were going, I'd record the main dialogue (performing live all appropriate sound effects e.g. foot falls or someone getting whapped with a crutch) into the primary recorder.

I didn't own a stopwatch and the egg-timer my mom used for her piano practice made a ding too loud to be much use as anything other than the ticking of a bomb about to go off (a handy effect to have ready access to!) so I'd always wait to start recording a section until a minute had just changed on the digital clock of the VCR, try to wind things down, quick, when the minute changed again. I became a dab hand at feeling out a scene, so nothing felt rushed and no air seemed dead.

Fade-ins and outs were a bit tricky, but in the end were easier to produce than having scene breaks indicated by a swell in music. I saved such tricks for special occasions and episode endings, mostly, as the execution of the complex technical manipulations necessary would often take an entire day, in and of themselves.

Produced an entire test program called Fancy-Flyer. The Elephant of Naja-Wan was the episode title. A freewheeling chronicle of a globe-trotting,

Indian Jones figure. After crashing in the artic, scarcely surviving the crucible of the elements (not to mention a seemingly kindly trapper who was in actuality a cannibalistic fiend hiding out from foreign bailiffs!) then descending into a volcano, he only narrowly escapes with his skin intact whilst succeeding in restoring tranquility to a race of peoples unsullied by the encroachment of Western civilization.

To avoid being pegged as too derivative, I had Fancy's partner lose an arm in a melee attack, but stopped short of having the wound be mortal. Death would've required an epilogue wherein Fancy addressed the emotional fallout, otherwise he'd come off cavalier, big time.

And this was just practice, after all. No need to tax my artistry to such silly extents for a trial balloon.

I DIDN'T KNOW ANY OF these kids. This was up at the Weird Park near the development's third entrance. Buzzing crackle from the metal tower the powerlines connected to, a junction box giving off a high whine which, on the whinging insistence of one of the kids, we took time out to investigate.

'Just so I know we aren't gonna be irradiated.'

I liked this guy. A tad reactionary, but his heart was in the right place.

One of his tagalongs, though, became more intolerable by the minute. For example:

Freeze Tag had gotten stale, so we'd switched over to a vigorous round or two of Television Tag. After first moaning enough we allowed movie titles to be utilized alongside television show titles, after petulantly insisting he could use sequels 'Halloween One! Halloween Two! Halloween Three! Halloween Four!' because 'They're different movies!!' (we tried to insist he at least needed to know the sub-titles of each, but he wore down or resolve there, too) he finally started insisting he ought be permitted to use character names, as well. Before long the rascal was simply calling out any old name 'Joey!' 'Barb!' 'Christopher!' 'Melanie!' and claiming they were members of the cast of a show we knew the name of but had never watched.

A genuine bozo, this shuck-and-jive artist, but could we do? Look up program listings in our spare time, hunt him down, dock him his various victories?

Eventually, I joined this motley lot for some wall-ball. Was kinda jealous how one of them lived in the house at the end of a row. They could whap the ball against the brick with impunity, twenty-four seven! In our neighborhood, all the end houses, save one, had sloping hills nuzzled up against them which made the game difficult to play. Several had spoil-sport neighbors dwelling inside, to boot, who made outlandish exaggerations concerning how loud the impact of the balls we used resounded interior their living rooms. They made no distinction between ball types - buncha liars expecting us to go along believing a tennis ball caused the same ruckus as a basketball, a semi-flat soccer ball, or a red rubber one someone had found laying around once upon a time and which was always left out, no specific individual claiming ownership of.

As we played, a peculiar thing went down:

Middle of the game - in the midst of me and these five other kids athletically jockeying around each other, throwing, dodging, catching, being struck in the head, ribs, wherever - I became aware of a seventh player, larger than the rest of us and handily taking a commanding lead. Suddenly, this interloper was clapping us to attention, dividing us into new teams.

Dale Beech.

I assumed he must be a regular round these parts, considering how the quintet I'd buddied with fell in with him lock-step. Except he didn't know the kids' names. Branded them with jocularly disparaging nicknames and otherwise razzed them after they first introduced themselves, proper.

This extended to me. 'And you - kid with the plant on his head - you're with me.'

I did a terrible job as his teammate. He seemed genuinely disgruntled about it. Though I felt I had excuses. I was self-conscious about my hair, in a general way, but had thought it looked fine today. His jibe had cut deep.

Plus his mere presence tweaked me out. When had anyone last seen, heard, or talked about Dale Beech?

I made casual inquiries over the next few days amongst my usual group and at school. The answers came in two flavors. Dale was either 'always around' or 'never around'. Was either 'everywhere' or 'nowhere'. Either 'on vacation' or 'in jail'. 'Dead' or 'playing Ms. Pac-Man at the Gourmet Grog'.

BERLIN KNOCKED ON OUR FRONT door to peddle his free periodical The Berlin Game Review. I admired the fella's gumption in not only continuing to produce this six-page front-and-back zine, but to venture door-to-door distributing it on a subscription basis.

Alvin and I, in private, wondered about him keeping subscribers. As he was going to hand free copies to all takers, regardless, why bother keeping a list of specific people?

But he wasn't doing any harm and the practice likely energized him to keep up the hard work of writing and publishing on a self-inflicted bi-monthly schedule.

Alvin had at one point been recruited to produce a two or three panel comic strip which would appear in the Review's back pages along with various Classifieds which we assumed were all dummy corporations. Adverts touting used games for sale, credited to different sellers we'd never heard of. All correspondence was to be sent care of Berlin.

The comic never materialized, though. Alvin could never think of any particularly video-game-based hijinx or zippy one-liners. Besides, with a lot of other things on his plate he couldn't go around doing pro bono work just on the strength of being Berlin's school chum.

While we flipped through our copies (Berlin insisted we each take one rather than share, as otherwise what was he gonna do with the whole stack?) we gabbed back-and-forth about the intricacy of Berlin's rating systems and the deep-dive analysis he gave to Capcom's Duck Tales - well on its way to being named Game Of The Year (the year of its release, an asterisk explained, was irrelevant - Berlin went by the year in which the game is reviewed) by both himself and the Reader's Poll (which, again, we assumed was nothing any living soul participated in, was merely done up to give the newsletter a patina of prestige).

Alvin started telling a story about Berlin. Such tales were repeated all around town, the kid a kind of celebrity for his dubious misadventures and awkward embarrassments he made no bones about sharing every nit and grit of for chuckles. And so it took me a moment to realize this wasn't a re-telling of events I'd been present for nor was any anecdote I was already familiar with, secondhand.

The gist was:

A day or two previous, everyone had been hanging out at the Little Park. An obstacle course had been concocted out of what was on hand - someone got all the swings going and challengers had to run past without getting whapped, jump from the fence to a tree branch, balance on the see-saw without falling while one fat kid (or else a few slimmer kids, in concert) flopped their weight on the opposite end et cetera.

Dale Beech was on hand and had, seemingly out of the clear blue sky, the impulse to take the green rubber ball being used to throw at people while they tried to hang from the monkey bars without falling and to give the bugger a tremendous kick which rocketed it absurdly skyward.

Cue Berlin, astride bicycle, turning the corner at the crest of the hill. He raised a hand to give everyone a jolly-jolly, corn-fed wave Hello as he began the semi-steep curve of the descent.

'And like it was timed - like Berlin was magnetic - the ball Dale kicked comes thundering down - Whappo! - nails Berlin splat on the head!' Immediately on impact, Alvin related with appropriate hilarity, Berlin bellowed 'Daddy!' and careened into the grass, head only narrowly missing the cement corner of the grated covering to a sewer tunnel.

Alvin told this story for yucks, the main point being to do his impression of Berlin's cry upon being struck. 'The timing was amazing!'

And, yes, I couldn't help laughing, knowing exactly how that good natured, hy-yuk hy-yuk 'Daddy!' would've sounded. Amused. Resigned. Devil-may-care.

Yet I couldn't keep a tiny chill creeping up me over how it was only now I was hearing this. I'd asked after Dale only two days prior and Alvin hadn't mentioned seeing him.

'Oh yeah - you were asking about Dale. I guess that's the last I saw him, then.'

I WAS COVERING OUTFIELD, LEANED against the fence of the Little Park designating a home run. Alvin was pitching, soft overhand as there wasn't room for a full wind up and underhand made things too easy. Donovan was at bat. Sundry neighborhood kids, the regulars and some randos, were filling positions or serving as fans in the rhetorical bleachers. On the two big-kid swings were Endie and Wally. Using one of the baby-swings as a platform, standing elevated, lightly swaying back-and-forth, was Dale Beech.

We were playing with a real baseball, not the usual tennis ball, and were using an aluminum bat Dale had brought from home so all of us were on heightened guard for new-fangled injuries our usual equipment couldn't produce.

So: how could it have happened?

We'd relate the fateful moment for weeks after, streamlining the most important actions down to these. Dig it:

Alvin pitched. Nice, clean, straight line.

Donovan gave a hulking swing, full bulbous weight really hupped to the effort.

There was a sound - Krak!! - of metal impacting ball-skin, just a ghost of tuning-fork ring to this. And then there was the second Krak!! Just as loud if slightly duller. From where I stood, clean sight-line down center-field to batter, the sounds overlapped. Krakkrak!!!

Donovan dropped the bat as though to run ...

...but didn't run.

The ball sailed over my head ...

... yet I made no effort to gauge its trajectory, note where it landed.

No one knew what had happened, but the unnatural sound had shut us all down.

A moment later, some little kid - we thought his name might be Benny - screamed. He sprang up like a B-movie scare, flailing, running a chicken loop, arms flapping as though mocking an epileptic. Screamed. He screamed! Scrambled out of the park with his brother booking it right behind him. Up the hill. Out of the neighborhood. The scream became ambulance pierce even as it silenced, well out of sight.

The facts of the prelude were simple to list: (one) those two had come down the hill on their bikes, had taken a position to watch the game (two) the little kid had moved in too close behind Donovan (three) Donovan, unawares, had giving the swing his collegiate best (four, five, six) bat hit ball then at full speed continued around colliding with the little kid's skull at the temple.

Binion swore he'd seen the kid's head caved in from the blow. No one doubted it. The words didn't so much put the image in our minds as brought harsh attention to how the image was already there.

A commotion like nobody's business of what on Earth were we going to do followed. We needed to get out of there! Donovan shook, ejaculating how it wasn't his fault to anyone who'd listen. Some scattered this way, some scattered that way, me amongst them.

As my group neared the top of the hill, Alvin agreed with Wally how running was fruitless. We'd need to look down the barrel of this and fess up what we knew. As we slowed, considering the implications of this, I glanced at the park. And saw Dale Beech. Still stirruped in the baby-swing, vaguely twirling, not seeming to've registered a thing.

No time to unpack this image, though, what with the harsh emotional aftermath of the accident and the difficult task of convincing Donovan he had to come with us to find the kid's house. The parents would need details for appropriate medical assistance to be procured.

'How will we know what house?' I asked.

'Follow the spilt brains, probably' Endie retorted.

But Donovan was bawling and in no mood for gags. Nor did he care for a kid called Tye's boneheaded and ill-timed mini-lecture on how ancient Egyptians had pulled brains out noses when mummifying their princes. Interesting, yes. Irrelevant, more.

Donovan became terrified he'd face years of incarceration for his actions, despite it being technically only negligent manslaughter and nevermind how extenuating the circumstances. He might've been right. Context was little matter in the eyes of a parent when their progeny's head had been walloped to paste. Juries were composed of parents.

A kid called Clive, very concerned, wondered aloud 'What if it's like that movie where when the mom opens the door she only has half a head?'

No one knew which movie he meant. But it seemed a salient point.

The sun bored a brightness down which somehow made us feel water-logged.

AS IF SPRINGTIME WASN'T SHAPING up harrowing enough, here we find Mrs. Terre (Social Studies teacher in tow, nodding Amens after every third word) nattering on about Earth Day.

What were the odds we'd caught wise to planetary destruction right in the nick of time? Where was this high-minded rhetoric last month, for example?

I kept these question to myself, tucked away with my skepticism over the assertion that if we acted now there was yet time to undo damages wrought. Not to suggest I was an outright naysayer. In a Pyrrhic way, definitely, I admitted it's important to protect the planet from the villainous practices of industrial smog, deforestation, and litterbugging.

'And noise pollution' some know-it-all sycophant chimed in, leading Mrs. Terre to riff on that tangentially related topic for another six minutes.

I didn't disagree with any of this, let me restate. It was just anyone who watched Captain Planet was hip to this gospel since forever ago. And I watched Captain Planet, big league. So it got in my craw, this girl's pat remark being treated as wizened - Mrs. Terre applauded the snoot like she'd been the one to identify the problem and coin the phrase!

What was all this yammer in aid of, anyway?

Well: What better way to combat the slash-and-burn operations decimating old growth forest than to have a poetry contest with tiered prizes?

Nothing could be better in the consensus driven opinion of a parent-teacher co-operative which'd put together a pamphlet to inform and inspire us.

To this end, we were introduced to The World's Mascot - a loveable, highly knowledgeable, and rather naively optimistic panda bear named Pie.

Our verse, in whichever form or meter we selected, had only one requirement - shoehorn in some mention of this panda. Ideally: make the entire composition a paean to the animal and her inevitable victory over humanity's shortcomings.

And what about this: here comes Mrs. Terre and some kid's mom who was tapped to oversee the Earth Day Assembly in a volunteer capacity. Beelined right up on me. Wink wink, they sincerely hoped I'd take some time to work up a poem for submission. They had a good feeling this occasion was my opportunity to shine.

Binion and I tossed a semi-deflated soccer ball back-and-forth at recess, secluded off from any of the main goings on. This was our spot, of late. Way in the corner of the permissible grounds, near a heating grate and a tree which had grown right around an old railroad spike and thus become a protected icon of the municipality.

He hoped I smelled a rat in Mrs. Terre's solicitation.

Of course I did! What flummoxed me was trying to wrap my head around how Mrs. Terre fancied, in her most unfettered dreams, I'd any intention of wasting one precious second of my highly valuable time.

Binion was glad one of us packed a rebel yell.

'Why? Are you writing a poem?'

His mom was gonna make him, I could bank on it!

'Since when're you a poet?'

It was just one of those things. He felt it in his bones.

I could relate. Sometimes my dad would suddenly insist on making corn-on-the-cob for dinner, having us all sit at the table in expectation we'd actually eat the stuff. When we didn't, he'd use his authority to have us sit there for hours, his heels preposterously dug into the hill he'd die on.

'It's a waiting game, when he gets these impulses. Usually if we weather it for three days his attention wanders and life snaps back to normal.'

Endie was bolstered to see I understood his ordeal.

Well ... maybe I'd write something. In solidarity.

'Only if you want' Endie insisted as the bell rung and we tromped toward line-up. He didn't want me to think he'd gone over to the other side, was acting as some kinda agent provocateur to rope me in, spare his own hide.

THE SPORADIC APPEARANCE OF THE ice cream truck was the only viable game in town to get one's hands on Garbage Pail Kids. Community mothers far and wide had deemed these collectable cards the thing to dub contraband. Even Collector's World wouldn't move packs to anyone not old enough to have driven to the store, themselves.

There was the option of procuring the cards off Wally, but no one much was up for climbing into bed with that unsavory character, even for a good cause. Beside which, Wally would only sell or trade his duplicates, effectively steamrolling his clientele's joy at dreaming they'd be first on the block to collect 'em all.

This afternoon, though, was anomalous. A harbinger of the changing winds. Patrick and I, armed with the required seventy-five cents to get ourselves a pack of cards each, had strolled to the adjacent neighborhood to loiter around for the truck. Less prying eyes to worry about, over there. Kids were respectful not to congregate if only looking to score ice cream lest the gaffe be blown. This spot was Black Market only.

Ice cream man claimed to be entirely out-of-stock. Could be he was truthful. Except it seemed we could see a box of packs next to the Batman pops with bubble gum eyes. Could be those boxes were empty. Except the ice cream man, to our faces, forcefully insisted he was fresh out and wouldn't let us get a word in edgewise concerning 'What about that box, there?' Quick as you like, he'd taken our money and tendered us each a soft-serve cone — vanilla and very liberal with the sprinkles, like the cream would collapse or keel over under the clustered weight of them all.

Off he drove while Patrick burst into tears and tore off toward his house to lodge an official complaint, in triplicate carbon, with his mommy.

Me? Se la vie, I made my aimless way along, gingerly mouthing my treat. Drifted along beneath the powerlines in the tall grass, a safe distance from the tree-line of the creek, eyeing the area near the Montesorri.

There'd been a drought of information concerning the whereabouts of Dale Beech, the past week. Some kids claimed their various older siblings said this, said that, but I was mistrustful. Why would everyone I asked have older brothers privy to some nugget of Dale Beech centric business, no two newswires ever the same?

No one seemed much concerned with the kid who'd had his head clobbered, either. Only time it came up was in the form of gallows jokes when Donovan was up to bat. One thing I certainly knew is how I'd seen who I thought was the brother of the victim drawing with chalk on the sidewalk and trying to figure out how to work a Transformer action figure. I'd watched him for a few minutes, increasingly uncertain was it the kid I was thinking.

As evening fell, I trotted toward home, chancing a glance at my shirtsleeve. A tick was crawling along it. Automatic, I jumped back a step, slapped at the intruder - WhapWhapWhap!! - wheeled around, peeling off my shirt, tottering over into an inelegant stumble, crawling as I stood, continuing to smack my exposed skin.

Careful inspection of my retrieved garment promised me I'd knocked the bloodsucker grassward - not anywhere in the shirt's folds nor on what I could see of my rawboned torso.

OUT CHEWING HIS CHAW, I came across the neighbor, Frank. My presence seemingly shook the cobwebs from whatever dull headspace he'd been
in. He lifted a soda can to his lips, excreted an amount of bilge, and reminded
me how he owned Super Mario Cart and that Alvin and I were welcome to
come over, any time. I thanked him kindly and was set to press on when he
asked after my dad.

Had my dad not been feeling well? What did he mean? Sneezing? 'He's always sneezing, from what I can tell. It's just white noise to me by now.'

Well, Frank was bucked up to hear this. Thing was, they'd had an adult
conversation regarding upper respiratory matters, Frank recommending a
brand of medication my dad had balked at. Here was the thing, though: while
Frank trusted my dad's medical acumen over his own lack of anything like
medical acumen, he harbored concerns and wanted to safeguard the old
man's health and vitality. 'I think he's a Future Person' Frank then hush-
hushed.

I nodded, hoping a nod was the best way to bring this encounter to a
prompt terminus.

Here's how this broke down: Frank had some cockamamie theory how
certain individuals from times-still-to-come travel back to various epochs
previous to theirs in order to spread learning unobtrusively into bygone society, hoping to germinate alternate timelines with wisdom so certain mass
tragedies their worlds had endured could be avoided. 'So I call them Future
People' he added as though the addition were necessary.

Pretty derivative theory, if you asked me. Tiddlywinks stuff - Frank was,
frankly, kinda half-witted when it came to quantum mechanics. But I supposed it was flattering to know my pop was thought to be in the ranks of these
learned and magnanimous travelers. Comforting, too, to know the man with
the gun safe who went parachuting in his spare time was scrutinizing my family's comings and goings to safeguard our pater from any possible Evil Future
People who might come back in time for sinister aims.

'Or even just jealous peers from our own time' Frank intoned with a note
of morbidity. 'We're savage. Murderous. There's no telling about us.'

Admittedly, I didn't spend a big chunk of time batting around the implications or unraveling the paradoxes and ethical quandaries inherent in the pos-
tulation. Though I did like how Frank had deftly sidestepped a lot of those
headaches by tacking on the 'alternate universe' bunko. No matter to him
how the presence of infinite alternate versions of our timeline mooted the
need to alter any one or the other of them - or, indeed, to project benevo-
lence at all as there would, by definition, exist infinite variant universes

wherein the benevolent gestures lead to their opposite intent coming to fruition as well as infinite variant dimensions where the most ghoulish enterprises somehow counterintuitively bring about peace and prosperity for all.

I told Alvin about all this. As usual, he cut to the quick of the matter with astute precision and sagacious wit. 'If there's infinite dimensions, how come it seems like the only movie channel-twenty ever shows is Jumpin' Jack Flash?' And the even funnier thing was how despite the fact Jumpin' Jack Flash was on television almost weekly, we'd never once gone through with watching it!

In the state of tranquility such chats with my brother tended to induce in me, I excused myself upstairs to bathe.

Chugging outpour of the tub faucet thrashing, overhead fan drowning out all but my interior monologue, I undressed. And then my body snapped in shock-horror. I bounced off the balls of my feet, whapped my back against the wall.

How in the name of God!?

Dead center of my chest, in the divot kung-fu movies had taught me was called the solar plexus, tucked right in there snug as you like and suckling to its vermin content, was a tick.

I glanced to the mirror, to my flesh, to the mirror, to my flesh, hoping it was all a mistake.

But no.

It must've purposefully taken some opportunity to get back onto me after I'd slapped it from my shirt. This couldn't be random! I'd shooed it off, put distance between it and I.

Why would it have bothered to return? Hadn't it only wound up on me because I'd been drifting though the tall grass where it dwelled?

This seemed personal. The thick scab of it entrenched to my flesh, burrowed in so that even if I plucked it out with my hands or with tweezers its head would remain subcutaneous and vital.

I watched it drink from me. Mortified.

I watched it and wondered: was it drinking? Or was it filling me with some of the juice its bulk showed it full to bursting with, already?

.APRIL.

THOUGH SHE NO LONGER RODE, my mom would hang around at The Horse Center, from time-to-time. Alvin or myself would gladly tag along. It was a holy place, this compound of stables, odd houses, dressage arena, and fields. In our formative years, due to one of those silly parental miscues, our dad, also a horseman, had thought we were with our mom while our mom had thought we'd been gathered up by dad and thus we'd found ourselves abandoned on the grounds for a stretch of eight hours on a rather stolid winter's day. The time had been wiled away throwing rocks at a black widow spider in its web at the lip of a frozen pond and in laughing at how the Center's free-roaming golden retriever would in mere seconds slobber sloppy the stones we lobbed for it to fetch, giddily barking for the next. Another time, the plowed snow out front of the main stable was piled so immense we clambered up to the roof. Peeping Tomed and eavesdrop through splintery windows for ages despite there being nothing of remote interest to see or to hear.

In the Tack Shop, my mom once bought me a very posh journal with a drawing of a fox on the cover. I'd utilized this dutifully for a time, often my mom suggesting prompts to investigate.

What would be better: Too much or too little?

My op-ed? Hedge your bets, people - proceed straight down the middle-path, same as like Socrates or Buddha might advise.

At present, I dug this journal off my shelf. Its spine was furry with dust where it crammed between some novels I'd never read and a pile of Star Trek action figures, many plundered of various limbs.

I found the front pages still filled with all manner of youthful scrawl, doodles of cats and skeletons. Perfectly ideal. This rubbish would put anyone off the sniff of the journal's new purpose: a chronicle of my life as a costumed vigilante.

Let's have a look at my initial declaration of intent: In times such like this, it behooves the common man to secret himself and to take risks of life and limb for the community health.

Pretty good, even if I had to be the only one to say so! Marvelously noble, all that. Reminded me of someone who'd in later life reluctantly accept the mantel of President based on the populace as a whole spontaneously beseeching them to rise to their historical moment.

Moving into specifics, I'd proclaimed: To this end, I have decided to print up business cards under the name Grady Walker and to distribute these throughout the development so that people might have a life-line.

Oh I'd wanted business cards ever since discovering the machine down at the post office could dispense them, made-to-order. I confessed a romantic thrill at this cloak-and-dagger, although in the normal run of things I preferred to keep well clear of skullduggery, in any form. But being a realist, I understood I'd have to keep this all to myself. My observations, adventures, what I came to know that others wouldn't (and likely would prefer to keep ignorant of even if they were informed). Besides: it'd be such a nuisance to explain every last thing to Johnny-come-Latelys in real time! The bulk of them playing perpetual catch-up and only willing to move to the meagerest action after committee and democratic consensus. Added to which: Alvin was on the cusp of a career in graphic design. Wasn't it the brotherly thing to shield him from the labyrinthine horrors I espied all around, intrigues and hellscapes budding like yeast?

To secure the environment from criminality and recklessness on my own was the least I could do! My God, of course it was.

And if not me, who?

THE WORKFLOW WAS MORE COMPLEX than a Bat-Signal, let's say that for starters. Such is the way of the world, no special allowances for vigilantism. Banality trumps fantasia. Nuance. Process. If something is going to work there has to be a way it does, no matter the toothaches.

The business cards: it was my intent to, on the sly, get these into citizen's mailboxes under cover of darkness. Since I didn't have my own phone number and seeing it would be disastrous to leave bread crumbs implicating my family in these extra-legal endeavors, the cards, in language succinct, informed people who desired me to take up the mantle of some cause to tack communications on the community bulletin board. Just whichever which way an individual felt comfortable. Leave personal phone number, for example, and I'd reach out to them. Or else details might be enclosed in an envelope. Nothing more was necessary than a sheet of paper listing a time and a place we could meet up face-to-face (though of course when I showed up I'd explain I was the plucky young intermediary and 'my boss' would think things over before accepting).

It'd all get sorted on the fly, as was likely the norm with any off-the-books justice.

Here, though, came a moment of curious existential reflection: First night going to distribute cards, it occurred to me how I'd honestly ought to've checked to be certain all comers had direct access to the bulletin board. Some such boards were under lock and key. In such case, any potential client could easily utilize Scotch tape to leave their info on the glass, but considering I didn't know the pressures each and every one of my neighbors might be under it was best to let the onus fall on me as far as keeping things well-oiled.

The bulb of the shed outside the board lit the area surrounding in a thick orange-nearly-brown, light the consistency of canned soup.

Yes. Simple cork board. Public access.

And just as I decided to affix a card to the board itself, it dawned on me how I coulda used this station as a place to've posted Hugo strips. The mailbox where the community newsletters were housed coulda equally served as a home to the stapled pages of a collected issue.

So why not do that!? No time like the present, wise men were known to say. I wasn't some dried out stick, after all - plenty of moxie left in me! Why not set aside this dangerous business of policing the masses incognito? Why not let the world at large fend for itself as had been the order of the day since time immemorial?

Returneth, Ichabod, to the bosom of Art! Make a Jim Dandy splash first locally and then inevitably charge ninety bucks a throw for original sketches - big man on campus a la Hugh Hanes!

By heaven, I'd do that very thing! And a whorl of desire coursed to my head
...

... then dropped. Burst in a beat to smithereens under the murk of these shadows swallowing up the pavement's black, the sidewalk's beige.

I'd tapped those accursed Hugo strips to sheets and walled them up in some Trapper Keeper! I wanted to laugh aloud recalling my fickle back-and-forth even while I'd been doing so. My impatience and numbskull frustration coupled with a bourgeois need for definitive and self-pitying symbolics had won the day.

So there it was. I'd made my bed, the die cast. And Fate in its inscrutable whimsy had brought me to this very bulletin board to show off how I'd un-forked the road, got myself lock-stock stuck into a lifetime treading the vio-lent and primrose path! What an origin story, eh? It was as though I'd truly become a comic book. A doodled man! Drifting panel-to-panel under the auspices of author and illustrator who dwelt entirely outside me.

GRADY WALKER, OBVIOUSLY, WAS MERELY Step One of an elabo-rate disguise. Commonsense dictated how - whether called Grady Walker, Ichabod Burlap, or Do-Dah Daisy - if some thug or spy met up with me in real life they'd recognize me later or show my face around back alleys. Some-how I'd be fingered and have the fatwah out on me, big league.

And so was born the notion of The Mongoose Rider.

Once Grady (viz me pretending to be Grady's kid assistant) had been given the scoop something was fouled up and a fixer was required, I'd hop on my bicycle (a Mongoose) don my favorite jacket (which hadn't fit precisely since second grade but was still cooler looking than any other garment I possessed) douse my safety helmet with a few squirts of working man's lighter fluid, strike a match - Fwoosh!! - then ride down on whichever perpetrator in a fury of nightmarish laughter which, with a bit of luck and depending on the breaks, would be such a shock to their miscreant system they'd not even re-tain wits enough to register I only weighed sixty pounds and came up to their navels, at best. In fact, such realities would only shore up my seeming some otherworldly wraith, a demonic manifestation of some ilk! No telling the ex-tremes of their confusion!

And nevermind if the entire masquerade was derivative or wasn't it - big deal! Fact were facts. And fact was: I'd honestly never read nor even much cared for the Ghost Rider character, even conceptually. And it wasn't as if a flaming head or riding a vehicle of some variety was the exclusive, copyright protected creation of Marvel Comics, now was it?

The laughter? Clearly an homage to The Shadow not cribbing! My credi-bility stood on its own considering I was a nine-year-old who owned pulp mags predating my birth four decades and could recite radio adverts for Blue Coal.

'Do we have lighter fluid?'

A simple enough inquiry but everyone seemed to require all breed of con-textualization before they'd give me a straight Yes or No.

I went with a vague 'I'm interested in the science of fire and have an idea for a cautious and controlled experiment'. When this didn't seem to pass the sniff test, I added 'Under strict laboratory conditions.'

But whatever. Not as though I couldn't snoop out where the stuff was hidden.

The shed in the backyard was the hottest lead I could scrounge up. I had a generalized memory how we'd once owned a lawnmower which ran on some flammable substance, at any rate. It also occurred to me how my mom's old gardening equipment might still be in there. Much of it could be repurposed into implements of self-defense with a little creativity and elbow grease.

The latch had rusted to the same dark brown as the mushy wood planks the shed was constructed of. A generic aroma of disuse and fungus notable from arm's length away. Some instinct warned me 'Watch out'. A sizzle of gloom and oppression whistled to-and-fro through my limbs.

Slowly, I opened the door. A soundless judder to it, like turning the page of something unreal but enormous. Lawnmower. Mulch bags. Rake. Trough. Spade. Ah! Damp box of long kitchen matches, there in the way back - might come in handy. Oil can? Oil burns, right?

But a slight rustle, a scratch, or a clicking to my left broke my concentration. I turned my head and ...

... my eyes, my mind, barely could process the sight.

What were these insects?

Thick as thumbs. Moist as gelatin corpse flesh. A pattern to their hides which gave a distinct sense they were covered in skin like that of a human. They produced a sensation I was looking at something which could rightly be described only as 'naked'. Twenty, thirty of them. Immobile. Waiting. A clot as tall and wide as me.

I yelped as I sprung back, in the same motion slamming shut the shed door in a gluey kabang! I heard the gathering of creatures expectorated from the door, clattering in amongst the bric-a-brac. And then, for a solid minute, I listened to the rat-tat-tat of the mongrels launching themselves in my direction, pulpy impacts to the soggy wood, a buckshot of them reaching to take me. It was almost a percussive hiss, a sound like split soda announcing their frustration, their agony and regret at not having taken me in their clutches while they'd had my turned back.

NOW: HERE WERE SOME FUNKY monkeyshines and Binion had the presence of mind and discretion enough to not even attempt pawning off some 'Look on the bright side' claptrap.

'No way, Ick - this has booby-trap written all over it.'

Here's what: end of the week, coming up on Earth Day, Mrs. Terre cluck-clucks her merry way on over to me as like all of sudden I'm the fruit of her womb. Tells me I'm being awarded Third Place in the Pie the Panda contest. No gag. Certificate of Merit and five coupons for personal pan pizzas at The Hut were mine! All the catch was was I'd have to walk up in front of God and everybody, recite the beastly tripe, and accept a round of applause.

No way out of it!

What a dastardly method of bringing me low in order she might strut her smug superiority.

'You think she knows you spat that poem out on the bus ride, last minute?'

'Come on, Binion! Out of the clear blue sky Mrs. Terre et al can't tell hawks from handsaws? They ex nihilo imagine I've been struck with the dum-dum stick and've grown ham fists and a tin ear?'

How was I to have the foggiest what their sick endgame's to be!? All I could say, with grim certainty, is they read the bloody thing, same as anyone might, and weren't such imbeciles they'd not know its gristle they're being fed.

Let me just say one thing: I have a bit too much dignity to be bought off with a bit of tickle to my pride and less than half-a-dozen mini-pizzas - so they can shove their prize wherever the shoving's good!

Alvin, that evening, concurred how the cunning thing would be to play possum. Don't let on I'm wise to their ploy. Here comes the day of the assembly, whereupon I'd - Oh dash it all! - be stricken with an intractable yet imprecise constellation of maladies which necessitated my being kept home to convalesce.

Slip the noose!

Alas, my complacency in the simple brilliance of this must've marked me by karma for a comeuppance.

My dad, retired cardiac surgeon and all around man of physic, would normally take me at my word I was feeling a touch green in the gills, let me spend a day in bed sweating things out. But no! This time of all times I had to be subjected to his interminable and somewhat archaic 'examination'.

Old man didn't muck about. Glass, mercury thermometer was taken from the twelve-year-old jug of rubbing alcohol. Had to sit on the sofa five solid minutes, forbade to even sip a breath through my mouth lest the reading be queered.

No fever.

But he was a savvy enough clinician to know illness might present in myriad ways. So he took a fat metal tablespoon, grabbed the flashlight (which never seemed to be used for anything but this, nor seemed ever to contain fresh batteries) and had me open wide. Clatter clatter the spoon clacked against teeth, my head tilted back harsh while he dug around. A real bit of spelunking! All the time deaf to my gagging protests and the growing reservoir of saliva under my tongue. Clatter clatter 'Stay still, Icky person' clatter clatter.

No evidence of 'white on the tonsil'.

Clean bill of health!

And so Mrs. Terre got to proudly usher me up to the stage to have my artistic reputation sullied in front of the entire student body and some deputy-comptroller loaned out to the school to legitimize our conscientious verve about giving a hoot, refusing to pollute, and all that jazz.

Maybe I could faint? Vomit? Thumb my nose at them by giving some firebrand speech about the futility of it all?

No. I lacked the requisite guts.

'Sometimes people try to make war / but they shouldn't try to settle the score' I began, wondering even myself what the devil such a line had to do with Earth Day. Not to mention - gah! - what an anemic rhyme! And quite a doltish sentiment as far as the complex reasons nations might wage militaristic campaigns against one another. But pressing on: 'Pie the Panda's here to say / she's gonna make sure we don't have a Doomsday'

Oh God, oh god on his throne - how could I have got myself cornered into this public execution?

'A LITTLE GAME OF RUSSIAN Roulette' Dr. Alvin prescribed. 'Just the curative for a young, world-weary chap such as our Ichabod Burlap.'

Afterward, we'd tromp over to Zeke's house to make prank calls.

Zeke's sounded like a hot ticket, to be sure. In my heart, though, I could do without the deadly game of chance.

'Too bad, so sad' Alvin chimed giddily whilst prepping the cups, at least one of which contained a mountebank.

He was devilishly refined in his prep work. Four cups, the heavier glass kind, textured, frosted so no telltales might show though (a shadow apparent from outside the receptacle had saved my sorry skin from a ghastly gullet-gulp, in the past). Each cup filled to exactly the same height with milk. And lastly, he laid a plump dollop of whipped cream overtop the liquid's surface, enough so no discoloration might give the game away.

'One cup poisoned or one cup safe?' I needed to know, seeing as he'd been sequestered in the kitchen more than long enough.

'One cup safe - be a man!'

'Then you have to drink all three as a forfeit if I hit Safe.'

Yes yes - he knew the rules, was a member of the board when they'd been drafted. Never fear, he'd take his lumps if things broke against him.

'What poisons?'

'You wanna know in front?'

Did I? 'Tell me' I sighed, nauseous enough with anticipation I'd probably puke even if I landed the clean cup.

'Cat Food.'

'Wet or dry?'

'Wet. Salmon Picnic.'

'Holy Lord - what else?'

'Mayonnaise and mustard mixed with some fishbones off a plate dad had under some cling-wrap.'

'This is outlandish! I can't drink chicken bones!'

But he was right - I should've thought of that before accepting the contest.

'And in the final rigged cup: three dead cockroaches.'

'You're lying!'

Not that there weren't roaches enough to choose from. They were legion, of late. A bowl of Honeycomb cereal I'd eaten had been fouled by two, just last week.

'Drink!'

And so I did ...

... but I don't much like to relive the particulars ...

Then Alvin took his go and hit the Safe cup. So I had to down the remaining duo of hazards - only he let me off the hook about the mayonnaise-fishbone bilge, knowing how afraid I was of condiments.

Down to Zeke's basement we journeyed. Not that crank calls were really my cuppa. Alvin and Zeke had gotten big league into the Jerky Boys lately, is what. I'd only ever heard one of their bits on Corn Between Your Teeth while driving home from mom's office.

It was tough to tell if our pranks came off as pranks or rather just seemed like kids asking questions of random businesses, genuinely confused about where they'd called.

By a stroke of sudden luck, a karate studio had an answering machine which picked up straight away, allowing Zeke to leave a twelve-message-long tirade in the voice of a chop-saki drunken master. He brayed on and on how 'My gung-fu's the best there is!' and many times named increasingly bizarre times and places for duels to be dueled.

This gave us the notion we'd like to record a zany greeting for Zeke's answering machine. He was sixteen and had his own phone with voicemail, so we figured it was nobody's business but ours. Recorded this and that until finally I hit on just the mixture of Texas medicine and railroad gin we jonesed for. From way across the room, in a kinda daffy voice, I belted out 'For fifty dollars, I can buy a girlfriend for an hour!'

Zeke thought this was the living end, boy howdy!

However, Zeke's mom saw matters in a different light based on her lifetime of experience in the trenches of nine-to-five. She made him erase the message as an investment in his future.

'What if one of the places you applied for a job called back and heard that?'

Good point, we guessed.

And then got very paranoid.

'That karate place won't call back, will they?'

It was unavoidably true the technology existed with which they could have captured the incoming number. We certainly shouldn't have used the house phone, hindsight made clear.

'Call back and apologize! Say your little brother was using the phone without your permission.'

But that seemed pretty thin.

No. Doomed. We felt it in our marrow.

Then after twenty minutes, Zeke seemed to have shook it off, grinned a que sera sera. 'Either way, it was all true, everything I said - my gung-fu is the best there is!'

His laughter made us feel hidden, free from whichever tentacle might be prowling for our meat.

ON THE FLIMSY HANGING SHELF above the washer and dryer units (sometimes in the empty box of fabric softener sheets, sometimes in a ceramic dish shaped like a palm which Alvin had fashioned in second grade) there'd be a collection of sundry coins, sometimes even crisp, faded bills. Laundered Money, my mom called this. Why she didn't pocket it for her trouble, who can say - not the sort of woman whose motives were easy to fathom.

I planned to splurge on some new comic books, figured why not scrounge up all the petty cash I could. Be able to start with as many back issues of Sleepwalker as possible. Or else (what's to stop me?) blow whatever boodle on that double-length, special edition Mister Miracle Steve Rude had the done the artwork for.

Thirty-five crumby little cents and the same old die-cast figurines which had been there since forever. I resigned myself to reading this as a signpost: Vacation Over. Back to the radio-show grind. Back to the hard knock life of selfless vigilantism.

Speaking of which: what ho!?

I happened to glance to the side - this in the exact instant I was forsaking all chance of respite or nepenthe - only to see an entire can of lighter fluid. Covered in a lustrous pelt of dust and coated in some substance thick as kitchen grease or dish soap. Holy cats, man - it was entirely full up! Plus a box of crisp, long kitchen matches, into the bargain!

I wasn't the uneducated sort to look gift horses in their mouths. Resolved, forthwith, to do a test dousing of my bike helmet so I'd have a whiff what kind of shock I'd give punks and lowlifes!

I hupped off from the stool I'd stepped on to retrieve the accelerant. The box of matches (still opened a tap) slipped my grip and the sticks skittled down under the washer.

Despite the grungy state of the floor (brown tile, textured like a Triscuit) and despite the proximity of my face to the rusted, circular drain in the room's center, I lay down to get a peek under, see how many matches I might rescue. Black as sack cloth down there. And I was too weakling to move the machines. So I improvised a tool from an unbent coat hanger, fiddled it into the space between washer-bottom and floor, gave a tense flick of my wrist and ...

... I'd wanted to exclaim 'Voila!' but instead choked on a shriek, sprung to my feet, and in the process struck my ribs but good against the wall-mounted crank-operated pencil-sharpener, promptly slipping on the pile of baby-powder like shavings covering the floor beneath it. Landed hard on my backside at the top of the three steps leading down into the room.

Three, four, five of those naked, thick insects I'd seen inside the tool shed. Able to give them more scrutiny, it was clear they were a patchwork of arachnid, cricket, and pill-bug. Legs plump but stiff, clitter-clatting amongst the spill of matchsticks.

Hardly thinking, I stamped my foot hard onto the tile, tensing up immediately, certain they'd spring into the air. They didn't budge. Stomped again and made an imprecise yelp meant to be 'Hey!' or 'Get lost!' No movement. So I growled 'Fine then - I warned you, rat bastard!' and brought a foot high then abruptly down, square atop one of the scum.

In the same instant my squish drove home, the other bugs leapt in all directions. Sounds of them hitting walls or shelved items - ting, plink, plit, ting - and the shivery flick of them leaping, again.

I twisted my weight hard, mopped my foot side-to-side to smear the carcass of the one I'd landed on. But when I lifted my foot, the mongrel was intact, alive, as though nothing had happened.

Maybe I have a curled foot or something?

I took deadly aim ... then with the point of my heel - Wham!!

Except this made me slip again, both from the impact and from fear. Back to the carpeted stair went my backside. And a glance to the floor confirmed no bug anymore where the bug had just been. No slick of gory mess. And no evidence of murder on my shoe bottom, either.

WALLY'S HOUSE WAS A PLACE no sane person would dwell. The residence was ensconced in dog feces, courtesy his loyal, unreliably tempered canine, Lupe. Hall tile, dining room carpet, along the walls up the staircases. We often told how there'd been batches of mud on the ceiling, as well. While that may've been a shared memory mendala effected into us, I'd with my own eyes seen a hardened crust of doggy diarrhea on the glass surface of the coffee table in his living room.

Wally himself was the sort of acquaintance who in small enough doses could pass for a friend. Here was someone who'd invite you over not to play videogames but to watch him play. Spoiled silly, he always had everything new and boat loads of rare items, exclusively. Oh sometimes he'd lend out a cartridge, but on such occasion it'd be 'for fifteen minutes' with a fee for the privilege, the vig starting at twenty-five cents each additional five minutes.

An avid comic collector who had a genuine subscription to umpteen titles, he'd purchase multiple copies of most things (one to read, handled with gloves, the other to 'keep in mint condition'). A savvy venture capitalist, to boot, he had, for example, bought twenty copies of the bagged, collector's edition of the premiere issue of X-Force, not to mention another twenty copies which allowed him to amass two complete sets of the trading cards, holograms included.

In his room, upstairs, stenched of corn chips, Laffy-Taffy, and mildew, he kept a separate box of the most oddball assortment of off-brand comics I'd ever heard of for guests to read. Which is what I was doing - leafing through an issue of Hong-Kong Fooey while (the reason we'd ventured into this cesspit) Alvin watched Wally play Pit Fighter for the Genesis.

As advertised, the game's graphics were state-of-the-art, photo-realistic. The gore was constant, gritty, and perfuse. It was like controlling flesh and bone combatants.

Since it was two-player, Alvin actually held a controller, having been permitted a go. Wally (maniacal and off-his-meds) was taking full advantage of how he'd had ages to master the controls, learn the intricate combos. He pulverized Alvin without allowing him a free round to get acclimated to punch, kick, jump gameplay. Insult to injury, in the few seconds it took for a round to officially reset, Wally would move his character back-and-forth over Alvin's defeated avatar, bellowing 'I'm dancing on your corpse!' corpse pronounced corp-see 'What's wrong - don't you like it when I dance on your corp-see?'

I wanted to lash out, lambast the malodorous jot - wanted to open one of his copies of Animal Man issue one, handle it without tweezers, give the spine a full crease! But I refrained from such undignified display. Readied myself to leave. Which is exactly when Wally, no solicitation, said 'Did I tell you about the foot that attacked Sylvester?'

'What foot?'

And Wally, no hint he'd ever acknowledge it was pure snake-oil he was peddling, told a story so fatty with detail and background context it could be nothing other than the product of an attention mad, only-child's need for perpetual center-stage.

In summary: a disembodied foot had got in through the chute leading from Sylvester's backyard to the basement (plausible, I admit) and had, middle of the night, snuck up the wood plank stairs to the main floor (also possible - Wally had the geography correct, anyway).

'Which foot?' Alvin asked. 'Needles? Barbed-wire?'

But no.

No.

'No' Wally said. 'This one was armed with a bazooka.'

IT WAS A GOOD JOB I bumped into Endie. He, like me, was of no mind to be suffered Wally's nincompoop fibs.

What could possess someone, we jointly wondered, to go so off the reservation they'd sense such sentences welling in their brainpan, feel saliva lacing their mouths to motion the words out, and not stay themselves before committing the drivel to posterity?

But I wished we hadn't asked. Because I was certain the answer lodged in the question. And frankly would rather not consider so creepy a proposition.

What could possess someone ...

Possess.

Possessed to relay false-narratives fed him by some entity, a mind which had jacked his.

Not unreasonable. These red-herrings and careless exaggerations spewed every which way but loose had some method to them.

Possession.

No. I wanted to forget it. And thankfully Endie was less invested than me, overall, and admittedly had sensational instincts for distraction. A level and serene head, just when I needed one most.

Not to say Endie didn't go in for some weird antics, all his own. Nor to suggest his house was shielded from its own gauge of peculiarity. Look in his fridge, right? He was offering me a drink but had to examine the plastic measuring jugs each liquid was housed in with meticulous care. Why? His family portioned beverages out, to the sip, each sip to the micron. Each cup was to be filled only so much and only so many cupfuls imbibed per day, per person.

My choices were milk (not 'skinny milk' - his familial language for 'skim' - but 'fat milk' which made me think unappetizingly of flies buzzing around an udder tugged raw) lime soda, extra-pulpy orange juice, or water. Nix-nix on the Hi-C which would obviously be what I'd request from a more obliging household.

'Sorry, Ick. There's only two Ecto-Coolers and three Purple Saurus Rex' (this latter flavor he pronounced Peppersaurus Rex which oddly made the drink sound all the more delectable, his lisping mispronunciation giving it a luscious mystique).

I'd have water, then. But could he let me have some of the slightly past sell-by Little Debbie snack cakes his dad brought home for free due to working stock at the grocery store?

Downstairs we played lesser-loved Nintendo games. Something I adored in Endie was his shared predilection for such outside-the-mainstream delights. We had a vigorous contest of Slalom, went an hour straight on Load Runner, tooled around with Dr. Chaos (though still couldn't figure what one was meant to achieve in it) and finally had the hoot of all time playing Flying Dragon - the finest, most true-to-life kung-fu game ever, no matter how viciously The Berlin Game Review had panned it once upon a time.

By the time evening had bleed into night, his parents only then realizing I was in their house and needed me to beat it back home, pronto, we'd spent hours forming a band called The Cheese Guys. Our songs were all approximately twenty seconds long, in some way or another to do with cheese.

We embraced upon my departure, promising to record the album, next day.

Alvin filled me in on what'd gone down with Wally after I'd brusquely departed. Pretty close to what I'd have reckoned. Wally claimed knowledge of additional Disembodied Parts. An unimaginative barf of 'a hand with a gun' and a 'head with a hand grenade.' Alvin scoffed how the kid had been playing too much Operation Wolf or Ikari Warriors.

I feinted agreement and begged off to sleep. Alvin didn't seem to make a thing about this, just tucked into some graphic novel after turning on the red clamp-lamp he'd somehow procured and affixed to his bunk.

I did my best to pretend my sleep real. Convince myself I was dreaming my thoughts, not responsible for their absurdities. Nothing more than slumbering synapses cracking off, sorting the day's events, catch-as-catch-can, to cobble a ramshackle narrative conceit from.

Certainly I didn't want to admit how, balderdash though it was, Wally's bazooka-foot terrified me. I felt tense, mortified at any thought of the thing. Not that physics allowed it could carry, let alone discharge, so bulky a piece of weaponry. Even if still attached to a portion of leg - even a leg entire - and if the bazooka had a sling strap.

It didn't matter. I was afraid to even open my eyes. Though behind closed lids I was petrified, regardless. Could see the vermin, so maliciously and with such patience, hopping those basements steps, one-at-a-time. Thup. Thup. Thup. Thup. Metallic weight of the bazooka somehow tensed aloft, controlled, neither banged nor brushed nor scraped against the walls or steps.

No sound whatever which might wise a victim to its deathly progress.

A DAY WENT BY IN joy and gladness.

Despite a touch of bother wherein Binion and I were observed by that goodie-goodie Safety Patrol (did she even have a switch for Off-Duty?) taking wizzes out into the tree-line of the woods during recess and were thus promptly trotted to the Principal's office for a pranging, things were looking nothing but up on all manner of fronts.

Besides: what did a duo such as Binion and myself care? This was the way deep bonds were formed - joint consequences for being caught with your flies down!

Alvin and I hiked to Collector's World as soon as we were home to investigate the rumor they had a small cache of Japanimation videocassettes for rent. Sure enough: squat half-dozen tapes adorned a stout shelf screwed in place above the main display wall. Akira. Vampire Hunter D. Bubblegum Crisis, volumes one-through-six. The riches and spices of the Orient! But even beached on our native shores they remained leagues out of reach.

To rent? Three bucks per night on top of twenty-dollars deposit! Minus a dollar for failure to rewind. Have to be over eighteen-years-old, regardless.

'But what about if people actually want to see them?' Alvin quipped and won a warmth of laughter which almost made it worth not being able to get our sweaty mitts on the things.

I browsed back issues of Punisher War Journal, listening to Alvin converse all swashbuckling with the grown-ups about his experience with Erol's Video, back in the day. Old story to me, but I always was keen for a retelling.

Alvin had rented a Dolph Lundgren film (Red Scorpion) a scant four days before the shop was to shutter for eternity.

'I went to return it, two days to spare - but inside, the joint was already gutted. Two plumbers or some kinda journeymen hanging out, nothing else.'

He'd rapped on the window, energetically pantomiming he needed to return the cassette.

'The plumbers didn't open the door or even come closer to the window, just made what I thought was a gesture of Go ahead, put it through the Returns slot.'

Despite this would plunk the movie on the being-peeled carpet, Alvin had done exactly that.

'The Collection Letters began arriving. For months! Demands for payment in amounts of three hundred, four hundred, five hundred dollars for failure to return rental property. Fees and Penalties snowballing! And for some unknown reason - a reason, if known, which would beggar reason! - the cost of Red Scorpion, itself, was two hundred-eighty bucks!'

How'd the saga end?

Alvin'd felt awful he was going to get my mom arrested due to his delinquency. He'd begged down the telephone with anonymous reprobates at the Collection Agency: couldn't he purchase a replacement copy from Suncoast Video for twelve crumby bucks and mail this in?

'I'll never forget how he'd put the hard word down: *the world don't turn on your bullshit kid - get square with us or else.*'

I was disappointed how, after the laugh that line garnered, Alvin abruptly switched course, leaving off the final act.

'Seriously - if I got you guys a note from my mom stating she'd cover any loss and in which she okays us renting, could we get a go at Akira?'

Shine dryly jibed how he couldn't imagine our mom would be game, based on the story he'd only just heard.

'You let me worry about corralling her - just what-if?'

Or - waitaminute! - couldn't we buy one of the tapes outright if we wrangled up twenty dollars?

Shine gave a raspberry thumbs-down, told Alvin to go pound sand so far as that little brainwave. 'That's why we rent it, capisce? This is a business, squirt - never mistake we'll-take-your-money for friendship.'

They all laughed. And I admired Alvin for being able to endure the currents of such jocular banter from cool older people so without bashfulness or outward ill-effect. I would've clammed up, found some excuse to leave. Alvin? He held the line, wits full enough about him to ask could he read the back of the cassette boxes - even struck a bargain to be shown the first five minutes of Akira on the store television 'Just to see if this slaw you all're slinging is even worth my bother.'

BUT THAT EVENING ... THAT NIGHT ... no ... tranquility was not engineered to endure.

As I reposed in the bathtub, the worm of incidents which had been brewing wriggled pasty and fat behind my eyes. I took to linking events, an even paced, causal chain. This to this to that to that. The creeps wouldn't leave me. Something beyond being hunted, quarried, stalked ...

How to make sense of anything?

Body parts disguised as fauna and flora - they'd have little call to butcher children! And once the initial rile of fight-or-flight was subdued, only a nimrod would persist in believing so insipid a fairy story.

All the signs were there ...

Piece-by-piece building bodies up ... infecting others to spread falsehoods, sew confusions, muddy all rational water with contradictory mumbo-jumbo ... an invasion physical and psychic ...

I sloshed in the crackle of popping bubbles scented of shea butter. An entire yet senseless understanding dawning, outskirting conscious understanding, a knowledge with weight but no language.

We were in the clutches of some malediction. A nuanced, leeching organism with myriad ways to transmit. Protozoa with tentacles! A venous network of burrows to make its way into us, flesh or else mind.

Mind! By God! Why did I think my thoughts any less vulnerable than my limbs or beating heart? It's no difference to this abomination - or at least I was a chump to blithely believe it might be!

I'd observed evidence, hadn't I? Even those who knew what was going on kept ignoring, forgetting, treating as a play-pretend, glad-handedly confuting the real with its inverse.

A million ways it could have penetrated my own brain and consciousness. What had I ever done to bulwark a defense against it?

Listening ... In me ... In me, listening to my thoughts ... Waiting for

realizations to wake in me before striking ... a spy which would leave me be
if deemed harmless (as this would all the better serve its devices!) but which
would report back, find use for me if I came to understand too keenly the
schematic of the snare I was in ...

Now I was thinking this. No undoing that! No way to unthink thoughts or
suggest those thoughts I'd thought were for chuckles now they'd been overheard.

But if I didn't think, I'd be as trapped as if I genuinely strove to think my
way clear!

Toweling off at the bathroom mirror, I felt spongy, as though I'd absorbed
the bathwater I'd soaked in, limbs moving in clunky Claymation.

'I can see you.'

What in the devil!?

'You do know I can see you, right?'

It was Alvin's voice. I stood there, naked, pacing in front of the toilet, and
muffled through the wall came Alvin's voice. 'Where are you, Alvin?'

'This isn't Alvin.'

But it was Alvin. And this wasn't funny. 'How can you see me?'

'I can see through the wall from here.'

Bingo! Give away! He was obviously in my dad's bathroom, which shared
a wall with the one I was in. So I ducked to one side, crouched in the bathtub's
corner.

'I can still see you.'

'How can you see me? Alvin - I'm serious! Can you really see me?'

'This isn't Alvin. And I can totally see you.'

Well, I could play this straight back in his face. I lifted firm my middle finger. Gestured it squarely at the wall above the toilet tank. 'Then what am I
doing?'

No beat missed came the retort 'You're giving me the finger.'

Enough was enough! A tremble coursed through me and I flung the bathroom door wide, bolting stark naked through the upstairs hall, into my parent's bedroom, through the door to my dad's bathing area ...

... and discovered it empty.

Empty!

'Alvin?' My stomach curdled, bowels shimmy-shook. I patted the walls,
attempting to sleuth the aperture through which I'd been observed.

But even had I found one - where was Alvin? Impossible for him to've
slipped out since last speaking. Any path he could've taken would've collided
us.

Suddenly wanting to be dressed, I sprinted back to the bathroom I'd only just vacated, yanking the spill of my clothes from the floor, pulling the garments on in my and Alvin's vacant bedroom. ' ...Alvin?'

Not two minutes passed before I heard the front door open and watched him enter. Brown paper bag filled with comic books in his hand.

'Where were you?'

'Dad drove me to Collector's World.'

But dad wasn't in the house. Nor did I see his parked car when I craned my head to glimpse out the window.

Alvin followed my glance. 'He had to go to his office, awhile.'

Despite the late hour, this was a common enough occurrence. Couldn't call him out there.

But: why hadn't Alvin gotten these comics when we were at the shop, earlier?

Clever, clever - an answer for everything. He'd left his money behind, back then. And, for authenticity, he now added how this time he'd grifted a few extra bucks off dad.

'You weren't just upstairs?' I didn't bother asking. He'd either genuinely not been or else had planned this out too insidiously. Plenty of old, empty brown comic bags downstairs to've concocted a dummy prop out of. I didn't know his full collection, so even if I inspected the titles there's no way to know whether they were new acquisitions or not.

'We good?' he asked with what seemed a sincerity same as sincerity had always sounded.

'Yep' I said back with what just sounded like Yep.

.MAY.

MY MOM: CARETAKER TO THE hilt. Kept my eyes opened to some of modern life's more arcane pitfalls. Instilled the appropriate fear of tapeworms and Debtor's Prisons, that's for starters.

The woman's solitary dream consisted of either Alvin or myself learning the piano. We didn't even need ascend to the ranks of concert virtuoso so long as we could achieve being 'people who enjoyed and appreciated the opportunities they'd been given'.

We belly-flopped on this count, all in a row. So she took lessons, now. Out of zealous parental spite ingeniously disguised as her own rekindled pursuit. At least this was the theory Alvin confided in me one night when he felt particularly guilty for not having made the grade.

A fifty-minute drive to her instructor's house. The trip to and from (on occasions I was lugged along) being a genuine highlight of a given week. This time, as was her wont, she was basking in talk radio. A disgraced former colonel who had quite the rabid following. Frank had warned me about this dude, though I could never find fault in anything he had to say over the airwaves. He used delightful words, besides. Referred to the current President's 'caravan of cronies'. I had a guffaw at that linguistic turn my mom seemed to appreciate (whether she was on the fearless host's side, I'd no idea).

Cronies. Cronies. The rough crumble of C into R - such a dry flavor, a bitter zest like coffee cake. Words were delicious. I remembered a time Alvin had spoken of geometry. Explaining the physical universe to some kid who I suppose had missed the memo. 'Everything has three dimensions. Width. Breadth. Heigdth.' That's just how he'd pronounced it. Heigdth.

This other kid tried correcting him. Alvin stood firm. Not only did I admire his not going kittenish in the face of this dolt's strong-arming, I knew he was correct. Aesthetic trumps all in language.

Cronies.

Heidgth.

The piano instructor, per usual, roamed his backyard, drinking what he claimed was iced tea, checking the tomatoes he for some queer reason grew himself. He had tons to say about all that and, same as always, lightly chided me over giving up my musical pursuits despite it'd been ages since I'd washed out.

Soon I was sat in the partitioned waiting area, my mom at the student bench handing over her practice tape. Instructor inserted the cassette. Hit Play. And soon, fading in slowly, the strains of the Moonlight Sonata plumped full the room. I froze. Felt my throat constrict as my voice, overtop the music, emanated from the radio speakers. Child's squeaky approximation of Vincent Price narration: *'It had rained for three weeks ... still the strangler at large in the corridors of the Bread Avenue Apartment Building ...'* Apartment made long, Aparta-ment *'... the corpses piled with steady meter ... one could keep time by the screams indicating ... another ... discovery ...'* And here a shriek - clanging, overlong, suddenly gone - Beethoven going loud, abruptly silenced, soon fading back up (I was proud of these volume effects, achieved by manipulating the knob of the background radio in tandem with my real-time performance)

I barged into the lesson area. All apologizes. Obviously I'd left my tape in the recorder. Simple oversight. A shared device. Cassettes all looked identical.

But wordlessly the instructor motioned me silent and shooed me back to the waiting area. I heard his chair squeak, compress, the ice in his beverage clink as he settled into a comfortable posture of audience. My mom whispered something. He whispered back.

From the radio:

'... Detective Caruthers!'

'Ma'am?'

'Look - do you see? In that corner?'

'The corner? Near those spilled boxes of old magazines with an oblong stain on the wall?'

'That's the one.'

' ... I see it.'

WHAT ELSE COULD I EXPECT? Why torture my peace-of-mind over how they'd listened and reacted? Like a mom and a former piano instructor? Like adults listening to a child's inconsequential pastime? An early attempt?

That's how they'd regarded the show, after all. Nostalgia coursing through them for their own youths, keepsakes tucked in boxes or time capsules.

Neither had asked to listen to the subsequent episodes. Neither were titillated, aching for storyline closure.

I lay on the bedroom floor. Quite the drama-lad. Bottom bunk too bougie for my funk.

I needed this disquiet sussed.

I was a kid, after all. They were factually unassailable there.

It was a radio show I'd put together in my bedroom. Also a true fact.

I'd performed every voice. Basically spit-balled the plot as I went. No second takes. Not a single re-working of scene.

I personally liked listening to it, sure. But I'd enjoy thinking about it as a finished product even if it remained incomplete. Similar to why I'd abandoned my piano career. Sit at the bench, stare at the keyboard, never plonk a mote? Imaginarium a concerto out of simplistic melodies? I'm your man! Indefatigable! Learn to read music? Muscularized my fingers with scales? Speed up my trills? Forget you, kimosabe!

Let's be serious a quick minute, shall we? At nine-years-old, didn't I already have a Trapper Keeper of disregarded 'early works'?

Of course. And discarded was where they belonged!

Was I seriously supposed be hot-to-trot over The Adventures of Ichabod or Hugo Plyankoff MD?

In no sane world! And that's even admitting the latter was a project I'd only recently considered Top-of-the-Pops!

Wasn't the reality me sitting around doing things but not actually doing them?

Here came Alvin, so I (the view of him perplexedly gazing down at me in upside-down from my worm's eye vantage) put it to him deathly: 'Isn't the reality I'm sitting around doing things but not actually doing them?'

How was he to know? Plus, he needed me to listen up about how weird Frank was. I knew (yes, yes - he knew I knew) how left-field Frank was, but this was a horse of different color.

Dig it: Alvin had been making his way home, crossing behind our row of houses, when Frank called to him from on the other side of one of the yard fences.

'How'd he know you were there?' These fences weren't mere slats, but solid walls of often wet wood already dry-rotted.

But this is what Alvin was saying! Weird.

So: he'd gone inside. Played Mario Kart while Frank drank beers and talked about inviting him along to a baseball game.

'Since when do you know from baseball?'

That bit was to do with how Frank was in discussions with his wife to have a baby and figured it would be good parenting practice. 'Anyway - to be polite, I asked after his gun safe. He said I couldn't see inside it - not that I'd asked - but did tell me how to make explosives.'

'How?'

'Mix some lighter fluid with a paste of nitrogen.'

'Where's a paste of nitrogen come from?'

'Exactly what I asked! Said you can get it from cat shit, bat shit, rat shit ...'

'Dog shit?'

'Exactly what I asked! Said dog shit doesn't work.'

I wasn't about to front off Frank was wrong, seeing as he was a military sub-commandant or something, but this intel struck me perplexing. Alvin seemed willing to roll with it, though. Figured it'd be a good job to make a bomb or two, just to have around in a pinch. Asked if I wanted to help him empty the litter box before dad got home from work.

ON THE SCHOOL FRONT, THE hits just kept on coming, didn't they?

The year was winding down, but a few big shebangs remained forthcoming. The Spring Chorus Concert was on deck. Every grade tasked with their little bit. Big league production! A cross-pollinated hybrid of interstitial vignettes limply plopped between musical numbers. All stops pulled out for a semblance of Broadway razzle-dazzle.

Chorus was not my thing during the best of times - and having gotten word from Binion he was moving away before the year officially ended made these times distinctly not those.

Binion and I, to speak it with candor, would be hard pressed, gun to our heads, to relate the loosest gist of the overall conceit of this extravaganza. Only knew our specific songs because we weren't nitwits and this production wasn't exactly on the magnitude Merrily We Roll Along. The lyrics the fourth graders were responsible for were no more than various onomatopoeia for laughter - then when those ran out we just literally sang words denoting various types of mirthful expression. As such:

Ha / ha-ha-ha / ha ha / ha ha ha / ho-ho-ho / ho-ho-ho / ho ho / ho-ho/ tee-hee / tee-hee / tee-hee / tee-hee / chuckle-chuckle-chuckle-chuckle / giggle-giggle-giggle-giggle.

So with that in mind, here's what went down: First of all, Binion and I weren't even singing at the time of the alleged incident. As was our habit (well documented considering how often we'd been cautioned over it) we were ignoring the entire endeavor, chatting amongst ourselves. Suddenly some girl wheels around brandishing j'accuse finger at me, bellowing to Ms.

Peabody 'Ichabod's calling me names!' Ms. Peabody, being already at the end of her wits about me, didn't bother with hearing out my side of the affair, just needed the formality of having the girl give her account.

Her claim: 'He's singing *Ho-ho-ho ho-ho-ho you are a Hoe!*'

Cue a chorus, no pun intended, of supporters all squealing affidavit evidence they'd heard me say it. 'And it's not the first time!' more than one added. Then to make it a real pecking party another shrieked 'Binion was telling him to stop but Ichabod wouldn't listen!' At this Binion was too gobsmacked to even formulate a word of defense or context for me.

Well, enough was enough. 'God send this toaster to Hell! I've had it up to my eyeballs with this joint and its libelous slurs. I don't even know this chick!'

I was told to exeunt the rehearsal bleachers and to go sit against the wall until I was ready to apologize.

'I'm ready to apologize, right now. Brandy - or whatever your name is - I'm sincerely sorry I implied you were a whore. Seriously.'

But this was strikes two and three in a ready-to-bake bundle, apparently, because Ms. Peabody felt like playing at semantical hair-splitting. 'You didn't imply it, Ichabod - you said it.' And now I'd said the actual word Whore which, in this universe, was worse than saying Hoe even though the terms were analogous.

And if I kept shining her on, Ms. Peabody told me I'd find myself unable to participate in the Chorus production, full stop.

'Oh promises, promises' I mumbled as I shouldered through the twin doors toward the Principal's office as ordered.

I WONDERED DID MICA ALWAYS hang round in lavatories. Was his off time at home spent squatted on the privy, dreaming up schemes? I also wondered 'Is this actually Mica?' But that was less to do with Mica, in specific, than with being the observational sort who figured this was a sensible question to have on deck concerning anyone.

'How's Dale?' I fairly hiccoughed by way of a dweeby Hello.

Mica was leaning on the sink lip. Bulbous glob of dispensed soap on the counter. I couldn't help but imagine he'd been the fella squirted it.

'You'd know.'

'Oh - I'd know? Is that the thing?'

He told me I might wanna watch out because people were talking about me.

Who? Everyone!? 'Everyone's one whole lotta people. No idea I was so

interesting. What're they saying, praytell?' I'd dropped all pretense of uri-
nating. Just stood in center echo of the chamber, hands to pockets in hopes
this fronted off a rebellious verve which might serve to disguise the gelatin
queasiness distending my belly.

'Bucha girls say you ate a fly out of a spider web.'

A flutter in my chest. Chirp of relief. 'That's only because I told people I
ate a fly out of a spider web.' Three weeks ago, or thereabouts. Blurted with
the vague dream it might make me out as intriguing to Nikki. She'd been
amongst a group of girls in Art class when one of them had asked 'Is it true
you ate a bug?'

Mica gave me the hairy eyeball. 'So you didn't eat a fly out of a spider web?'

How to play this? 'Who's asking?'

'I'm asking.'

Yes, yes - very droll I was sure. But I held my tongue, yet. Who would this
conversation filter to? Maybe Nikki had, it'd turn out, found something re-
markable in me. 'He's some Jack-the-lad who not only eats a bug but can
admit it without feeling lowdown.' Such humble braggadocio might be
swoon worthy. Fair's fair: I wouldn't give a hoot had she eaten a bug. Say she
broke the ice with telling me about it? I'd not only not hold it against her, it'd
serve nicely as the cornerstone of our bourgeoning intimacy.

'I ate a fly. Out of a spider web. Bank on it.' And I reiterated, as previous,
it'd been a particular web everyone knew about near the custodian's door in
the sixth-grade hall.

'No you didn't' this bum gloated, ready to go spill the beans.

'Look Mica: okay. I didn't. I'll come clean on that. But why don't we go
ahead and keep that between the two of us?'

'You're a liar, man.'

I'd lost the thread of was I or wasn't I or which one cast me in the more
desirable light. I should start avoiding school toilets, I thought.

And odd timing (could he read my mind?) Mica said 'Nina told everyone
about seeing your thingy when you took that leak one recess.'

It was Nina who'd grassed me out? I'd never've put her down as a wiretap-
per. 'You've got a big mouth, Mica.'

'So I've heard.'

So he's heard? What could that mean considering he'd said it in such a
loaded tone? My mind rolodexed until it hit on the only option exactly as
Mica pulled his mind reader bit again.

'I'll tell Dale you said Hi.'

'Listen Mica - for real, I did eat that fly.' This was the only way I could
think to respond. The world had looped topsy-turvy.

Mica emphatically spit into the plop of hand soap then dispensed a sinewy few more splats on top.

I was left alone. Wondering should I clean up the mess. Otherwise, I'd wind up in the frame for having caused it, wouldn't I?

MY MOM WAS IN THE front yard of Donovan's house. She and Donovan's mom posed in parental postures associated always with speaking sotto voce about serious matters. For whatever reason, this conversation was occurring out of doors whilst drinking limeade.

I braced for a button-holing. No doubt official report of my day's misdeeds had wound round to the homestead. Though turns out, if so, it didn't much matter.

'Have you seen Ezekiel?'

Couldn't recollect the most recent time I'd laid eyes on Ezekiel, no.

Not as school?

'I wouldn't see him at school.' He was in first grade. Acquaintance at best. Really in the Venn overlap of flat-out-stranger. If he was even who I was picturing.

My answer seemed all that was required of me so I continued on home.

Alvin was pouring a fresh bowl of Honeycomb into the remaining milk of his previous bowl. Yes, I assured him, of course I was still down for the big game of Guns which was planned for the afternoon. Ideally, it'd become Flashlight Tag, come evening. Except we'd have to borrow flashlights from someone, if it came to that. Only one in the house was part of dad's ragtag medical kit.

Alvin asked had I seen Ezekiel, anywhere.

'What's he got? The winning ticket? Why's everyone asking?'

Alvin had asked only because he didn't know my mom had already. She'd also asked him, no clue why.

When we got to Donovan's, Endie and some kid I knew the brother of were also there along with Wally - and someone who I think was called Ryan rounded out the group. We were informed how the hard word had come down: a parental committee had decreed we were no longer allowed to play Guns.

'Why not?'

'Some flim-flam about with everything going on they'd rather not have us out killing each other.'

'What do they expect us to do all afternoon, then?'

All moot court, of course. We soon got bored trying out logically secure arguments which, to a sane jury, would win us our cause, made up our minds to play past it.

The kid called Ryan suggested we change the game of Guns to either Mutants or Nintendo Guys. When the explanation of Nintendo Guys indicated it was the exact same as Mutants (except instead of choosing mutant abilities to wield you choose a character from a Nintendo game to be) we sagely gaveled in how we'd combine the games by allowing players to be either mutants or whoever they felt like being from Nintendo.

Proviso: try to avoid being someone who used a gun.

We weren't certain how gung-ho the parents were about the whole firearms thing. Letter of the law or spirit? Could we point our fingers like pistols? Arrange our arms as though enacting the kickback of shotguns? Might Bang or Boom be spake as sound effect without fear of punitive measure?

Side problem: Donovan wanted to be Bomber Man.

'Using timer-bombs' he quickly explained when he saw our collective faces go quizzical as to how the logistics of this choice would go within actual gameplay.

But timer-bombs put him a peculiar gray-area. If he set a bomb trap, pantomimed depressing a plunger device when someone wandered into his snare, could he explode them?

We'd go along with it, of course. After all, landmines were a regular part of any worthwhile game of Guns. Moreover, it was a stone blast to sometimes act out you'd stepped on a pressure mine, even if no one technically claimed they'd set one up. Very pleasurable to face down certain doom as the enemy caught you exposed, to pray they got near enough the explosion from your stepping off would take them down with you.

'Go ahead and do it' was the verdict on the timer-bombs. If an adult came poking around and issued a writ, he could say how it's not a bomb but a mechanism which sent electric current through the ground.

Yessir. We all concurred this was the pat way to handle such a grim eventuality.

AN HOUR INTO THE FIRST campaign - teams assigned, territories demarcated, powers selected - a trio of kids, none of whom seemed directly connected to the other, ambled across the battlefield. They kind of piddled about there, making it impossible for any member of either team to leave our concealed posts or to wage any meaningful offensive.

Both sides got the idea. Under gestures of truce we dispatched representatives to see what was the score with these interlopers. Within minutes, they were brought up to speed on the rules of engagement, selected avatars, and

were divvied up onto team A or B. All except one kid who asked could he be
a Yojimbo, take his own chances procuring mercenary work, perhaps attack
both teams with equanimity. This lad was a true cipher: zero connection to
the other two and no one recognized him from school. But - sure, whatever
- we said he could do as his little heart desired and we'd incorporate it as fea-
sibly as we were able. This oddball then immediately took off running, became more and more remote a spot on the horizon line, disappeared behind
an area of houses our games never ventured anywhere near.

No time to dwell on this beyond the requisite shrugs and befuddled 'Maybe
he went home to get something?' we dove into the game, headlong.

A dozen children, aged seven to sixteen, coursing the veins of the neighborhood, we repeatedly screeched out the identifier words for our powers.

Fireball! Fireball! Fireball!

Electroshock! Electroshock!

Ice! Ice! Ice!

Shatter bomb! Shatter bomb!

Some abilities were more complex (Time Freeze! Ripple Mist! Poison Music!) but, seasoned pros the lot of us, we could act out the appropriate response to any and all new power abruptly shouted into the mix. All on the
honor system. If someone shot Sonic Stabs at you from the distance and you
were weaving and dodging it went without saying the dodges were legitimate. And sometimes, for the communal simpatico, someone would act out
being hit in the shoulder from a distant Thunder Star (a kind of propulsive,
explosive shuriken) gladly writhing on the ground as their assailant moved in
for the kill. Perhaps a teammate, meantime, tried to defend with Armor
Wind! or Crack-Ka-Boom! (I assumed this was a kind of fantastic quaking
force which disrupted the senses of everyone in proximity except the individual wielding it) and, well, it would be sorted out on the fly, most often to
the satisfaction of all parties.

The neighborhood adults - walking dogs, tinkering with loose planks on
their verandas – paid us little mind. Sometimes one even seemed pleased
we'd selected their bushes to hide out in, often for upward of fifteen minutes.

I was hidden in just such a manner, three hours into combat. Loyalties were
vastly shifted, team-to-team, and a rather heady plotline had developed concerning the team I was not on erecting a Hydrogen Time Bomb (meaning it
would 'blow up time' not that it was on a timer, even though, in many respects, it was on a timer) by the business park currently under construction
over the hill across from the bus stop.

I caught sight of the kid Yojimbo making a sudden mad dash from the cover
of the trees at the top of hill. He was barreling down on Endie. As he

advanced, this kid was screaming 'Neuter power! Neuter power! Neuter Power!' and enacting rather arcane, semi-spiritual looking gestures with his noodley arms. Endie must've been as confused as I was (and I saw several other players stop short to gawk at this sudden spectacle) because as the kid bore down on him he froze, stammering as though absolutely perplexed how to react to the assault. 'Neuter power! Neuter power!' the kid persisted in bellowing. Becoming giddy. High pitched. Manic. 'Neuter power!'

Endie (good sport, most likely freaked out of his right mind) finally clutched himself here and there and allowed the kid to stand overtop his bested form, whipping hands around and cock-crowing 'Neuter Power! Neurter power! Neuter power!'

This didn't stop until Alvin and an older kid called Patrice gave time-out gestures and made their way over to sort out heads from tails.

THESE WERE BULLETS. REAL MCCOYS.

'Bullet shells' Wally corrected. We had to grudgingly admit his accuracy.

'But that means there were bullets' Donovan chimed in to save our collective face.

'A clip full' Endie estimated while Alvin laid them side-by-side for an official count. We reckoned Endie had hit it on the nose.

Query: what's a spent clip of bullet casings doing all over the bare concrete floor of an unfinished room in an office park under construction?

There were obvious answers. They just seemed too big city, overtly cinematic, to have direct bearing on the here and now.

Fact one: bullet shells equals bullets - you don't get them any other way.

Fact two: spent shells mean, de facto, shots had been fired.

A firearm had been discharged. Here. In this room. Many times over

Wally tried to gadfly how the rounds could've been expended elsewhere, the shells then spilled here for nonspecific reasons. But this was about as relevant as snooty philosophically navel gazing such like 'we don't know all men are mortal, we only know every man has been, thus far'. Wally ate humble pie on that. So we were magnanimous enough to tell him how he was correct in the way that if this were an essay we'd give him a good grade.

Everyone fanned out to see if we could gain entry to any of the rooms with doors. Some of us went to bellies, crawling meticulously to bloodhound out further evidence. Could be a murder, quite brutal, had taken place only recently! Killer had dragged the body off to stash it, meant to return for the shells, but our arrival had hamstrung him.

'Where's the blood?'

Wally again. And this time I took the time out to sideline him, dressing down the smarty-pants but good. 'Coulda been a sheath of plastic laid out, body shot close range. Think a professional cleaner's gonna croak someone and leave blood spatter!'

This cowed the rascal. He seemed to be more genuine in his investigations from then on, no more of his smug armchair detecting.

But, speaking seriously: was there a non-lethal explanation for this?

'Someone used the room to blow off steam? Frank says guns are relaxing' Alvin offered though didn't seem invested in selling this scenario against the slightest skepticism.

He, like me, was stuck on the real haunt of this situation. Namely: 'Where did the bullets hit if they didn't hit someone?'

No sign of holes, anywhere. And were they fired out the door - say into the grass of the hill across the parking lot - why would the shooter have bothered hiking out to this half-built office park instead of any remote field?

What I didn't say: Everyone kept assuming the shooter was assailing some-one - but what if the shots had popped off in defense? What if there weren't bodies because the bullets had been worthless? Say whatever had been shot at had dragged the shooter off with it after gaining the upper hand?

Our search spread to the nearby dumpsters. No carcasses to speak of, but whole loads of broken fax machines, printers, bulky computer monitors.

'Why would these be here if this building is new?' Wally seemed to need to know with urgency. I mean, I agreed it was a sound question, but it dis-turbed me how he gave it precedence over the probable homicide.

'You'll never make sergeant at this rate' I didn't bother to quip.

Meantime: Alvin, Donovan, and Endie were sorting through the half-dozen high-class lingerie catalogues found inside a bag of shredded docu-ments.

ENDIE STUCK WITH ME WHEN the group parted company. The majority of the others headed to re-establish The Pack Rats, toot suite. The hidey-hole had fallen out of use since some hooligans had ferreted out the stashed porn mag, absconded with it, and generally made a wreck of things. But now there was a common idol to protect and not a moment to lose!

It hadn't taken any sweet talking for Endie to hang back. His mind trol-leyed the same track as mine, what with our shared history.

This office park adjoined another sewer opening. At the end of an un-tended field, down a sharp slope of hill, was a swampy reservoir, leakage from the tunnel what fed the fetid divot its pulpy moisture. The entrance-mouth was typically only visible from interior a passing vehicle. Even then, due to weather, much of the time the area was plump with water and the sight of collected geese or the sinuous weeds were more noteworthy than the gaping maw. An entrance-mouth tall enough a grown man could walk upright in and out it, not even stooping his shoulders. But (Endie pointed out while we finished our scoot down the hill) the circular aperture had a grate over it.

Except here that was. Torn from its casing. Rusted and covered in bird droppings, plastic bags clung under lumps of scabby poop.

We glared down the dark gullet. And it was then Endie, quite offhand, whispered 'Who is Ezekiel, anyway?'

What did he know about Ezekiel?

Nothing. It's just his dad had been curious had he seen the kid around. 'I don't even know him, but my dad thought I might.'

'You know Ezekiel. First grader who won a tapdancing award.'

Endie's face was unguardedly baffled. First off, the tap-dancer was in second grade. 'And his name's Kale. Kale Davies.'

Even as he pronounced the K of Kale I knew he was correct. 'Then who's the first grader?'

'There's no first grader.'

Yes ... with Kale's name in place, any inkling of an Ezekiel vanished from me. 'Then ... who is Ezekiel?' I asked. But trailed off on the name. Jostled Endie to look up the hill. 'Isn't that Neuter Power?'

And there was another kid with him who neither of us recognized. The both of them loitering there with no apparent cause beyond kicking at clumps of something and watching us.

'Why're they watching us?'

Again in tandem, Endie landed on the same grim truth I did: It was nothing to do with us.

'They're just waiting to get in the tunnel' I whispered.

No other explanation covered all available facts.

So as though it didn't mean a thing to us, we clambered back up the hill. At the top, we assumed body language suggesting jocular ribaldry, paly conversation, and crossed to the trees near the bus stop where we took cover.

Surest thing you know, when we returned to the lip of the reservoir, Neuter Power and his cohort were nowhere to be seen.

So we waited.

Waited.

Dusk settled proper. The streetlamps lining the road nearby slowly glimmered on their orange.

The kids never exited. And we weren't for one minute gonna entertain the notion they'd popped through a manhole somewhere in the middle of a neighborhood.

The both of us remained on our bellies, cloaked in some high grass. 'You said something about making bombs?' Endie whispered.

'Bombs?'

'You can make bombs with dog shit?'

'No - only three-letter animals that rhyme. Their poop is nitrogen rich.'

Well, Endie reckoned some bombs might not be bad thinking. Times like these.

THE HOUSE WAS HUMID. STILL. The empty rooms seemed garments long seeded with mildew. The churn of the dishwasher, its mildly acrid fragrance of artificial citrus, whorled through the matted air, a kind of aromatic clot coursing the household's veins. From out back - a rough, percussive mumble due to the windows being closed - came the high-pitched whinging of some child.

'You can't do that! You can't do that! You can't do that!'

Antagonistic laughter from several other voices.

I wanted to move to the pane. Have a look.

'You can't do that! You can't do that!'

Desired any distraction, really.

'You can't do that!'

But at the top of the basement steps, I took a stabilizing breath, started down, the 'You can't do that!' ending abruptly 'You can't—' almost as though its purpose was spent.

The laundry room.

I'd not been down since the discovery of those insects.

Light switch in the hallway. Flick. The mute, sour brown of the single bulb did its usual gig hardly illuminating anything at all. Though it produced light, it served more to thicken the outskirting shadows, added lurk to the dark's sum total.

Bombs would be a good idea. And there was cat waste aplenty. For the time being, I'd need a small sampling, only. Just enough to test whether Frank wasn't getting his jollies yanking the cranks of schoolkids.

The main issue was lighter fluid. I didn't even know whether my mom or dad put the cannister back on the shelf after finding it on the floor all those months back. Seemed the sort of thing they'd have at least done basic fact gathering about. Could be they'd asked Alvin, he'd had no clue about it, they'd let the matter drop but kept suspicions of him. Perhaps they'd put it together it was to do with me but as the accelerant had been retrieved without incident it was deemed no harm no foul.

Who knows with them, really ...

I felt dozens upon dozens of compacted eyes on me. Though how was I to know if these critters even had those. Maybe they were blind. I somehow felt they were, as this trait would make them all the more odious. Pictured antennae doubling as tongues, rough as those of a cat. Imagined they lacked mouths ... they were mouths ... entire body opening exactly in half to close around prey, their vital organs solid like gums to grind victims down ...

Unsettling how it was the bugs themselves I feared. If only I knew what body part they turned into, which weapon they'd wield, I would be fearful of that. But as things stood, it was just them.

No sign of the fluid bottle. Typical.

Where would it have gone? Would a parent keep it in this room, merely shelved in another spot? Or would it have been relocated, outright?

Then: a click from the shelves. Over in the pitch something had struck a piece of anonymous clutter. Now the silence was too purposeful to trust.

I reached for the only weapon available - an unopened box of dryer sheets. And I waited.

Waited.

Waited.

It would take some few paces, only - split second at most - to sprint to the door. Two more seconds would have me up the steps with door slammed shut behind me.

But whatever was there knew this all too well. Likely salivating for me to make a break whereupon it would flit out like a frog's tongue and have me.

Waited.

Waited.

In an inspiration, I flung the box I held into the darkness. My intention had been to book it out of there in the confusion, but a horrific ruckus caused my treacherous body to tense up. Items fell. Items broke. I sweated, aghast at my idiot move. How the devil would I explain this?

'The bugs' I'd say.

Except in my mind's eye I could already hear my mom's exceptionally rational observation 'Bugs are completely harmless' besting my equally true but far more conceptual retort 'Horror is a kind of harm!'

As though on instinct - paradoxically self-preservational and apt to get me slaughtered - I moved into the dark corner to start making straight the disaster.

And that's when I found the boxcutter. Dense and metallic. Somewhat rusted. A switch manipulated with thumb - click click click - made the blade inch out - tick tick tick - made the blade retreat.

Positively exquisite.

MOM'S CAR WAS IN THE lot. Dad's wasn't. Coming up on ten o'clock at night. The inverse of what I'd expected.

I took another loop through the house to prove without reservation it was only myself and Alvin there.

Alvin: in the basement eating chicken tenders, using a fork to chip at frozen lemon-lime Gatorade in a tall plastic cup, watching television through crumby reception.

Me: standing there verifying.

Alvin knew mom wasn't at work. 'She's upstairs.' And when I informed him otherwise, he followed me to see for himself.

We telephoned my dad's office to discover he was there. As excuse for calling, Alvin asked could he bring home two particular types of cereal and also requested some Mama Celeste pizzas.

'Ask for some for me, too.'

But the call was over.

We sat in semi-darkness at the dining room table. What light there was slipped in through the narrow kitchen via the living room. But with only one of the three bulbs under the fan operational and the dimmer switch slid down the illumination was phantasmal.

Alvin soon poured himself some Cookie Crisp and began leafing through pages he dug from a manilla envelope.

'What're those?'

Didn't I remember when we'd gone to some friend of our dad's house? The woman's niece was a wannabe cartoonist?

I did remember. Vaguely. Exactly the way one remembers something that didn't necessarily happen.

He handed some of the papers across. Photocopies of various runs of her comic strip. She'd been vibrant with hopes of syndication. Alvin wondered if she'd ever struck gold. Would we ever have means of knowing? 'They wouldn't necessarily be in The Post' was what he was driving at. It was the first time I'd considered how The Post wasn't the only newspaper there was.

I didn't much care for the comics. Maybe the humor was too grown-up. Maybe they weren't meant to be humorous.

Maybe a lot of things.

Maybe I should tell Alvin about the boxcutter. The bombs. The kitchen knife I'd slipped from the silverware drawer, hidden upstairs in an old school-box.

Eleven o'clock came and went.

Mom still hadn't returned.

We decided she'd maybe gone to Donovan's house. His mom was the only other parent she ever much interacted with. We'd pieced together they'd been friends since before Christ. Or maybe not. Alvin thought I'd told him so and I thought Alvin had told me. In the long run, there was little chance it mattered.

Like all the other dwellings in the neighborhood, Donovan's had no windows lit. Not even the walkway light was on. The entire night seemed lifeless.

'Did you hear that?'

I hadn't.

Alvin tensed to attention, finger held aloft to gesture me silent. 'Listen.'

First one voice. Distant. Then another. Distant. Then a few voices together.

'Ezekiel!'

'E-zeeee-key-elllll!'

'Uh-ze-ee-ee-ki-hull!'

This chorus continued. A kind of cricket song interrupted by the odd cicada rattle or throaty croak of a toad.

We immediately altered postures for creeping. Made our way to the back yard where we took sentry at the edge of the pricker bushes beneath the powerlines.

'Ezekiel!'

'Ezekiel!'

From our duck blind, the voices were identifiable. Frank. Donovan's mom. Our mom. Some man. Some man. Some woman. Another. Many more, further on down into the tar thick black of the field.

'Ezekiel!'

'Ezekiel!'

'Ezekiel!'

Neither one of use spoke while we observed for a solid fifteen minutes. Twenty minutes. Thirty. More. Forever, it seemed.

All down into the tall grass, to the creek's tree-line, flashlight beams traced slow arcs. Flickered up. Down. Traced slow arcs. Flickered up. Down. Streams crossing, catching in the fog, casting gloomy, oversized shadows while the voices called out for Ezekiel. A methodically combing of the lukewarm night growing chill. Flashlights blinked also from inside the woods. Whit-whit-whit as trees obscured them or they were blocked by the other bodies in the grass.

The flashlights, I could tell, were mostly trained toward the soil. Only seemed to raise, drift side-to-side, teeter and dance, when a grown-up would stop, breathe in, boom out 'Ezekiel!' with voice hoarse from throat tight at the top of arched back.

The voices seemed complacent. Assured the boy was simply somewhere. All it was was a matter of determining the function of an unknown quantity. A peculiar calm to it all. Even a dribble of boredom.

Alvin and I didn't comment once back inside. Sleepy in the tip-toeing blue of the basement television, its sound mute. The film we didn't know the name of played in front of us, sound-tracked with our chewing and the languid squegs of the chocolate milk we swallowed.

.JUNE.

ALVIN AND I MADE QUIZZICAL expressions at each other but kept schtum. The landscape out the backseat windows changed as our dad ventured us further and inexplicably into Olde Towne. Here was an area I'd only visited on a field trip in first grade, the purpose of it lost to my memory, mysterious as this current impromptu errand.

Front passenger seat: a woman we'd never laid on eyes on. She seemed to have no historical relationship to our dad which might explain her presence or why he was playing the dutiful chauffer. Mumbling to herself quite a bit. When she wasn't, she'd be relating a narrative I could only suppose made sense to someone with my dad's medical expertise and adult understanding of the world.

To me? She was gobbledygook incarnate. Reminded me of Monacci. Kinda wondered had she won a Secret Movie Theater ticket via bare-knuckle com bat. Or maybe she was an usher there.

After an interminable duration (dad seldom used air-conditioni' though he allowed us to open the windows it remained an op' bright, stovetop warm day) we let this woman off on some ano' outside what was once a working train station but now existe' ist attraction. Yokels could photograph a disused engine gift shop, so-called, the sort hocking locally produced shirts proclaiming the wearers loved this or that str'

Back on some roads Alvin and I recognized, fif' senger debarked, the whole thing felt almost abruptly remember we were on hand. Ask' going.

'I thought we're going home?' Alvin chirpe' headed after buying doughnuts and wasting four do.'

I B'
cupi'
thank'
I'd in'
though '
nabbed a'
tary of som'
just his uncl'
around here,'

a Robocop arcade game (lousy console which seemed engineered to not allow players to proceed past thirty seconds of Level One under any circumstance).

Dad consider this. Drove on another five minutes. Then seemed to reckon he'd better hip us wise to what all about the woman. 'That person was crazy' he opened with, flat fact.

We laughed. Seemed a bit bold a pronouncement considering he'd known her the mere length of time she'd sat at the shop counter. Not to mention during those two, three minutes he'd seemed occupied, as usual, with his important sheets of mathematical scrawl.

He counterpointed how, for a man of his clinical pedigree 'It is possible to tell if a person is crazy from the way they order their coffee.' He dolled this assertation up with an anecdotal digression consisting of a trio of non-consecutive incidents circa the nineteen-forties when he'd be doing his residency in Argentina.

There might be some truth to his boast. No call to dismiss the old man out of hand. True statement: she'd ordered coffee. Thus, he wasn't weaving his observation from whole cloth.

However: Alvin and I joshed that we weren't certain 'crazy' was an officially sanctioned psychological distinction. He admitted we had the core of a sound rebuttal, there. In fact, he'd need to conduct a few diagnostic appointments with her to 'determine which type of crazy she is'. In a general way, though, he stood by his quick-draw analysis with an admirable confidence.

Soon, his swagger absolutely won me over. Woman was a loon. He'd done the civic thing. Must be.

Alvin seemed less sold but was smart enough to use saying 'Very interesting, dad - I see what you mean' as slick segue into scamming could we stop by the bookstore, maybe get something if it wasn't too expensive.

'PASSED THE LITTLE PARK, enacting a pantomime of being quite oc-
∙d with rehearsal for a scene in a play, too busy to suffer intrusions,
all the same.

itially been curious to join what I took to be bout of Freeze Tag, even
didn't recognize a single participant save some kid who'd once
Science award. He'd garnered a classroom visit from some secre-
≥ secretary of someone in the Federal Avionic Program (or maybe
∙ stopped by, I was hazy on certain facts). Since when he lived
' hadn't a clue.

My mind had changed when I overheard two older kids (frames almost like adults) clapping whilst boisterously announcing the game was being altered to Smear the Queer. Without any sports ball to designate the titular queer, a pinecone would be used. Anyone not made of the right stuff was asked to scram on home to wet their sissy beds. The science kid was ridiculed by poorly done clucks and br-wawks as I finished tiptoeing away.

I kept up my monologue, letting it become a rather meta-soliloquy explaining why I was giving a soliloquy. I crossed the road, up the hill, taking quick peek whether any actual construction was going on at the office park site. Climbed into the control seat of a small crane. Tried the door of an asphalt paving machine, but it was locked solid.

The room where the spent bullet shells had been now boasted full glass doors, also locked. Forehead to one, I made out how inner walls denoting office units were in place. One outside door had the name of either a financial firm or a dentistry practice stenciled to it. The blinds of these windows heavy down, mock-wooden. Electronic badge-swipe device secured against unauthorized ingress.

Who'd wound up keeping those shells?

I was miffed they hadn't been distributed evenly amongst all members of the discovery party. I'd likely never lay eyes on one, again. Though it'd be worth checking out The Pack Rats lair. Could be they were kept as a communal belonging, like with the underthings catalogues. I desired, at least, to know how it felt to hold one.

Of late, the sidewalks had been thick with caterpillars. Out of the clear blue hundreds (thousands it must've been, all tallied) of fuzzy, verdant green, sometimes soot-grey, little buggers littered the neighborhood. I'd gotten into the habit of all but tapdancing my way along. Motion a gameplay. Hopscotch. Superstition. Break-your-mother's-back.

Pavement of the parking lots had a crust of scabs, like a big skinned knee, dozens of unfortunate lepidoptera euclea who'd gotten smooshed, popped by the grind of vehicle rolling by. Burst, juicy innards baked to a crisp in the sun, washed gooey with sudden drifts of rain.

My attention was drawn to a kid some distance off. He was positioned beside his bike. Seemed to be having a jolly swing of a time lifting the front wheel high (like a pop-a-wheelie) then letting it drop (bounce bounce bounce). He'd scoot ahead a step. Lift tire. Drop. Bounce bounce bounce. Got near enough to make out the exact nature of his activity just as he straddled the bike and undertook the same sequences of actions but in the position of rider. Feet planted on the ground to allow the lift, drop, bounce bounce bounce.

He was bursting caterpillars. One-by-one. A mechanized progression. Whole of the walkway to his house a massacre. Lift. Drop. Bounce bounce bounce. I could see several adults out. Others in windows. He was as visible to them as to me. Lift. Drop. Bounce bounce bounce.

I didn't really stop, as transfixing as it was. But as I walked, I felt I was still watching. All desire to check on the bullet shells gone. Mind fixated on what I'd witnessed. Daydreamed watching him proceed around the loop of neighborhood sidewalk until nightfall. Other kids joining him.

And I felt an almost physical pull in my thighs to get out my Mongoose.

Lift the tire.

Let it drop.

Know the sound, feel, the reality of being astraddle the bounce bounce bounce.

WHILE BINION KEPT THE CUBBY under his desktop tidier than I did mine, by a length, I'd never observed it entirely empty. We'd only a handful of schooldays left, but still there were activities, reasons to be stocked with staple supplies. Plus: zero other desk cubbies stood empty. Also: hadn't there been plenty in there, just last week?

Thursday had been an early dismissal. Binion hadn't done anything different than normal. Friday ... had he been absent?

Oh what could I do about it, regardless?

I had things which required all my immediate attentions. Namely: I needed to conceal the weapons I'd snuck from home. I'd fashioned sheaths out of notebook paper and invisible tape for both boxcutter and serrated kitchen knife. I now secreted them under the enormous mess of outdated worksheets, project folders, and sundry Weekly Readers I'd let collect since whenever we'd last done a clean out.

No bombs. I'd written that pipedream off. Frank was bonkers. I'd have to face facts, there.

Plus: remember my only other attempt at anything requiring precision chemistry? Dig it: I'd convinced my mom to purchase me a chemistry set because I'd liked the look of the little vials the powdered or crystalline elements were kept in. As far as experiments, I'd done little more than mixing random things together, liberally adding water, hopeful for a reaction worth my precious time. Boners, all around. Though in some kinda deranged fugue I'd convinced myself I'd invented 'a compound which could douse fire swifter than water'. Tested it via setting billets of paper aflame, pouring water on one, my concoction on another, feeling out which seemed to extinguish the crackle first.

It'd been Binion who'd soberly reminded me 'Isn't the main ingredient of your potion water, though?'

'Water with stuff in it' I'd tried to argue. But seeing his point, the wind went out of my sails.

In any event, it boiled down to fractions of a second and those'd been tiny, laboratory controlled blazes. Not the stuff of grants or patents.

Where was Binion, today?

By the switch to Math class, I was anxious. He was to bring his weaponry for a final inspection, too. There was no way he'd gone lily-livered, so something must be afoot.

Mr. Podmore was substituting for Mrs. Terre, though she'd left robust instructions for him. Poor chump little more than her mouthpiece. He gave me a perplexed sniffle when I asked after my friend.

'He and his dad took everything home Friday, didn't they? I think they're in California.'

This clod had a jumbled handle on the facts, so I went to set him straight. Maybe he'd like to tell me how on Earth my best friend would have dropped the ball as to telling me I'd never see him again? All I got was a restatement of the company line with a generic buck-up remark how he was certain my pal would keep in touch.

No percentage in agitating myself with Mrs. Terre's stooge proxy, I returned to my desk.

Let's try to suss this out ... No member of the institution could be trusted to dish the straight scoop ... it was down to logic.

I'd seen Binion Thursday. We'd been full steam ahead about being here today, sorting things for our final assault. Sorting out, moreover, what precisely this final assault would be comprised of.

Friday, he'd been ill.

His departure must've been sudden. And heartless at that! His parents didn't even allow him farewells? I admitted I didn't know them well, but they'd never come off as bloodless fiends.

No ... no ... Something was rotten in the state of Denmark. Too many happenstance pointed in one direction to ignore. I was always the first to agree the plural of coincidence isn't murder ... but times like these? They turn one thinking. Must be some reason it once upon a time was coined the exception proves the rule.

SLOW TRAIN COMING, BUT SPINNY Johnson of Harlem Globetrotters fame proved well worth the wait - and how! What a treasure! Nevermind being a top notch comic personality both in his prepared material and his on-the-fly crowd work (working with random children pulled from the audience, no less!) the chap was bounds more inspirational than he had any call to be. His refrain, laced throughout his cut-up antics and moments of sober poignancy, came in the form of a mantra his grandmother had related to him throughout his humble upbringing. 'What your mind can conceive, your heart can believe, you can achieve.' Remarkably succinct considering the vastness such a be-boppy, easily memorized nugget of sagacity contained.

I was so enamored by this talented-athlete-cum-all-around-man-of-the-people, I regretted ever poo-pooing the suggestion of bringing scratch paper to nab his autograph. Nearly all others in attendance had come prepared.

In this connection, I asked to be excused to the toilet. All a clever feint, in fact! I used the stolen moments to dash to my homeroom, whereupon I intended to retrieve my nice, cloth covered, blue three-ring binder for him to sign. I drew a circle on it in permanent marker, which I intended to alter into a clean illustration of a basketball once his John Hancock was set to the center. Underneath his autograph, it was my intention to copy out in fair hand the succulent little trio of rhyming phrase which had so moved me.

While at my desk, though, better just quick give the double-check my weapons hadn't up and walked off. Plunged hand under the junk pile where I'd quite on purpose secured them with a hearty shove earlier.

Under the pile ...

... as far back as could be ...

... knife ... knife and boxcutter ...

Felt my stomach turn over, acrid build-up like swamp gas fill me, skin souring, draining of blood, and goose-pimpling while queasy sweat pressed out my forehead. Considering my typical pallor and gangliness, I'd no idea how livid I must've come across. Thankfully, no one there to regard me.

Checked again.

Again.

Again.

What in the name of the great good Lord could it possibly mean!?

Boxcutter. Gone. Kitchen knife. Gone.

This could be no zany mistake - no mama, don't even think so sideways! I'd practiced digging the blades free a few times just after stowing them. They're disappearance could only be the result of someone's conscious hand.

Needless to say my nerve was ashamble, mind on the blink. But with the grave realization Spinny was only fielding autographs for a few minutes, I

managed to snap out of it. He's a man who can't afford dawdling around a
cow-town grade school for my shirker pleasure!

Down the gymnasium corridor, nick of time. Spinny exited the gym (thun-
derous whoops and applause belching out with him, silencing as the doors
shut) and bestowed me a polite nod. I stammeringly explained I'd been kept
in the toilet longer than anticipated. 'Some malady which genetically afflicts
me' (he nodded in very sincere understanding as I prattled) 'but your message moved me profoundly and I'd be sincerely privileged if you'd still be
willing to autograph my binder'. No problem there. His handler had a fresh
red marker at the ready. What a brilliant stroke of aesthetic luck! The red
would stand out aces on the denim blue of the binder and drawing the quota-
tion in black would serve to accent the authenticity of the autograph - put any
doubting Thomas' snide assumptions to rest.

As he signed, magnanimously repeating the poem aloud, the gym door
opened to the general dismissal of everyone. Spinny finished with me, turned
to amaze the gawkers afresh with a last twirl of ball on his fingertip, bopped
then from his shoulder to his head to the back of his palm where it somehow
stuck, smackdab presto!

Soon I was left standing there while exiting traffic coursed around my terrified, flabbergasted, spiritually empty frame.

RATIONALITY INTACT ENOUGH TO NOT press my luck, I refrained
from remarking how Mr. Podmore would lack a leg to stand on were I to
demand he explain just what the devil he'd been playing at, nosing around in
my desk. Supposed I ought thank my lucky starts it'd been this fop who'd
found me out rather than Mrs. Terre. No doubt my (albeit brilliant) excuse
'The knife's just to cut the apple in my lunch' would not've held up were she
my interlocutor.

Podmore took me at my word. However, he did have to insist on a second
explanation which would cover the boxcutter - an item he referred to with
pantomime of extending the blade and the sound effect of chik-chik.

Had me dead to rights there. Not even I was brazen enough to front off
there might be a traditionally acceptable reason for such a mortal device to
be hidden in the desk of a fourth grade classroom.

Podmore laid out if I wanted the things back, I'd have to arrange with my
parents about it (leaving it uncertain whether any official dispatch outlining
the day's events had been put in the post alerting them). He then released me
out to recess.

My calm had a disquieted limp. Could I have walked away from this unscathed? Why? How? On the strength it was end-of-the-year and what teacher with a jot of wit would want to be bothered with such loony tunes?

Only thing for it was: keep my head down, steer clear of pranks, no hijinks for the remainder of the week. Putting this resolution into prompt practice, I kept to the outskirts of the play fields. Up the hill. Over near the tree with the railroad spike through it.

There I sat, still catching my breath, when what should I see but Mica, some caravan of nondescript cronies in tow, making directly toward me. Mica brandished a plump length of rope, the sort used for climbing in gym class. 'Where'd he get his hands on that?' I was still vaguely trying to sort when he and his henchmen were upon me. They formed a half-circle which robbed me of any easy means of egress.

Mica somehow knew I'd brought what he referred to as 'a bunch of ninja knives' onto school grounds.

'How do you hear about it?' I demanded.

But he had a head of steam up, barreled right past my calls for points-of-order. 'It's like this: we can't have turkey necks like you bringing in assassination stuff to school' he said while casually tossing one end of his rope high over the extra-tall chin-up bar near at hand 'so now we're going to have to hang you.'

Just then I noticed how the end of the rope drooling over the gallows' crossbar was not a proper hangman's noose, but had been tied into an open circle. 'Mica, you can't hang me. First of all, it's school property. And it's broad daylight, beside.'

Nice try - but this could not be let slide. Justice demanded disallowing any flimsy excuses about cutting apples at lunch. 'You can just bite an apple. Even worst case you don't need a boxcutter to slice any apple I've ever tasted!'

This was getting wildly out of wing. Couldn't we work toward a non-violent compromise?

'You made your bed.'

'You're for real going to string me up right during recess?'

He spat on the ground and scuffed where they loogie'd plopped so there'd be no mistake about he would.

Thankfully, his cohorts lacked the inherent zeal to actually commit homicide in front of countless kickball field witness. Thankfully, much of the longer grass around me was actually attached to small, wild onions I was able to yank from the soil to brandish self-defensively. The entire stand-off promptly morphed into a kind of free-for-all tussle with all manner of randos joining in for the zippy satisfaction of whapping each other with the miniature vegetables.

And soon enough the fracas wound down to everyone having a contest to see who could do the best jump kick against the backstop of the ball field.

THE EMBLEM ALVIN DESIGNED FOR the swim team was breathtaking. Simplicity itself, at a glance, yet I wondered if given years to tinker would I have it in me to craft such a dazzler.

The team was called The Stingrays. Which is what he'd rendered to the hilt. Precision black with some few artful additions of white accenting the beast's skin to make this image more than some shoestring silhouette. All set against the perfect blue of imaginary water. Precisely what a swimming pool looked like in the mind's eye. Platonic crisp, sharp, refreshing. Palpable impression of the stabbing cold of a first dive in mingled with the warmth achieved from having been at swim for hours beneath the sun. This enclosed within a thick black diamond outlined by a black diamond, thin, space between the two a blue the meagerest shiver fairer than the main.

'It makes me want to join the team except I'm absolutely never going to!'

Alvin guffawed, immediately recounting the abysmal bellyacher I'd been when mom had insisted I participate two summers previous. Gah! The ludicrous showings I'd made during the few meets the poor coach had been forced by circumstance to let me race in.

Alvin was earnestly chuffed by my reaction to the sweatshirt.

Sadly neither he nor those close to him would receive any discount. One freebie plus the pay he'd received was the boodle in full. 'The life of a freelancer' he said, breathing a sigh like the peal of Spartan triumph.

Soon we were walking the area in back of the neighborhood houses, working up a dull sweat, picking at dry bark from certain trees we passed, fingers cemented together from pine sap inside twenty minutes.

According to Alvin, his heart's new aim was to become a lifeguard. Pound-for-pound he was trim enough and had the stoic mind for such responsibility. 'But are you legally old enough to save a life?'

He could start as an apprentice, maybe. Or sit around taking the pool passes, handing them back out. Sweetening the pot, he was already privy how to check chlorine levels.

I deeply hoped it all shook out in his favor.

He confessed it was mostly daydream. High schoolers went in for the job in droves. Lots of wheeling and dealing behind-the-scenes. He just couldn't compete with that. Still: might be worth a go ingratiating himself, even off the books. Hang around all summer, give it a year, two years, become something of an inevitability, ascension assured.

I failed to see life moving forward according to any design other than exactly that.

The more we chatted the more it was revealed how much there was to look forward to in the coming months. Realities I hadn't been the least bit cognizant of two minutes prior but which, now I was hearing of them, knew certainly would become fixations.

Did I remember Michael Dudikoff from American Ninja and Avenging Force? What a question! Not only was he in all my favorite movies but when mom took me to the hairdresser we requested 'The Michael Dudikoff.' Well, it so happened the chap had a television program called Cobra set to premiere. Some kinda cross between Street Justice and Knight Rider. 'Or anyway - he drives a slick car. And he must do ninjutsu or why else cast Michael Dudikoff, right?'

Right. He was absolutely right!

And what would I say were he to tell me a movie about Bruce Lee was set to hit theatres, come summer? Or how about: Shine at Collector's World had it on good authority there was a flick about The Shadow in the offing!

I nodded and nodded while we wasted an entire afternoon gloating about how the world favored us, obviously moved in accordance to our whims! Our fancies were the mother's teat all enterprises suckled for sustenance.

Later on, even a long bath couldn't get three of my fingers un-cemented from each other. Fused with tree sap. As though I had a fin. Had turned alien. Become something new. More myself than myself. Fantastically grotesque.

LAST FEW DAYS OF SCHOOL the only things going were group projects, free periods, and (due to the weather) indoor recess. Thankfully the projects, so-called, were voluntary. Buncha busywork while teachers milked the clock or whatever their angle was. Aides didn't even oversee the majority of each day's activities. Students were deputized. It was time to shine for Safety Patrols and kiss-ups!

In large part to keep myself distracted, I'd thrown myself headlong into a new comic book project. It was that or face up to the emotions associated with all I'd be through of late. I wanted shut of run-ins with the supernatural, with friends traipsing to the other side of the continent without leaving method of dropping them a line. This new mag was to be a game changer. No more doodle art shortcuts. Nope. I was gonna work on things! Overhead perspective! Foreshortened posing! The figures were all gonna be rendered anatomically correct - or if they were robots, they'd be complex robots, retaining their intricate details, panel-to-panel.

In many ways it was a knock-off of Nexus, up to and including its store-brand lifts of storyline particulars - and certain bits of the dialogue were straight up purloined. Except for some minor changes to insignia and the fact my character required an energy pack connected by wires to wrist devices in order to wield his energy blasts he was, for all intents and purposes, just a poor man's Horatio Hellpop. For goodness sake - he was even from 'the planet Plum' which an asterisk explained was pronounced peh-loom (this an obvious homage to the moon of Ylum, pronounced eye-lum per an asterisk in the first issue of Baron and Rude's original three issue black-and-white run).

But what of it? Forward by any means, eh? If Steve Rude could draw OMAC in college, I could crib Nexus in grade school! Who was gonna keep the populace on their side if they started advocating I ought be looked down the nose at!?

To save headache, I skipped any semblance of origin story, starting off with the third issue of the series. And to cement this illusion, I included asterisks after certain dialogue and connected these to explanatory notes claiming how matters being referenced had gone down in some previous issue.

The adventure picked up in extreme media res. Our hero was trapped in the clouds which, handily enough, was the title of the chapter: Trapped In The Clouds.

Some curious classmates moseyed over, here and there, all quite generous in lobbing praise on my abilities as an illustrator. I kept it humble. Quick to mention how much better my older brother was. Quick to name drop my adventures with Hugh Hanes, though taking care to paint those circumstances so I'd come out in the finest light possible. Not that these philistines knew Hugh Hanes from Adam. I wondered why I ran myself ragged with such sophistication and layered in-reference.

Who but me would care? Who was any of this for? Did posterity exist? I thought so. But: why did I think so? Nobody had directly claimed as much to me, had they? To the contrary: I'd just assumed it. A dream. Perhaps mine and mine alone. An arrogant assumption that anyone cared about anything merely because I cared with such fever about it all.

———————————————

CHECK IT OUT, CHECK IT out: in some kinda trance I'd completed eight solid pages in-a-row. Some of the most whiz-bang sequential illustration of my career. An entire issue of Thun-Dar ready for inking which, really, ought be a cakewalk.

As the jury was still out on the character name, I was cautious to avoid tracing in pen any instance of it appearing.

But then, why not? Sure! Thun-Dar it would remain!

Say people thought it a bit silly at first? Say it didn't strictly make sense on account of he didn't really have anything to do, per se, with thunder or even with particularly loud sounds? Once a readership developed, they'd gloss past all that!

Having started at issue three was a blessing here, too. If the grousers started bringing me down, I could always make them feel ignorant for not knowing the true reason Thun-Dar was called Thun-Dar. It was 'something explained in the lost issues' all to do with a piece of his private history. So there!

I worked through the night on the living room floor. Even when I realized it'd been a mistake to have drawn on the fronts and backs of pages (text and illustration from the one kind of bled through to the other, in a few places making panels a bit untidy) I took it on the chin, refusing to become disconsolate.

Alvin made a carnivalesque to-do of how impressed he was at my Herculean effort and rapid turn-around, nevermind the content. Pouring himself some Corn Chex, liberally spooning on sugar, he set to reading.

There was a particular bit he would come to which took all my self-control not to squeal out a spoiler for in advance ...

... Thun-Dar has failed thrice in drilling down through whatever these mysterious clouds were ... believes he's come upon a scientific discovery which will turn the tide in his favor ... must hurry lest these armored foes he's never encountered before return in legion ... who are they? ... he cannot plumb the reason for their rabid hatred of him nor even how they know he's called Thun-Dar ... ... he alights to the clouds, reaching for an instrument panel ... a shadow covers him ... ... a sound such as no man had ever heard (KwarKwarque!) jolts him ...

The panel at the low corner of right-hand page depicts an up-close of Thun-Dar's terrified visage, imperative word bubble exclaiming 'What in Hell--!' thus forcing the reader to brace for the page turn ...

... and ...

...there! A full page spread of a Thunder Eagle! Talons primed, wings at full span! The beast looms over our hero, he too awed by the sight to comprehend what is about to happen. An extraordinary artwork! Bold and mortifying! Inked to perfection - shaded with sublime insight to achieve three dimensional pop! Oh a marvel of perspective! It gave off the seasick feeling of Thun-Dar bending backward and the swoosh of the suggested assail the animal's posture promised ...

'I think you spelled Eagle wrong.'

... think I ... spelled ... 'No. I checked before I inked.' I had. I'd checked it. Before I'd inked.

'How do you think you spell eagle?'

'E A G ...' I had checked it '... L ...' before '...E ..?' I'd inked.

Well I was right about that. '... but ...' Alvin said, clenching teeth.

How could this be? No!! 'I checked it before I inked!' I yarled desperately. 'It was spelled wrong and I ...'

Except I hadn't! I'd been too fatigued, too caught up, too proud of myself for noticing, for double checking, making the effort, doing the professional thing ...

A Thunder Eagel. There it was! Permanent ink for all to see the boner of!

Alvin tried to brace me up. Made a joke of trying to think how else Eagel might be pronounced. 'Maybe another asterisk would take the curse off it?' he joshed, chucking my shoulder.

'I'd also meant to call it a Lightning Eagle ...' All that business of Thun-Dar's name must've gotten addled up in my sleep deprived brain.

Alvin's suggestion: what about filling in the block letters stark black? Should be no trick altering capital L to capital E. 'The L's another matter ... Maybe put an exclamation bubble around it? Crosshatch shading behind the black letters? Bob's your uncle, no one the wiser.'

I was too overcome with emotion to thank him. He was a genius.

But I? Oh here sat the schmuck of the contemporary age. Because to black in the block letters would concentrate too much ink, make a mess of the lead-in page on opposite side of the sheet.

There was always something. Some vicious saboteur seeded in my fore-brain to remind me I was exactly not who I thought.

A WALK AFTER NIGHTFALL. THOUGHTS of my failures roiled, though didn't work up any kind of lather. If anything, it was humorous. Life's pre-dictability. Putting it all out there, no punch pulled, I was a reliably clock-work mechanism, was I not?

This latest business, misspelling eagle?

Here's what - one of my earliest memories: Writing a birthday card for my mom (maybe a Mother's Day card - some celebration of her). After saluta-tion and an illustration of the cats we lived with at that specific epoch, I summed things up: I love you and I hope you are well.

Except, as my mom promptly pointed out, I'd spelled hope H O P.

Flustering embarrassment. Regret a fizz in my head. Tried slickly retconning 'You're not seeing what I meant, mom. Knowing you're well makes me hop. I hop - poetically we leave implied the word when - you are well.'

Naw. She saw clean through the ruse.

What did I care, in any event? Wouldn't typos, slippages like those appreciate over the years? Who wants to look back at their oeuvre to find it machine wrought, buffed, pristine?

Additional effort would merely sniff out new crannies for mistakes, besides. A mug's game, so far as I could tell.

Was I impressing if impressing meant sluffing off my own skin? Some kind of horror show! Knowing it wasn't me who'd dazzled the throng I'd dazzled, so called - and if I discovered others were bowled over by what I'd done prior I'd have to confess I'd unbecome the entity responsible, was pulling a posture of being it still only once they'd made it definitively worth my while.

A bogus lifestyle, however you gussie it up.

As I rounded up a hill, I noted a kid, maybe my age, I'd never known lived in the corner house. We all believed it was only an old woman and the nurse who changed her bandages bi-weekly residing there.

He crouched, gingerly tilting a saltshaker. Enough just some few flakes dropped at a time. Half-a-dozen slugs were below him. Coils resembling sucked orange slices. Clearly he'd been as long-winded killing those as he was being with his current victim.

When he addressed me, it struck me I'd been thinking of myself as only my observations of him - a peeping ether, as if I were nothing, he only a thought of mine.

'Did you know that kid Ezekiel?'

Ezekiel? 'What about Ezekiel?'

'You don't know what happened?'

'He disappeared' I immediately shrugged.

The slug he was working on ticked another tap of its enclosing demise. 'Disappeared?'

'Disappeared ... few weeks ago.'

Not according to this kid's brother.

He suddenly full on shook the saltshaker, as though greedily seasoning a baked potato. The slug went taut, petrified in the space of a blink. And as he teasingly started in on another he explained 'My brother said they found him down in the sewer. Over there.' Nosed out beyond me. Past the field. The tall grass. Telephone lines. Montessori. My skin began to crawl. My eyes to water. The new slug gave a writhe suggesting it knew from watching its cousins' fate what was in store for it. A second coy dusting of salt tip-tap-tip-tapped its pelt.

This information about Ezekiel was no surprise to me, of course, though some speck of my heart had held out hope his fate had been something less gruesome. I drew in a breath, prepped to give this latecomer the scoop, wise him how to best avoid certain pitfalls.

He blurted ahead of me 'There was an old woman living in there.'

'Old woman ... living where ...?'

'In the tunnel. My brother said she wandered off from an old folk's home.'

I said nothing. The slug suffered another jolt of salt.

'The kid, Ezekiel? Been bringing her food. Thought she was his mom's ghost.' Kid looked at me flat. 'No one knows how she got down there.' Killing dose, all at once, over the slug. 'She was dead the last time he went to feed her. Found him sleeping next to her, all cuddled up.'

He stood. Extended the saltshaker to me. Licked lips like did I want a go.

I took the container by rote. 'You know that's utterly preposterous, right?' I sneered, spilling salt off blindly to one side.

He snatched the container back. Shoved me. Called me 'Dick cheese' then barked 'What's preposterous?'

'Your lie' I snarled. 'You and your brother's lie.'

A DAY. SOMETIME AFTER. WHO knows when ...

The sort of heat to the sky made one think about the end of the world. Sort of brightness made anyone you mentioned this to admit you might be onto something.

School had been out for ages. I'd taken to walking the grounds. Back behind the building, areas off-limits during the year. Where dumpsters were tucked. Large shuttered entryways for delivery trucks.

The playground seemed derelict. Almost a science fiction.

Obviously it could be utilized by all comers, but other than hoodlum evidences (cigarettes, soda cans, every once-in-awhile an inside-out tennis ball) there was little sign anyone but me ventured by.

I liked putting my face to the outside of the grid-lined windows. Peered into the corridor outside the gymnasium doors. Liked to meander under the overhang to the main entrance doors, too. One time there'd been adults in suits, three of whom waved at me in gleeful Hiyas I'd recoiled from.

A sign for the school, just outside the fenced in area of the kindergarten playground, had manipulatable letters which spelled Have a Terrific

Summer! I drew blanks coming up with anything puckish to rearrange them into.

I supposed it made sense for the world to leave off coming to this school park. Who wants to be reminded of school? Plus: there were better parks within spitting distance. One, a proper outdoor athletic cooperative. Upkept baseball diamonds. Snack hut. Water fountains. Soccer fields with lines painted on the ground, nets left in the goalposts. You could put coins into a slot and turn on the field lights. Those dozen large bulbs glaring their overwrought illumination, cold and insectoid. Another, we used to call the Log Park. Until some wise-guy sweet talked a town hall meeting armed with enough signatures garnered from a door-to-door petition to see the log constructions dismantled. New, garish, multicolored fibrous plastic monstrosities were erected in their stead.

Word around the campfire was such blights were coming soon to my neighborhood. A beautification project. Though if one were to take Frank's information as fact, our development was actually procuring posh play equipment like at Burger King. Habitrails, he called these. The word reminded me of sawdust shavings, the acrid scent of newspaper shreds urinated on by domesticated rabbits.

This day, I was laid on the ground. No one tended the grass, so it'd died, silent and dignified. The soil left exposed had baked itself into fissures until the first solid rain came, left the field a disc of dandruff consistency, entirely featureless.

I imagined the world had died. It didn't seem bad. To be one of the few left, knowing we'd lived past life. Nothing but to wait. My thoughts might even be the same as they were now. Why not? Lay on the disc of a dead world. Lay pretending you're only pretending.

The insistence of sunlight made it impossible to keep my eyes closed. Through my clothes it was as though my back's flesh could detect the crawl of ants, writhe of worms, thick strangle of cicadas feet down into the soil.

When I sat up, my open eyes revealed the world under a chemical smear, a haze like from chlorine over all I saw. Eyes coated with a sour-milk cataract.

A noise off at the tree line. Over-distinct snap. Stick cracked purposefully in two.

At first, I saw nothing. But with enough noise of rustle, enough squinting, and now on my hands and knees, I made out, yes, there was something. I'd expected a kid. Distinctly expected a child my age. And so initially thought I saw exactly that. But in just a blink, two stinging blinks, focus revealed it was a deer. Paused in its grazing. Looking at me. It turned away as though to address some other presence standing nearby. Returned to expressionlessly regarding me. Another deer soon stepped to the tree-line. Then they both moved out from the shade. Stirred up dust from the jogging path which encircled the playground entire.

They must've gotten enough out of looking at me because soon they moved back into the woods. Only maybe I heard a clatter of them trotting away. Only maybe. Or maybe they were suddenly gone.

I was too occupied wondering what I'd thought of them. They were either terrifying, inconsequential, or I couldn't think what else.

CPSIA information can be obtained
at www.ICGtesting.com
Printed in the USA
LVHW031258140520
655613LV00020B/2209